head of English at a school in Surrey. *Jamboy* is his third novel
for Oxford Uni

Other books by Will Gatti

Sea Dance

Abe's Team

Jamboy

Will Gatti

OXFORD
UNIVERSITY PRESS

For Annie
who is in the garden right now.

OXFORD
UNIVERSITY PRESS

Great Clarendon Street, Oxford OX2 6DP

Oxford University Press is a department of the University of Oxford.
It furthers the University's objective of excellence in research, scholarship,
and education by publishing worldwide in

Oxford New York
Auckland Bangkok Buenos Aires
Cape Town Chennai Dar es Salaam Delhi Hong Kong Istanbul
Karachi Kolkata Kuala Lumpur Madrid Melbourne Mexico City Mumbai
Nairobi São Paulo Shanghai Taipei Tokyo Toronto

Oxford is a registered trade mark of Oxford University Press
in the UK and in certain other countries

British Library Cataloguing in Publication Data available

ISBN 0 19 275273 1

1 3 5 7 9 10 8 6 4 2

Typeset by AFS Image Setters Ltd, Glasgow

Printed in Great Britain by
Cox & Wyman Ltd, Reading, Berkshire

PART ONE

IS NOWHERE SAFE?

ONE

The moon was full and bright and cast a pale light down into the empty street; and it was just as well there was a moon because all the street lights were dead. Everything was dead. Nothing shifted, nothing stirred; there wasn't even a cat slinking along a garden wall. Nothing, except the soft murmur of a still sea against a shingle shore.

And then, down near the street corner, something strange happened: the air glistened, bulged, and then, quite suddenly, ripped; a raggedy up-and-down tear about four feet long, and about two feet above the pavement. There was a momentary howling sound that seemed to come from a long way away, and two figures tumbled out of that gap in the night air and fell with an awkward clatter onto the ground. Behind and a little above them, that same long rip in the darkness shimmered for a second and then was gone.

'That,' muttered the boy, who was on his hands and knees, 'was what I would call extreme.' He shook his head. 'Are we safe, Alicia?'

'Of course we are, Nasfali, don't fuss,' said the second figure, a girl with short black hair, wearing a neat grey suit. She was already on her feet, dusting her hands, then quickly looking up and down the street, as if half expecting to see someone or something waiting for her. She was older than the boy, pale faced and serious. She had a silver ring in her nose and seven more in her right ear. For some reason the smart clothes and the punk rings looked a little odd together; not that it mattered for there was no one there to see and even if there had been, she didn't look the sort of person who would put up with comments on her appearance.

'Is it a good scheme?' said the boy. He was as dark as she was pale. Ebrahim Nasfahl Ma'halli was his name, though she, Alicia Dunne, called him Nasfali. His English friends had called him Abe. He was half Egyptian and his mother was a witch. He was thirteen but looked a couple of years older than that.

'I have already told you it's a good scheme.'

'I know, but that was then . . . ' He broke off and looked around. He seemed to be operating a little more slowly than her. 'Where are we? Is it England? You didn't say . . . '

'Of course I did.'

'Where are we?'

'Hove, near Prackton Hall, and that's where we have to go. This way.' And she marched to the end of the street and turned the corner.

And stopped so abruptly that Abe, who was hard on her heels, bumped into her back. She didn't snap or tell him off, just very quietly and very calmly said: 'Nasfali, the other way.'

'I'm sorry . . . ' He was on the verge of telling her that the way she had saved the team had been truly magnificent, when he peered over her shoulder and saw why she had stopped.

It was a vast, sweaty-faced figure, with black beady eyes and a chest the size of a keg of beer, and it was called a Lakin. It leaned down and forward: 'Oh,' it breathed spittily, 'it's a jamboy. We've been lookin' for yer, jamboy.'

Once upon a time Lakin had just been a smelly, mean-minded, heavy-bellied cook working in the kitchens of Abe's school. Then Mrs Dunne, in a powerful knot of foul magic, had multiplied this one man into an army of greasy chefs. Lakin disliked everything but most of all he hated boys.

Abe froze—this Lakin knew who he was! Alicia didn't hesitate. She snapped her fingers in front of the monstrous man's face and then pointed to the right: 'There!' she snapped. 'There!'

The Lakin grunted and turned his head. Instantly Alicia and Abe pelted down the street in the opposite direction. The oldest trick in the book but the Lakin, dangerous and disgusting as he was, was not very smart.

'Oi!' roared the Lakin. 'I'll smack yer! I'll roast yer on a spit! Come 'ere, yer jamboy.'

The two young people ignored his shouts and skipped across an overgrown front garden and over a back wall, into an alley. Behind them they could hear the crash and slap of heavy feet and a mindless roaring from the Lakin.

'Stop,' wheezed Alicia.

'No,' said Abe. 'Keep going. There might be more of them.'

There were.

The roar twisted into a thin, nerve-scratching howl as the Lakin sensed it was losing them. Instantly the howling was answered by another off to the left, and further away another, and behind them another and another. Alicia grimaced. 'The place is stuffed with them.' The alley turned out to be a dead end. Alicia slumped against the wall and held her aching sides, while Abe cast around for a way out, but there wasn't one.

'Why is the place stuffed with them, Alicia?'

'I don't know, do I?' she said crossly.

A fat shape lumbered into the alley and with a grunt started towards them.

'Here!' Abe made his hands into a step and levered Alicia up so that she could scrabble up the wall. The moment she was safe, he ran back about ten paces and then charged the wall and just had enough momentum to catch the top. Alicia grabbed his wrist, and while he kicked, she hauled him up and out of reach of the Lakin's hands.

They dropped down on the other side of the wall and the howling started up again.

'Can't you do something?'

She shook her head. 'Too tired. Go.' She gestured for him to start off again.

He set off, aware of Alicia wheezing along but always just behind him. He ran blindly, zigzagging through the unfamiliar streets until the Lakin howls grew fainter.

Abe slowed his pace. They turned onto a main street and with the full moon shining down like a spotlight they jogged down the pavement past one shattered storefront after another. It seemed to Abe as if there had been a riot or war or something else disastrous.

Alicia drew up beside him and put her hand on his arm to stop him. 'I know where we are,' she wheezed.

'What?'

'I know where we are. Been here before. It's not Hove. Friend worked here in a café. Came to a party here.' She started walking again.

'But you said it was Hove.' The team was gone; he had left behind his father; he'd left Egypt when he'd spent his entire life trying to get there—he had left all that to come with her because of her scheme, because she had said that they had to get back to Britain. He had done that and now it seemed she didn't have anything sorted at all.

'Well, we're in Worthing, just up the coast a bit. Not far off. You probably jogged me.'

'I didn't do anything.'

'No,' Alicia sniffed. 'You didn't, did you.'

Ahead of them the moon shone down on a still sea.

At the front they turned right and then hurried along until she pointed out what she had been looking for: beach huts. 'Perfect. We'll be safe in one of these.'

They broke into one, made a kind of nest out of mouldy chair cushions, and then, leaving the door slightly ajar so that they could see the moon, they settled down. But though they were worn out by their escape neither of them could sleep. Outside they could hear the soft breathing of the sea up against the shingle. 'You've changed, Nasfali,' she said. 'You look older.'

'And wiser?'

'I didn't say that.'

'You've changed too.'

'I know,' she said flatly. 'I found out a lot of things while you were in Cairo,' she said. 'A lot of things . . .'

'Magic?'

'Yeah. Loads of it.' She tucked up her knees and clasped them in her arms. 'I found out what your mum stole from Egypt. A book. Really old. It's full of secret things, I think, all to do with magic, power, and stuff like that. It must have been kept hidden away since forever, different people looking after it. Your dad must have been the last guardian.

'I don't know how your mum and mine found out about it but the sisters have it now. The weird thing, Nasfali, is that they don't do anything with it; just sit on it. They're like . . . I don't know . . . they just like to hoard things, I think. Stop anyone else from having anything that's precious. They're too stupid or lazy to work out the secrets in the book but I found out one thing. That's how I got the team back to 1942. At least, that's how I think I did it; I had to do a bit of guessing,' she admitted. 'But it was wicked anyway, wasn't it? I liked doing that.'

Abe recalled how the old men, right in the last moments of their championship game, had seemed to change, become visibly younger, before fading away into thin air. She said they had gone back in time, back to their families, back so they could live their lives properly. It had been a great and a mysterious thing that Alicia had done but it was a shame, too. The victory would have been so good. There would have been a cup, television, hundreds of reporters, and sponsorship. Huge amounts of money from sponsorship. He would have been rich . . . but Alicia had done the right thing, because just as the last of the team was disappearing the witches of Britain had come turning and twisting out of the night sky, right over the football stadium. Another few seconds and they would all have had it.

'Yes,' he agreed. 'It was the very stuff of a legend, Alicia. We were like a mirage in the desert. They thought they had us, and then, poff, we were no longer there.' But there was something else, something that didn't seem at all right. 'Why didn't you use your great power on the Lakin? We wouldn't have had to run then, would we?'

Alicia shrugged. 'Dunno. Didn't think of it, I suppose. Things aren't quite the way I thought they would be.'

'But your scheme,' said Abe, 'you still have that?'

'Oh yeah, of course. We get the book away from the witches; I learn loads more magic, and we get things back the way they were before, before they started meddling with everything. You'll see. It won't be so hard.'

'Good,' said Abe. 'I shouldn't like things to be so hard.'

Out of the darkness came a long-drawn-out howling. The Lakins were still hunting for them.

Two

It was the crunching of feet on shingle that woke Abe. A Lakin! He lay very still. If you don't move they can't see you, was the panicky thought that flickered through his head.

'Don't be silly,' hissed Alicia out of the darkness.

How did she do that? He hadn't spoken, had he? Had he?

Outside, the crunching seemed to go on and on. There couldn't be just one, there had to be hundreds and hundreds of them. Either that or some monster had wallowed out of the deep and was eating up the beach. But that didn't seem likely. And there was something else, too, like the murmur of voices, and here and there a sharp crack, like the snap of a dry stick.

'What's happening?' he whispered.

'How should I know?' He sensed her shuffling into a different position and then in a muffled voice, she said, 'Too early. G'back to sleep, Nasfali.'

How could he? There was an army out there. Carefully, he twisted himself round so he could peer out of the door. The moon had disappeared and the sky was pitch black, except for the thinnest of grey lines down on the horizon. It wouldn't be long before dawn, but it still took Abe's eyes a while to adjust to the darkness, and then he saw them: shape after dark shape coming from somewhere off to his right and crunching down onto the beach, moving slowly, heading straight towards the sea. Whoever they were, they clearly weren't interested in searching beach huts.

'I think we shall be all right,' he said quietly. Silence. 'Alicia?' There was a faint snuffling snore and then silence again. 'I'll keep watch then.' He pulled one of the covers round his shoulders and positioned himself cross-legged, just where the door was slightly ajar. It was a summer night, but cold after Egypt. He shivered and waited for the dawn to come.

At first there were pale streaks above the grey line on the horizon, and then thin smears of pink and orange and, as the darkness faded into light, Abe rubbed his disbelieving eyes. Zigzagging down the beach in a long, winding column were hundreds and hundreds of people, all patiently huddled down onto the hard shingle, suitcases and bags and bundles stacked around them. Out on the sea were moored dinghies of every shape and size imaginable; and further out still Abe could see the grey hull of a large steamer.

People, dinghies, a steamer . . . so many people leaving. Were they running away? Like Moses from Egypt? An exodus? The nearest group were no more than thirty feet from where he crouched hidden from view. He'd ask. It was too strange, and with so many people around, there surely couldn't be any trouble from Lakins.

With the rising sun, there was more movement: some got up and stretched; down at the shore families were picking up their bags and standing ready; a small motor launch had already nosed into shallow water and four figures, their boots round their necks and their suitcases balanced on their heads, were wading out to it.

'Alicia,' he hissed. 'Look at this! What do you think is happening? Shall I go out and talk to them?'

'No.'

At that moment three Lakins crunched past their door, no more than five paces from them; white nylon shirts stretched over barrel chests and larder-sized bellies, shirtsleeves rolled up over tattooed forearms, and each of them had a thick black whip gripped in their right hand. One had the lash draped like a thin snake across his shoulder, the others trailed theirs along the shingle so that they jiggled and wriggled and seemed horribly alive. The waiting families stared ahead. They looked tired and frightened.

Now he could see that there were many more Lakins moving up and down the lines of waiting people, questioning a group here and there. 'They're looking for something,' murmured Abe.

'You mean someone. Haven't you noticed yet, Nasfali? Look.'

He looked and then looked again. 'They are mostly boys my age, aren't they?'

A Lakin on the far side of the column of people snapped his long bullwhip a second time, and twenty feet away from him a boy, who had moved a little bit too far out from the others, gave a shout of pain and clutched his arm where the tip of the whip had stung him.

'Back yer go,' growled the Lakin, and the boy ducked back into line.

'They're like you, aren't they, Nasfali? All the boys That's what it is,' murmured Alicia and she gave him an appraising look. 'Mother always thought you were special.'

'Thank you.'

'That's why she disliked you so much. You know, I think that whoever is in charge here is getting rid of all the boys your age. Expelling them!' She snapped her fingers. 'That's it! They're getting rid of anyone who might be you. They're frightened of you, Nasfali. They believe you're the enemy! You should be flattered, Nasfali.'

He didn't feel flattered. 'They don't want me, but they want you.'

'Oh, probably.'

More families and groups of boys were wading out to the small boats now, and all across the still blue sea there was a constant traffic of vessels, pulling to and from the steamer.

Alicia had moved back away from the door and was cautiously tapping the back wall. 'Yes!'

'What?'

'See if any of them are near.'

The nearest Lakin was more than twenty paces away. 'It's safe. What are you going to do?'

Alicia stood, leaned both hands against the back wall, then gave the bottom plank a sharp kick and it came clear away from where it had been nailed. She levered it out, then pulled the two above it away and immediately wriggled through.

Abe followed. Behind the line of huts they were out of sight of anyone on the beach though, up on the road, they could see a loose group of people, leaning on railings, watching what was happening down below. Alicia frowned. 'Walk casually, Nasfali, and no one will pay us any attention. Here.' She offered him her arm and the two of them sauntered onto the road.

'What about Lakins?' murmured Abe.

'All on the beach.'

'You don't think they're still hunting us then?'

'Can you see any up here?'

'No, but . . .'

'Well then,' she sniffed, 'stop fussing.'

As they passed by, Alicia stopped, pretending to be engrossed by the scene too. The watchers were a poor looking bunch: shabby clothes, holes in the elbows of their jackets, and grizzled pinched faces.

'Excuse me,' said Alicia turning to the woman beside her, 'what's going on exactly?'

'Eh? Exactly? Exactly what are you on about? Everyone knows about this lot.' She looked suspiciously at Alicia. 'Don't you come from roun' here?' Then she noticed Abe. 'And what's he doin' here? Should be on the beach with the rest of them.'

'No, he shouldn't,' said Alicia firmly. 'You don't mean that, do you?'

The woman blinked stupidly. 'No, course not. It's them down there what ought to be on the beach and good riddance to them.' She fell silent for a moment. 'You on your holidays?'

'Yes, staying with my auntie.'

'Good. Good. Don't want outsiders round here. Only bring trouble, they do.'

Down below them on the beach, whips cracked and the lines slowly moved forward.

'What did you say your auntie's name was?' said the woman Alicia had first spoken to.

'I didn't,' said Alicia. 'But I think you probably know who she is, don't you?'

The woman took a step backwards, her sullen and suspicious face tightening suddenly with the shock of recognition. 'One of them, aren't you?' The others picked up her words. 'One of them. Sorry, miss.' One after another, they turned and dispersed, crossing the road and making their way back through the side streets into the town.

'What did they mean "one of them"?' asked Abe when they had been left on their own.

'Haven't got the faintest,' said Alicia.

'And what was that about your aunt?'

'Just made it up. Did the trick though, didn't it, Nasfali?'

'Yes. You are quite exceptional, Alicia.'

Alicia sniffed dismissively. 'Exceptional! After going to Egypt is that all you can say?'

'Well . . . '

'Don't bother, Nasfali, let's just find the railway station. We need to get to Hove quickly.' She looked up and down the tatty and practically deserted sea front. There were no cars, no buses, no wardens, no police—only the exodus on the beach and the witches' Lakins. She sniffed. But differently, her head tilted back slightly, catching some current in the sea air. Then, without another word, she turned and briskly crossed the road and Abe had to run to catch up with her.

'Do you know where the station is?'

'Of course.'

THREE

Alicia led the way through a series of deserted side streets, walking quickly, right here, left there, never hesitating, across what, at one time, must have been a main shopping street, though the shop windows were either boarded or smashed. What had happened here? Abe had the odd feeling that these smashed shopfronts looked like gaping mouths with broken teeth. He shuddered and, not meaning to, heard himself mutter, 'Dentists.'

'What did you say?'

'Ah.' He gave a quick half-step to catch up with her. 'Hunger, Alicia. I'm very hungry.'

'That's not what you said. Here.' She abruptly turned in through the doorway of a big store. Their feet crunched on broken glass. 'Shortcut.' Without shoppers, and servers, and bottles, and bags, and drapey things, and racks and rails, the unlit space was gloomy and threatening. The sort of place that Lakins might have as a dirty sleeping-nest.

Abe shivered and kept close to Alicia. A small voice kept telling him that they would be safer outside; too many places in here where a person could get jumped.

At that moment, he caught the edge of a movement, and a quick scuffling sound, over to his right. He stopped. There it was again. And then a small shape scuttled on hands and knees from behind a screen to a doorway to a changing room. 'Did you see that?' he whispered. 'Can't have been more than six or seven. What do you reckon? Sleeping rough? Let's see if it can tell us anything.'

Alicia shook her head.

'Why not? I mean it's not like there is a tourist information office that we can just pop into, is there. I mean, where is everyone, Alicia? Did you do something, when you sent the team back to 1942? Did you do something weird, break some law of magic or something?' She bit her lip, frowned, looked as if she were about to say something and then shrugged. 'I've been away a month, that's all,' said Abe. 'My mother and your mother and the rest of the witches, they can't have changed everything, not in that time, can they?'

'My mother is gone,' said Alicia flatly, but she was only paying half attention to him.

'This is like a witch's prison,' said Abe, 'nothing but rubbish.'

'Of course, that's what they're like. You can hardly have forgotten, Nasfali. This is why we have come back.'

More scuttling and shifting shapes, and then, quite clearly, Abe saw a little hooded head and the pale face of a staring child, girl this time, before it ducked away out of sight. Why should she hide from them? They meant her no harm.

'They like children,' said Alicia. 'Girls.'

'They? Lakins?'

'The witches. Make them slaves. Use them. I don't know.' Then they were through the store and out in the open again. The glimpse of the child seemed to have upset her.

After ten minutes' fast walking, the streets began to change slightly. There were the odd signs of life, smoke drifting from a chimney, the occasional person in a doorway, watching them pass, two women wheeling a cart stacked up with potatoes. Not a car though, nor a coach or bus, nor a plane leaving a trail of white across the blue sky. They saw two Lakins but they were moving off in the opposite direction to them. Perhaps they had been forgotten. Abe relaxed slightly.

'Do you think there'll be any trains?' said Abe.

'People have to get round, somehow,' said Alicia. 'Bound to use trains.'

It seemed as if she was right, because as they neared

the station they could see people going in. Inside Abe and Alicia found a couple of dishevelled looking men in shabby British Rail uniforms in the ticket office. One of them was boiling water on a little camping stove and the other was polishing the inside of the window with a leather rag.

'When's the next train to Hove?' asked Alicia.

'Depends.'

'What do you mean?'

At that moment there was the clanging of a bell coming from the main part of the station.

'That's her coming in now. 'Scuse us.' And both he and the man behind him buttoned their jackets and hurried out through a side door onto the platform.

Alicia and Abe followed them in. The station concourse was surprisingly full of men and women—no children, though—all surging towards one of the platforms.

'Number nine,' said Alicia. 'Hurry.'

They squeezed through the crowd, causing some angry muttering as they passed.

'Mind yourself, sonny.'

'Beach holiday for you, sunshine, when she gets a hold o' you.'

But neither of them paid attention. All they wanted to do was find a seat and get out of Worthing as quickly as they could. However, no sooner had they reached the barrier leading to platform nine, than they both wished they hadn't pushed their way through quite so eagerly.

'Oh!' said Alicia.

'Flaming pharaoh!' breathed Abe. 'It is not possible . . . '

But it was.

Steadily approaching their platform was a single railway carriage painted a dark and bloody red. There was no engine, unless the hundred or so miserable looking wretches straining at the two long cables by which they were hauling this coach along the line counted as one.

Lakins were evident everywhere, snapping and cracking their whips across the bowed backs of the slaves.

The crowd broke into polite applause as the carriage door opened and a figure stepped out and began to walk towards them.

Grey. Trouser suited. Shiny black hair.

'Suppose it's my mother?' said Abe quietly. 'What do we do?'

'Change of plan,' said Alicia and instantly shoved her way between a large woman who was clapping with grim energy and a dark-bearded man whose eyes were on the exhausted slaves now being rounded up onto the neighbouring platform.

'That's it,' he was muttering. 'That's the way.'

The bearded man became aware of them. 'They're looking for snappers like you,' he muttered. 'You're the age they don't like and all, and you got a bit of colour on you. They don't like that neither.' His eyes shifted to Alicia. 'You're more like one of them, which is an odd thing.'

'I might look it,' said Alicia stiffly, 'but I am not one of them, I am one of me.' Gripping Abe's wrist she tugged him back through the crowd before the man decided that it was worth his while to call out to a Lakin. 'Trains,' she said firmly once they were outside, 'are not an option.'

From inside the station they could hear an eruption of shrill screams and the rounder howling of Lakins.

'Do we run?' said Abe.

'We do,' said Alicia.

FOUR

'It's dangerous.'

'It doesn't look at all dangerous. Just . . . long.' Alicia tossed the small sack she had had slung over her shoulder down onto the roadway. Then she sat down and took off her black lace-up boots. 'My feet hurt.' She massaged her left foot and then leaned back on her hands and wiggled her toes. 'I don't like running. Why is it that when I'm with you, Nasfali, I always end up running!'

The Lakins had burst out of the station after them, howling like a pack of mad dogs, and Abe and Alicia had had to run through half of Worthing before they finally lost them. And now, with the town a good two hours' trudge behind them, they were both tired and hungry. Abe was still anxious. The cracked and weed-scarred dual carriageway that they were walking along stretched ahead, curving up into the Downs. On either side of the road the land was wild. Scrubby thickets of thorn and elder pressed in around them.

The high point of Chanctonbury Ring, the old celtic fort, was off to the right and that was where they were heading. Alicia had reckoned they would be all right on the deserted roadway but Abe had it fixed in his mind that they should get up high, that they would be safer on the top of the Downs, and away from the coast.

'Why?' said Alicia.

He didn't know 'why'; some things you knew and that was it. 'It is a thing I have,' he said. 'I know. This is it.'

'You are peculiar, Nasfali.' She gave him an owlish look. It made him feel uncomfortable. 'Like a vision?' she said abruptly.

'No, not really.'

'Why are you smiling?'

'I'm not.' He turned away, and scanned the scrubby bushes for any sign of movement. 'Perhaps this is something I have from my mother,' he said. 'Perhaps I am a bit like you, after all.'

'I do not think so; you're a boy.' She went back to massaging her feet.

His eye lifted to the skyline. 'It is an old way,' he said suddenly. 'Up at the top. I bet you. A safe path. From ancient times.' He thought of the Great Pyramid of Giza, how his father had called it a place of power. Perhaps he, Ebrahim Nasfahl Ma'halli, could sense these things.

'And another thing,' said Abe. 'I don't think they like lonely places. They're always in towns, aren't they, cities, loads of people round them. I think their magic needs people, children, husbands who don't question them. They want slaves to pull them around in trains that don't work. Stupid. But that is their power.' He stopped suddenly, surprised at himself. 'You knew all this?'

She shrugged. 'Sort of.'

'There's something else, isn't there?'

'All right,' she said in that matter-of-fact way she had. 'If you must know, it's more than needing people like my stupid father to boss around. Much more.' She pulled on her boots and tightened the laces. 'They need people because they steal from them, not money and stuff like that but, I don't know, strength, or character maybe.'

'Their will,' nodded Abe. 'Free will. Yes, I can see how they do this.'

'Yeah, well, that's it then. It's like feeding, that's all. Builds them up, makes them strong. The stronger they are, the more magic they have.'

A crow flapped overhead and gave a rasping cry. 'Da?' It sounded like a question to Abe and for some reason that he couldn't fathom he thought of Stokely. Stokely had lived somewhere near the Downs.

'We should keep going,' said Abe.

Reluctantly she stood up and they walked on in silence,

apart from the crunch of Alicia's boots on the hard broken road.

'Stop looking so worried, Nasfali. There's no one following us.'

It was true that they hadn't seen anyone for hours. The last person they had spoken to had been at a miserable little market, where Alicia had exchanged her silver eyebrow ring for supplies. The woman at the fruit stall had taken the ring, wiped it on her sleeve, and held it up to her eye. 'Silver,' she'd said. 'They like silver, they do, silver and gold.' Then she'd let them help themselves. Abe thought it was lucky that Alicia wore so many rings; at least it meant they wouldn't starve, for the time being anyway.

She rooted in her sack and pulled out an apple and a lump of hard cheese. She studied the cheese with distaste. 'What I need,' she said, 'is chips. Not an apple.' She took a bite.

'You know,' she said after a while, 'I am tempted. You know, be a queen and all that.'

Abe glanced at her. She seemed taller, paler, her expression now haughty, cold. She turned her head, catching his wondering gaze, and seemed to look right through him.

'I might be terrible, mightn't I? Is that what you were thinking?'

It was what Abe had been about to be thinking. 'Of course not, Alicia, but . . .'

She gave one of her dismissive snorts. 'Oh, I could be, and why not? A terrible queen. I could give those stupid witches a thorough kicking. You could be my partner.' He could feel her eyes on him, but he kept his on the road ahead. He thought he could see a trail off to the right that would lead to high ground. 'There would be plenty of opportunities for you to devise grand business schemes. You would like that, wouldn't you?'

'Are you serious?'

She didn't answer his question. Instead she said: 'I don't think you know how to have fun, Nasfali, do you?'

He blinked and wiped his eyes. She seemed to have changed again, no longer so tall, no longer so pale.

'Nasfali, I asked you if you knew how to have fun?'

'Yes,' he said. 'I was thinking.' Seeing his team play had been fun. 'It is perhaps hard to believe,' he said, 'but I think I miss Griffin and Stokely and the others.'

It was hard to believe; they had been so annoying as only thirteen-year-old boys can be, except worse because they were so old on the outside.

'No,' she said. 'It's not hard. They were sweet.'

'Well, I wouldn't have called them that, but they were . . . ' He searched for the right word for that gang of troublesome, cheeky, funny old men . . . 'they were OK.'

'As OK as camels in the desert? As OK as an oasis of sweet grass and shady fig trees? As OK . . . '

Abe stopped and stared at her. 'Alicia!'

'What is it?'

'You're teasing me and you don't do that. You don't make jokes and you don't tease.'

'No, I don't do I?' She shrugged. 'I must be changing.'

'So you don't really want to be their queen?'

'Of course not,' she sniffed. 'Whatever made you think that?'

The climb up to Chanctonbury Ring was steep and hard-going. They had to push their way through scrub and bush, and brambles plucked at their arms and snagged their feet. And it suddenly felt cooler, too, as if the sun had been turned off. Pockets of thin scraggy mist drifted in around them, fingering their faces, cold and grey, making it hard to see, making it hard to keep to the way. They struggled on, sweating and shivering, hoping that once up on the Ring they would be clear of the mist and be able to make a camp for the night.

Eventually they scrambled past the steep banks that had once been the walls of the old celtic fort and then into the plantation of oaks that crowned the summit of the hill. A silvery grey sea of mist, lit by the sinking sun, lipped their island. It was beautiful, thought Abe, but lonely, an oasis. A faint, faint breeze stirred the leaves over his head, and fine threads of silver twisted away from the mist's surface and drifted towards the ring of trees before fading in the evening air. Was it safe, though?

'That's it!' Alicia flopped down and pulled out from her bag the heel of a loaf of bread, a tin of tuna that had a 'best before' date on it of 2001, and a second-hand tin opener that they had picked up at the shabby market. 'Only a year out of date,' said Alicia regarding the tin with some distaste, 'and it's fish.'

'Fish from the Nile, and dates,' said Abe, 'a veritable feast.' Veritable was a good word, he wondered where he had heard it.

'Tuna don't come from the Nile,' said Alicia, 'and I'm cold.' She sniffed the open tin, broke a piece of bread, hooked her finger into the tuna and scooped some onto the bread and handed it to Abe who took it and ate hungrily. Alicia wiped her fishy finger on the grass and closed the tin.

'Aren't you going to eat?'

She shook her head. 'Not hungry.' She shivered. 'I don't like outdoor stuff. Girl Guides and camping shops . . . '

'Camping's all right,' said Abe. He had, in fact, just been thinking how fine it was to be where they were, an adventure, a veritable adventure in which he, son of the great Ma'halli of Cairo, would lead Alicia Dunne to her destiny and there would be a crushing defeat for the Sisters of Britain.

'Don't be so sad, Nasfali, of course it's not all right. It's just the sort of stuff my dad liked. A total loser. Still, you probably do like this, don't you, Nasfali, out in the damp, nothing to sleep on.' Abe kept his mouth shut. 'I suppose it's a boy's thing,' she sighed. 'Go and get some wood for a fire.'

He was about to protest but somehow he found himself turning away and doing what he was told.

There was plenty of kindling around so it didn't take him long to bring back an armful, which he heaped up in front of Alicia, but not too close to the tree. Then he went off to find some larger branches to feed into the fire once it had got going. It would be good to sleep by a fire, and it did seem safe up where they were.

'Well,' he said when he returned for the second time and Alicia hadn't moved. 'How are we going to start it without matches? Have you got anything to make a spark?'

She furrowed her brow and scowled at the little pile of heaped kindling and there was a crack and yellow and orange flame rippled over the wood and then snapped into a true blaze.

'Magic!' Abe was surprised. 'I thought we weren't going to.'

'Goodness' sake, it's only a little fire and we're miles away from anyone. You sometimes disappoint me, Nasfali. Put on that big branch, my toes are cold.'

He did and then squatted down on the opposite side of the fire to her and together they sat in silence, gazing into the swirls of flame, enjoying the warmth on their faces.

Perhaps she was right, thought Abe, about the fire anyway. And about retrieving the book from Prackton Hall, but what then? He remembered something his father had said: how magic was made up of action and consequence. You change something here and then somewhere else there is an effect, perhaps not the one intended. What had been the effect of Alicia pulling apart the threads of time and finding a tear through which she could pass Jonson and Thomas, Jack, and Jissop and gentle, thoughtful Stokely and all the others back to their homes and well out of the reach of the witches?

The answer, when it came to Abe, was so blindingly obvious he couldn't believe it hadn't struck him from the moment he had seen that extraordinary queuing on the beach, and then the derelict town, and the hauling of the railway carriage. All these changes hadn't happened as the result of Alicia's battle against her mother. No. The half-empty town, overgrown fields, and the ruined roadway, these things couldn't have decayed in . . . how long had he been away? Two months, perhaps. It was Alicia had caused it all. She had broken some law of magic, something so serious that it had changed everything. She had changed time, turned it back and set it spinning forwards again but so that things had taken a different course. That had to be it.

If they found the book, Abe decided, it should go back to Egypt, back into the care of his father, its rightful guardian. That would be the safest, certainly. He would tell her, now. 'Alicia,' he began.

'What?' She glared at him across the flames. 'You are going to blame me, aren't you? All this because of me. Well, what was I supposed to do, tell me that? Do nothing? Let my mum and all her sisters get away with all their mischief, wreck everything? Just put my head under a pillow, like you, and pretend all the bad things would go away?'

'I wasn't going to blame you,' lied Abe. 'It was just . . . '

'Yes you were.'

'Oh!' Abe threw his hands up in the air. He was cross too. 'How do you always know what I am thinking? It's not right. My thoughts are mine. Nobody should go sneaking about in here.' He tapped his forehead. 'Nobody! But it is just what "they" can do, isn't it?'

'See!' she exclaimed. 'I was right. I knew I was right. You do blame me.'

'But it is because of you.'

'So you think I'm one of them, do you?'

'No.' Abe pulled a face. 'Of course I don't mean that. You're different, I know that. We don't have to argue.'

She hunched her shoulders. 'I don't like it out here.'

'It's safe,' said Abe. 'You were right. Just starting a little fire; they are not going to notice that, not from so far away. But we do have to think what we are going to do.'

'Oh, we've decided that. We'll get the book and we'll find a safe house somewhere where I can study it and then we'll defeat them and put things back.' Her shoulders suddenly sagged and she wiped the back of her hand across her forehead. 'I feel so tired. I think I'll try to sleep.'

Abe lay back and stared up through a gap in the branches of the oak tree to where a thin moon hung delicately in the black sky. He hadn't told her what he really thought about the book, that it was dangerous and should go back to Egypt.

He thought he heard her say, 'Don't worry about me,' but her sleepy voice was a vague murmur from the other side of the sinking fire and he wasn't sure. There was something else too, a murmur, a shift in the stillness, the soft press of a foot on damp grass. He couldn't hear anything but he sensed something or someone, moving closer. He sat up, the hair prickling on his neck and wished now that they hadn't lit a fire, it made the shadows so much blacker. He held his breath so that he could concentrate.

Nothing.

He sat up and looked around.

Nothing.

He pulled up his knees and hugged them and stared into the glowing caverns of the fire's smouldering embers. Do not be so fearful, he told himself. Alicia would know if it wasn't right. She would not sleep if it was dangerous. No. But if only they were not quite so alone. It made him think of the team. Where were they now? If he and Alicia came across them, would they even remember all that time ago what had happened to them: the spell and the rescue, the great game and then the going back? Perhaps it would have seemed just a strange dream to them. Perhaps it wouldn't be right to dig them out of whatever lives they were now leading. Except if they were alive they, like everyone else in Britain, were under the heel of these witch women. Perhaps they could help; that was a thought. They would be bound to be willing. Hadn't he and Alicia rescued them in the first place?

That thought stirred another. Stokely. In the coach, they had driven this way to find Stokely's home, that had been up close to the Downs. Ashington, he remembered. It wouldn't be so out of their way to go there and see.

He found the thought comforting and unclasped his knees and lay down again. A refuge. A safe house. That was the thing. He closed his eyes and at that very moment the darkness erupted into the scuffling padding of feet, a thick smell of oniony sweat, and rough hands grabbing the sack with their precious supplies which he had been using as a pillow. He instinctively held onto the bag.

FIVE

'Give it up, eh,' muttered a rough voice, but Abe didn't let go of the bag, and the next second he was reeling backwards from a smack on the chin that made his teeth buzz.

'Shine a light,' growled a voice and the fire was kicked into life again. 'Hold the girl. She's the one's got silver.'

'Alicia!' Abe shouted a too-late warning and had a thick arm clamped round his neck. The next second a rag stuffed into his mouth. He saw two figures, both men, lifting Alicia to her feet. She stood between them, seemingly still half asleep, her head hanging down, the glint of firelight on the rings on her ears and nose.

'Pull 'em off her, she don't need that many.'

They were rougher and more ragged than the beggars Abe had seen in Cairo's city of the dead. Their leader wore a shaggy sheepskin waistcoat, belted with string, and torn trousers that ended midway down his calves. His head was a wild mop of bushy hair and his eyes glittered from a blackened stubbly face. The rest—it was hard to be sure exactly how many there were—looked much the same, wild and dirty and with faces blackened. By their voices he could tell that at least two were women. It was one of them who faced Alicia and tilted her chin to peer at her rings.

'All right, dearie,' Abe heard her say, 'let's be having them, then.' She didn't sound aggressive, just matter of fact, a little tired, more like a mother than a mugger. She moved Alicia's head to one side so that she could begin to undo the earrings.

Abe tried to wriggle free from the grip of the man who had him in a neck-lock but the man just squeezed a little tighter and Abe found himself fighting for breath. 'Steady now,' murmured his captor.

How could he be steady? Alicia's rings were all they had; without them they would starve. And why was she doing nothing? There was no one holding her.

The leader of the group moved over to stand beside the woman. 'What are you then?' he growled. 'You're not them-people are you? Because it's certain you're not us-people neither.'

Alicia made no response.

'But you got all this silver,' continued the ruffian. 'So the question is, are you one of them?'

Abe stiffened. There was a different tone in his voice. It was thick with dislike. Who knows what people like this would or could do? The others murmured to each other and moved a little closer. Even the woman paused.

Perhaps Alicia heard him too for suddenly she stiffened and then shook her head free from the woman's hands. 'Stop it, now!' Her voice was icy sharp, and seemed to slash at them like a knife. The woman flinched, throwing her hands protectively across her face; the man, though, didn't move.

'Well now,' he said. 'Woke up, have you? Well, you don't need to fret . . . ' Abe never saw the signal, nor the figure gliding in from the shadow behind Alicia; he just glimpsed the club poised over her head and then there was a crack and her head snapped forward and she collapsed to her knees and to the ground.

'Never known one of them-people to come up this way before.' The leader nodded to the man who had struck Alicia and then turned Alicia over with the toe of his boot. 'Finish with the rings and we'll be out of here . . . '

Abe didn't think; he moved. He wrenched himself free from the loosened grip of his captor and before anyone could stop him, he had leapt across the smouldering embers of the fire and was standing astride poor Alicia. 'What have you done!' He was furious and frightened. His chest hammered and his hands trembled so much that he tightened them into fists. He expected the man with the staff to whack him at any second but he didn't care about that. It was the leader he faced. 'What have you done?' he repeated. 'You thief!' Then he saw the pencil-thin line of blood running from Alicia's ear down the edge of her cheek to her chin and he felt suddenly cold. 'You have killed her,' he said numbly.

'What's she to you?' said the man. 'Them-people, them foul-swat sisters, don't truck with young lads or no one but theyselves. So what's this she to you?'

'She's a friend,' said Abe, he kept his voice steady, 'and she was the only hope this country had.'

'Them-people don't give hope,' growled the man, 'they suck it out of we.' He made a sign with his hand, and the gang picked up Abe's bag, the woman handed over the rings she'd removed from Alicia before she'd been struck, and then they turned and melted into the trees.

It was only when he was alone that he registered that under his fingers he could feel a strong steady pulse, and when he put his head close to hers he could just hear that faint pig-like snoring noise she made when she was deeply asleep. And they hadn't even taken all the rings from her ear, either. He stared down at her admiringly. She had such calmness. She could have raged at them and used magic, sent them hurling into the night, but she had fooled them instead.

He ripped the cuff from his shirt and damped it in the wet grass at the edge of the hill and wiped away the thin streak of blood. Then he used some of the grass as a compress where she had been hit. It was not so serious; she would have a bruise, that was all. Then he sat down to watch over her.

SIX

'I am sorry, Nasfali.'
    'You've burnt my eyebrows!'
    'Yes, I expect I did. Sorry.'

Had Abe not been feeling quite so battered and singed he might well have remarked how surprising it was to hear the vision apologizing. As it was he was more concerned by the crispy feel of his eyebrows and by the quite extraordinary sight of the oak tree on the outer edge of the ring ablaze in a roar of spiralling flames, a beacon which only the blind beggars of Sussex would fail to see. The heat pressed out at them, the flickering light shoved weird shadows and splashes of firelight into the wooded inner part of the circle of trees where Abe and Alicia sheltered. It made Abe think of Hell and he half expected imps with forks and tails to come prancing out of the furnace to stab and prick him and generally make life even worse than it was at this moment.

Slowly, he got to his feet. 'We should move,' he said. 'We should get as far away from here as we can. If this doesn't bring all your mother's friends down on us like a plague of hornets I don't know what will.'

'A tree does take a long time to burn,' said Alicia. She didn't seem inclined to move.

'Yes,' said Abe impatiently, 'the more chance that more people will see it. Why did you do it, anyway? That gang had been gone about half an hour when you came to. I was watching over you, you know.' He wanted to say guarding because it sounded better but the truth was he felt he should have done better guarding before they were robbed, not after.

'I was cross,' said Alicia. 'It just happened, so don't go on about it. I suppose I was about to do something just at the moment I got hit and so whatever the something was happened when I woke up.'

'Something?' said Abe. 'That is a very fine something, a burning tree. Next time when you are going to do one of your somethings, Alicia, perhaps you can make sure that I am not in danger. I could have been like that tree.'

'Don't be so silly.' She stood up and dusted her hands. 'I would never do that to you.'

'How do you know? If these things just "happen" when you get cross, anyone could be hurt. You are very dangerous, Alicia.'

'Yes,' she said simply, 'I suppose I am, but it has got us out of trouble a couple of times, hasn't it?'

'Yes.' Abe had to agree. The first time she had used this wild magic of hers, it had enabled them—Alicia, himself, and the team of old men—to escape from the witches when it had seemed certain they would all be turned to worms or into a photograph and hung on a wall for ever · and ever. She'd exploded with zigzagging lightning of blue flame; cars had exploded; her mother and the rest of the witches had howled louder than all the dogs of Britain. One of them had been hurled through a hole ripped in the night. She had been marvellous and terrifying. Twenty minutes ago she had just been terrifying. 'We'll go,' he said decisively.

'All right, but you were the one who said it was safe up here.' She felt both her ears. 'They didn't get all the rings. I suppose that's something but if I find those smelly bearded thieves again, I'll frizzle them. Which way, Nasfali? You're the trailfinder.'

At that moment there was a tearing crack and the top half of the blazing tree slowly folded down on itself. As if, thought Abe, it was making a bow. 'Everything else is going to catch fire,' he said. 'Can't you do anything about it. If you started it you should be able to put it out.'

'I should, shouldn't I,' said Alicia, 'but I am just not sure how.' She stared at the fire and frowned. Nothing happened. 'I can't concentrate,' she said. 'There's someone coming and I can't concentrate on a stupid tree. Let's just leave it. Trees grow again, don't they. Which way?'

'East, I suppose,' said Abe, nervously glancing up at the night sky half expecting the sisters of Britain to come riddling down at them like black ash. 'But I can't see the North Star because of the flames. Let's just take a chance, come on.'

He led the way through the centre of the ring and away from the trees, then followed the raised mound, the old fort wall, until he came to a gap and a path. Hoping it didn't lead back down to the road but along the high downs, he said, 'We'll take a chance on this.'

'We're too late. I can hear horses.'

Abe could hear them too; hard to tell how many. Wasn't it too steep to ride? He could hear the scuffle of hoof on stone, and the snorting breath of a straining animal.

'Back,' he whispered. 'We'll slip down the other side.' Lakins, he thought. Could it be Lakins on horseback, drawn by Alicia's magic? No. No, Lakins didn't ride. Who then?

Keeping low, so they didn't show a silhouette against the sky, they scurried back round to where Abe reckoned they had first climbed up and onto the ring. But just as they came up to the edge, one, two, three horsemen breasted the rise. Their mounts, eyes rolling white at the sight of the fire, snorted and whinnied until they were reined in and settled by their riders. Abe and Alicia turned but again too late—coming up behind them was another rider, and from the far side two more came threading through the trees. The riders closed in around them. Abe and Alicia stood still and waited.

'Shouldn't you do something?' whispered Abe.

'You mean another tree?' said Alicia, not bothering to keep her voice quiet at all. 'I thought you disapproved of that. Or do you mean a different sort of something . . .'

'That'll do.'

It was one of the riders who had spoken but it was hard to tell which one: they simply looked like dark figures on horseback, six of them. The horses seemed very large to Abe. The riders, their faces lost in shadow, sat motionless.

Alicia ignored the man's command. 'I don't think we need worry about these people, Nasfali, they are certainly nothing to do with my mother, and my bet is they are nothing to do with thieves either.' She pitched her voice a little louder. 'You're not thieves, are you?'

'That's ripe,' said one of the riders.

'No,' said the one who had spoken first and who edged his horse a little closer to Abe and Alicia. 'Are you? You look like out-people to me, scruffs, strays. We keep a lookout for such as you. Arsonists and suchlike.' He pointed to the tree. 'You did that.'

'No,' said Abe instinctively.

'Oh yes,' said Alicia as if he hadn't spoken, 'I did. But it was an accident.'

The horse snorted and stamped as if irritated by Alicia's cool answer.

'Accident?' exclaimed the leader. 'Takes more than a few sparks from a campfire to set a blaze like this. What's your game?'

'Hang 'em.'

'Make an example.'

One of the riders to Abe's right nudged his horse a little closer and seemed to be peering at them and Abe thought he heard him chuckle a quiet, raspy, 'He-he-he.'

Were they serious? They couldn't be. Alicia, however, didn't seem bothered. 'Not a game at all. We were attacked. I was hit on the head and we were robbed. If you're looking for robbers you should be hunting them, not holding us.'

The man leaned forward and pushed back the hood of his cape so that Abe could see his face for the first time. A young man, serious but not aggressive. A man of authority. Not a ruffian. 'How many?' he said.

'Five, six. They took our food supplies and some silver rings that I had.'

'That so?' He swung down from his horse and walked towards them. 'Let's see the injury then.'

Alicia turned her head sideways.

'Nasty bump, missy. Let's see your hands.'

To Abe's surprise Alicia meekly did what she was told.

'You too,' he said to Abe and then barely glanced at them when Abe held his out. His eyes were on Alicia.

'I know her.' It was the rider to Abe's right, the one with the elderly, raspy voice. He chuckled again. 'Him too. Know them both. Know them both.'

'That's enough, Uncle. You promised you would be quiet if you came out with us.'

'Righto, Ralphy.'

'Knows everyone, silly old fool,' muttered one of the others.

'Quiet.' The tone was firm. The young man clearly was used to leading this group and to having them obey him without question. 'You better come with us,' he said to Abe and Alicia. 'Give you shelter for the night and help you on your way tomorrow if we can.' He turned to the riders. 'Walter.'

'Sir.'

'Barnaby.'

'Sir.'

'Stay up here till the tree falls, and then beat out the fire. Don't want to lose the whole plantation. Though I reckon we'll have rain by morning anyhow. Matthew. Luke. Take the roundway back, see if you pick up signs of that gang of out-people this girl speaks of. Be wary. Don't tangle. Just note where they be and then head home. We'll scout for them tomorrow.' He swung himself up onto his horse and offered a hand to Alicia. 'You can ride behind me, missy.'

'Wicked,' said Alicia, but Abe didn't think the man heard, which he felt was probably just as well.

'What about me?'

'You can ride behind Uncle. It's nothing but a half hour to the farm. You can tell us your full story when we're there.'

The man called Uncle leaned down and offered Abe a bony hand and then with a surprisingly hard grip yanked him up and immediately wheeled the horse about and followed Ralph and Alicia who had started their scrambling descent. 'Hold tight.'

'Thank you,' said Abe and then gripped the man's waist as the horse made a lurch and then steadied. 'How can you see?' he asked. With their backs to the flaming tree, the night seemed as dark as pitch.

'Plenty of carrots,' said the man with his raspy chuckle. 'Home again, home again, jiggety jig.'

It seemed a long and uncomfortable half hour to Abe. They followed a thin track to the disused road and then forded a small stream and skirted a heavy black wood from which they caught a pungent musky scent that had the two horses throwing back their heads and snorting with fright. Then they climbed again, crossed an open meadow, and there, lit up like a liner, was what the young man had called 'the farm'. Abe had a curious feeling that he had been there before. Once again he thought of the team and Stokely, the one whose family had lived in Sussex. But his home had been nothing like this. This was more a fortress than a farm. The main building was circled by a high wooden stockade. A voice challenged them when they came to the gate.

'It's me, Ralph,' said the young man. 'The others will be following. And we're bringing in a pair of strays that we'll put up for the night.'

'Very good, sir.'

The gate creaked open and they rode in and up to the main door where they dismounted. Uncle led the horses off to the stable, still cheerfully muttering to himself, while Ralph showed them into the building. 'This is what we call a Friend's House,' he said. 'There are not so many of them now but it's said you can make your way the length and breadth of the country finding shelter in one of these. Come into the meeting hall.'

'Well,' said Alicia, taking in the deep fireplace and the chairs layered in sheepskin and the long table with a smoke-stained cauldron of something hot and sweet-smelling steaming on it. 'This is more what I had in mind than that horrible outdoors camping you like so much, Nasfali.'

To Abe, the room looked almost like one of those illustrated books of how people lived in medieval times. Almost but not quite. There were light bulbs for a start which hummed very faintly and there was glass in the windows. But there was also a rough, home-made feel to the place: hewn benches, bare boards underfoot, a brightly dyed tapestry on the wall of dogs hunting a sharp-toothed black pig such as Abe had never seen but recognized as a wild boar, and a half-completed tapestry stretched on a frame.

Ralph invited them to sit and served them stew and big chunks of crumbly brown bread. They gorged themselves and sopped up the juice with the bread. Meanwhile the room gradually filled around them with men and women; no children or people their age. Some joined them at the table, others took the chairs or leaned against the wall, talking quietly among themselves but watching them, waiting for them to finish. Abe looked around for the one they had called 'Uncle' but though there were a number of older people he wasn't sure that he was one of them.

'Thank you,' said Alicia eventually, pushing her bowl away. 'I was ravenous. We haven't eaten properly for days.'

At that moment the door opened again and an elderly woman came into the room. She was flanked on one side by a younger woman and on the other by a man who seemed elderly too but Abe couldn't see him properly. It was the old woman who caught his attention: she was charcoal-haired with a strong, kindly face but with the most piercing eyes and the blackest and thickest of eyebrows he had ever seen. She was obviously important because instantly everyone in the room stopped talking. But she wasn't dressed as an old person should be. She was wearing an oily blue sweater with a crew neck and old blue jeans with splashes of paint on them. She came to the head of the table and Ralph stood up.

'This is they, Aunt Ida, the strays that set fire to Chanctonbury Ring.'

'I can see them,' she said, 'I can see them plain as day and they are not from hereabouts nor from anyplace this side of the south country. And you, miss, I can tell you are not one of us folk, isn't that right?'

All eyes in the room focused on Alicia who sat pale faced, her eyes shadowed with tiredness, but quite calm as she looked straight back at the woman called Ida. 'No, I am different to you. So is Nasfali. More different than you could ever imagine, I suspect.'

Abe nodded. Yes, he was very different, not quite like Alicia, of course, but parents just made you different, didn't they, particularly if one of them was a witch.

Ida's attention turned to him. 'Oh,' she said, 'of course, the boy. A pair. How old are you, boy?'

'Thirteen but . . . ' he hesitated . . . 'perhaps fifteen . . . ' His voice trailed into silence. It was too difficult to explain that he had given a couple of years of his life to Jonson. He and his father had cheated death, just for a little, and then, of course, Jonson had escaped back through time to his childhood, so he had done all right, and Abe hadn't minded looking a couple of years older.

She gave a half smile. 'Uncle has no idea how old he is, either. Do you, Uncle?'

The elderly man who had come in with Ida pulled up

a seat for her, and as he did so he winked at Abe and Abe felt as if he had been flapped in the face with a smelly wet towel. It was him! Of course, it was him. He should have known from his first words up there on the ring. 'Somewhere between thirteen and a hundred and forty at the last count,' and the old man chuckled quietly to himself. Then, a little shyly, he said, 'Hello, skipper. Hello, Miss Dunne.' And he turned to Ida and said, 'And he's half Egyptian, Ida, that's pretty jolly different, wouldn't you say.'

Alicia, as soon as the old man had spoken, was sitting up ramrod straight, gazing at him. 'Stokely,' she breathed. 'How thoroughly wicked. Nasfali, are you impressed?'

'Very, and indeed most thoroughly impressed,' exclaimed Abe, jumping to his feet and vigorously shaking Stokely by the hand.

'Now we are going to have some sport,' said Stokely. 'You just wait and see, Ida. I told you about these two, didn't I?'

'Yes,' she said. 'Many, many times.'

SEVEN

If the people of the house had previously thought Stokely's stories were just the ramblings of a dotty old man, they listened carefully now. He took them from when the last goal had been scored against the Italians at the great match in front of the pyramid at Giza to the moment of their homecoming.

'It was like chucking off stinky old clothes,' he said, trying to explain what it felt like to lose the wrinkles and aching bones of old age and become young again, and springy as a whippet. 'We were jumping and giving three blinking great cheers and when I jumped my feet just jolly well didn't touch the ground again. It was like going up for ever.' He paused. 'It was you, Miss Dunne, wasn't it?' Alicia nodded. 'I knew it. You always promised you'd get us home. So I was positive it was you because when that funny peculiar bit was over we weren't together, me and the rest of the chaps, but I was in front of my own front door and my mum was there and so was dear old Ida. Except she wasn't old then, were you, you dear old thing,' he said and patted her on the arm.

'We're both old now, Uncle.'

'My sister,' he said admiringly. 'Total sprog then, but she's the mum now. Have to watch my p's and q's.' For a fleeting moment Abe wondered where Stokely kept his p's and q's and why they needed watching and then Stokely continued.

'It was the summer holidays and everything was nearly perfect, except because of the war all the dads were away. Griffin came over once—he was contacting all the team— making everyone promise never to talk about what had happened because it was too confusing. Griffin had said that if we tried to explain about the spell and being dumped in a photograph no one would believe us. They would think we were bonkers and lock us away. So it was total hush-hush,' and he tapped his nose and closed one eye so that Alicia would be perfectly clear what hush-hush meant. He then told them how once that summer ended, the happy days were over.

Back at Prackton Hall the team were together again so life should have been bearable but it wasn't. Deadly Delia, Alicia's horrible mother, made each day a misery even though they did their darndest to be nice. Nothing went right: the war went on, and on and on, the terms became longer, the years rolled by, and the team didn't do so well. Not at all.

'Dim,' said Stokely. 'All of us in the team seemed to be jolly jolly dim. Couldn't pass a single bally exam.'

Bally, thought Abe, somehow comforted by the sound of the odd words the team always used.

Then, one by one, Stokely told them, the team began to bunk off school. It wasn't planned; they didn't even discuss it with each other but they just couldn't hack it any longer: they were always on washing-up duty and shoe polishing each time they failed a test. They were made to stand in the corridor. They were beaten. They used to say that they'd had more laughs stuck up on the wall watching Abe being punished.

While the others had slipped away home, Jonson, Thomas, and himself had hung on, didn't really know why, they just had. They learned later that it hadn't been happy times for the others though. Being older, sixteen now, their mothers and fathers thought they should be working or helping in the war effort. But the boys didn't get jobs. How could they? They wanted to play football and have fun and so eventually they drifted away from their homes and lost touch with each other.

'They kept telling us to grow up,' he said. 'What does that mean? It doesn't mean anything, does it? You can't just grow up like that. You just are, aren't you, Miss Dunne?'

'Yes,' she said, 'we all just "are", Stokely.'

But Abe sat there wondering why the boys hadn't grown up. Was it the change, Alicia's tampering with the laws of time? Had that stopped them from being like other young boys? Or was it Mrs Dunne's fault? She was the one who had cast the first spell, locked them for sixty years in a photograph.

To Abe, Stokely seemed no different at all from when he had last seen him and yet he had lived practically a whole lifetime since then. There he was, hair just as grey, thick wild eyebrows and that way of ducking his head when he talked, and breaking into little chuckles for no real reason. But he had seen the world change in a way that was entirely different to all the history that Abe had ever learned.

'At last we couldn't put up with it either,' continued Stokely. 'Thomas told us that he was going and if we wanted we could come with him. I thought it was a cracking idea because I'd always loved Thomas's stories about being allowed to drive his dad's tractor. So we packed our bags, stuffed dressing gowns down our beds, and in the middle of one night we did a major bunk. Luckily for us Thomas's old mother and father were happy to have the three of us living on their farm, because the work was hard and they needed our help.

'We jolly well did work too: we milked and cleaned; we mended stone walls in the fields—Jonson was good at that—and herded sheep too—Thomas had a knack with the dogs; but we still larked about, and that was all right. Nobody minded us up there on that hill farm and Mr and Mrs T were as nice a mum and dad as anyone could hope for.

'When the war finally ended,' Stokely said, 'there was quite a ballyhoo and all sorts of celebrations that we heard about on the wireless. It seemed everyone was terribly happy—old Mrs Thomas certainly was, though all she said was: "Well, this is a wonderful thing now, isn't it."

As it turned out, it wasn't such a wonderful thing because once the soldiers started to come home and there was a general election the sisters started taking over. Parliament and what not,' Stokely said. 'Spies and very peculiar things happening. Didn't care too much about it but there you are. Perfectly ghastly and everything tumbled backwards. We ran out of petrol, then diesel, so that put paid to the tractor. Mrs T couldn't get the food she wanted from the shop and then the wireless conked out. Never listened to one since either.

'However, the really big change for us came when Thomas's dad went off down the mountain one day, taking sheep to market, and he never came back. Nobody told us what had happened to him but Thomas's mum became fearfully sad. She went into her room and wouldn't come out. We brought her her favourite food, you know, but she wouldn't eat a thing,' he said. 'And she was such a nice woman. She knitted me a jumper.

'By the end of the week poor Mrs Thomas was dead. We buried her in the orchard beneath her favourite tree. And that was really the end of it all. The three of us tried hard but we couldn't manage the business, the bills and the harvest and buying and selling sheep. It all became very leaky: lambs died, we had no money to buy food, the windows got so dirty we couldn't see out and we never could find our socks. Thomas didn't talk at all and Jonno said that he was fed up not knowing anything and he wanted to go somewhere where he could read lots. But he wouldn't leave Thomas, though, not on his own.

'You know I just got so miserable that one morning I got up to milk the cow—we only had one left by that time—couldn't find it in the field where it should have been and somehow I kept walking. Someone gave me a lift in a lorry and a few days later I found myself back in Sussex walking up to my home and there was Ida, which was splendid because I needed a bath and was really jolly tired of being on my own. Should have come here first, I know. Shouldn't have gone off with Thomas and Jonno but they were always my special chums.'

He stopped and ducked his head to chuckle. 'And I knew we would see you again, you and the skipper. Me, Thomas, and Jonno often said it would all come out all right in the end, when we found the skipper and Miss Dunne. Of course, we only whispered it because it was a secret, and we didn't want anyone to know and think we were thoroughly bonkers. Ida did think I was a bit bonkers but she's a decent old thing, if a bit fierce.' He waved his bony hands around, somehow including everyone in the room. 'They're all terribly decent here, but . . . ' He winked and tapped his nose, and lowered his voice, 'Ralph's bossy.' Stokely subsided into his quiet little chuckle, nodding his head and blinking his eyes.

'The others,' said Alicia, 'what happened to them? Did you ever see them again?'

Griffin, Roberts, Chivers, thought Abe, remembering how he had been made to stand down in the corridor in front of their team photograph, 1942, chanting their names like the evening call to prayer. Thomas, Stokely, Bittern, Pike and Johnson, Jissop, Jack and Gannet.

'Oh, Jonno went to Oxford,' said Stokely. 'Always talked about it. He wrote me a letter and told me that Thomas had joined him there. Jonno's really clever, you know, used to think an awful lot, made him a bit absent minded. Did I ever write back to him, Ida? I hope I did.'

Ida didn't answer. She was watching Alicia.

'And the others?'

'Oh, don't really know,' said Stokely, quietly chuckling to himself. 'Not seen a whisker in a fair while . . . Jonson said he was being a bit of a Sherlock Holmes, trying to trace them all. He might know a thing or two.'

Abe looked at him and had the odd feeling that Stokely wasn't quite telling them everything he knew. At that moment Stokely caught his eye. 'Maybe now, eh, skipper, maybe now we'll all get together again.' He tapped the side of his nose and gave a wink. Then he turned to Alicia. 'And you're bound to need us, Miss Dunne, aren't you?'

Alicia smiled. 'We'll see.'

'Stop there! You'll decide nothing, young miss,' said Ida. 'Not till there is a talking in this hall. I tell you that now. No one is going outside the bounds unless there is a fierce good reason.' There was a murmur of agreement to this.

'But, Ida,' protested old Stokely, 'this is *the* Miss Dunne. You can't get all waxy . . . '

'Uncle, you've had your say. You know the rules.' Ida looked sternly at her brother.

'Rules,' grumbled Stokely. 'There's always rules. Fed up to the back teeth with them . . . ' but his voice dropped, and his head dropped, and his complaining sank into a sleepy mumble.

Ida watched him, though not unkindly, and when Stokely's chin was well and truly resting on his chest and his eyes were fast shut, she turned back to Alicia and Abe. There was something bird-like about her—not frail but fierce: jet black eyes that glinted in the light, and a beaky nose. A desert eagle, thought Abe, a match for the sisters. She folded her hands and rested them on her knees. 'We folk up here on the safe Downs must be careful. We have to watch all the time, else the danger is that we'll lose what we have. Even Uncle knows that. My family thought he was soft in the head and none of us knew what to make of his stories but it looks like there's truth in them after all. My reckoning is that he is not so much soft as he belongs to another time, not this here and this now. I blame the sisters and their filthy magic, polluting the country, making life impossible.' She eyed Alicia. 'But they leave us alone up here for the time being though there seems neither rhyme nor reason as to why they do.'

'They get caught up by little things,' said Alicia, 'and then they can't see anything else. They're stupid but they're also dangerous. Aren't they, Nasfali?'

'Indeed,' said Abe, 'as are the snakes of the desert.'

'Yes,' Ida interrupted. 'Well, I imagine that you should know, young miss. You have a pointy look about you. So much so that I would say that you could be one of they sisters yourself.'

There was a stir in the room: couples glanced at each other; one or two, Abe saw, crossed their fingers; others touched an amulet worn round the neck and next to the skin. This is what they had to deal with the power of the witches: good-luck signs and charms. It wasn't much.

Over by the door were two heavy looking men, grizzly, with black spade-shaped beards and thick hairy forearms. They didn't look as if they needed good luck charms. Their expressions were less than friendly and one of them was hefting a black club. Abe glanced round the room to see if there was another exit. There wasn't.

Alicia, however, ignored the stir. 'Yes,' she said, 'of course I am. I would have thought it was very obvious. But,' she said, raising her voice, so that everyone could hear clearly, 'I am not with them and nor is Nasfali. We want to put things right.'

'What's "right"?' said Ralph, speaking for the first time. 'We've learned to live and let live. What do you propose to change, missy? Get rid of the out-people and they witches? Clean the scrub-lands of their dirt magic . . . '

Abe wasn't sure he understood exactly what Ralph meant other than things were a mess, but Alicia was her usual businesslike self. 'I mean make it better,' said Alicia. 'Break their power, if we can.'

'I see,' said Ida, 'and how will you do that?'

Alicia didn't tell them about the great book that Abe's mother had stolen, instead she described how all the witches learned their magic from books which they kept in a library in Prackton Hall so they were going to go there and destroy the library. Simple. 'No books,' said Alicia, 'no new spells and so they won't be able to train any of their children. It will break the chain.' It sounded reasonable to Abe; it just wasn't what he and she had planned.

'I see,' said Ida again, though Abe had the feeling that when she said this it meant something completely different.

'And they sisters will let you go into this place, Prackton, just like that?' Ralph shook his head. 'I've been there. Walter was with me, weren't you, Walt?'

Abe recognized one of the riders who had surrounded them up on the Ring. 'I was,' he said, 'and never again, I hope.'

'Never again is right,' said Ralph. 'Brighton's where they-people breed. Witches, slaves, and armies of that monster. It was a war camp,' he said. 'Hammering and burning and marching and more ruins than buildings. I tell you there may be no walls round the town but it's a fort all the same, fort or prison, depending on whether you want to get in or out.'

'How did you get in then?'

'They called a big meeting—that's why we went. Someone had to. They wanted all the farmers to come in. Witches got to eat like other folk, I reckon. It was business so they let us in and they let most of us out again too.'

'So farmers make deliveries into the town?'

'They do.'

Alicia's eyes lit up. 'Well, there's our way then.'

'Not for us-people,' said Ralph, looking at Ida. 'We agreed on it long ago. Those that live on safe land, stay on safe land. We don't go near any towns, and I told you the witches, the sisters as you call them, keep out of the country, round hereabouts anyways.'

'But will you at least help us to get there?' asked Alicia. 'Nasfali is hopeless at finding his way. Ask him, he's only any good in the desert and things like that. It would take years if it were just the two of us.'

'Excuse me!' This was not so at all. He had led her safely

out of the town and up onto the Downs. He appealed to Ralph. 'Was I right to take the high ground?'

'High ground is best,' Ralph agreed, 'but that's where you meet out-folk, as you did. Small bands of them all over, thieving, scraping a living. Can't blame them for not wanting to go into the towns but they cause us a headache. We're always driving them away.'

Abe remembered the way they had drifted out of the trees as silent as shadows. Organized they would be quite a force. He stored the thought away in the back of his mind.

'So,' said Alicia, looking intently at Ralph, and Abe could tell that she was trying to use some power on him, 'will you help us? Will you?' He shifted and looked uncomfortable.

Ida suddenly rapped her knuckle on the table. 'That will do,' she said sharply. 'We'll have none of that here, thank you.'

Alicia sat back, a little startled, Abe thought, at being spoken to like that, but she nodded as if accepting what the old woman had said.

Ida then leaned back and looked around the room which seemed to be an understood signal that anyone could ask questions now. Immediately one of the young women said: 'You can't use magic? If you're one of they-people, I reckon you can fly.' Others in the room nodded their agreement, and murmured. They didn't like having Alicia there, a witch in their friendly house. They were nervous. Only Ida and Stokely didn't seem to mind.

'If I use any of what you call magic, they will find me. We have to surprise them.'

'If you be one of they-people,' said one of the others, 'why don't you be with them?'

'I didn't choose to be what I am,' said Alicia with uncharacteristic patience. 'My mother was or maybe still is my enemy. They want me to join them but I never shall.'

There it was, simply said, and the people in the room liked hearing it.

For the third time, Alicia asked her question, and this time she directed it to Ida. 'Will you help? What we want to do is for the best, I promise you.'

'Sometimes,' said Ida, 'the road to hell is paved with good intentions, but if nothing is tried, nothing will change. We will take you as far as we can.'

Stokely opened his eyes. Abe had the feeling he had been listening all the time. 'And I shall help,' said Stokely. 'I know the best way to Brighton.'

'You're not going anywhere,' said Ida, 'except to bed.'

'He could do it,' said Ralph. 'Uncle is one of my best riders, Ida. You know that.'

'I shall sleep on it,' said Ida and then, with some difficulty, she rose to her feet. Stokely stood too. 'The meeting is over,' she said and then closed her eyes. 'Bless this house,' she said quietly.

'Bless this house,' echoed all the people in the room.

'You,' she said to Abe. 'Take my arm. We'll go up to my studio. Uncle, you will come too and your Miss Dunne. I would like a word in private, if you don't mind.'

Abe offered her his arm and she gripped it with a surprisingly tight grip. 'Are you the reason the witches are hunting down boys?' she asked quietly as they headed out of the room.

'I think I might be,' said Abe. 'Alicia's mother never liked me very much, nor did my own.'

'Whyever not?' said Ida.

EIGHT

O ranges.

He blinked as Stokely held up the storm lantern he'd been carrying and revealed the room to them: a floor planked and spattered with gobs and blobs of paint and odd patches of carpet, and every surface scattered with jars and cracked saucers, little boxes, rags and scraps of paper. And oranges. 'Ida's den,' he said proudly.

Oranges. Everywhere. All over the wall, paintings of oranges: oranges in bowls, oranges on plates, oranges sliced in half, and so oozing with juice that Abe felt his mouth water, and one giant orange smack in the middle of the wall blazing on a sky-blue canvas, like the sun scorching high above Cairo. And stacked in a corner more paintings. What was this? It was so late, they had walked so far, his legs ached and his eyes ached and all these oranges made him feel dizzy. What was this place they had come to, this safe house, with its bounds that its riders patrolled; and who was this wiry old woman, this sister of Stokely, who ruled the house and the riders, and whom the witches left alone?

'Sit,' said Ida, indicating the two hard-backed chairs and a scruffy sofa placed in the centre of the cluttered room.

He took one end of the sofa and Alicia the other and watched as Ida reached up and adjusted the wick on a second lamp hooked up on a central beam. He sniffed suddenly. It wasn't paint or the canvas and oils, but something else; a thought more than a smell, a feeling more than a thought, a whisper of feeling. And up here it felt somehow different to downstairs. 'Ida's den.' He rubbed a knuckle in his eye and then without meaning to sniffed again, loudly. 'Sorry,' he muttered, aware of Alicia glancing at him. What was it? Something he couldn't quite catch. Power? She couldn't be like them, could she, like the sisters? After all she was a sister, Stokely's sister . . . his mind was beginning to rattle in circles. Of course, being a sister didn't mean she was a witch, that would make no sense . . . like all these oranges. Her hands were not those of an old person—they were hard, bony but weathered, brown not spotty. He remembered the tight grip on his arm. She would keep a tight grip on them all.

'Now, we can speak plain.' Ida took the chair opposite them. Stokely folded himself down onto the second chair, his eyes permanently wrinkled into a secret smile. Ida didn't smile. 'I don't usually let anyone in here, apart from Uncle.' She folded her hands in her lap and looked straight at Alicia.

He sensed Alicia bristling with tension. 'Why us then?'

Why did she have to sound so rude? 'It is a kindness, Alicia, hospitality. Isn't it?' Abe appealed to Stokely who nodded his agreement. There was no reason to fight; they needed Ida's help.

'Because,' said Ida evenly, 'you can do none of your pointy harm up here.'

That was it. Abe could almost hear the sound of sharp claws scratching the air. He closed his eyes. 'What harm exactly do you think I mean to do?' The hiss of a curved scimitar drawn from its scabbard.

'I don't know that your kind ever mean to do harm . . . '

'They're not my kind. I told you that before.'

'You did but even though you say it, you're not sure, are you? You are not sure that it is so. Can you put hand on heart and swear?'

'If I was their kind, I wouldn't be here, would I? Your doubting us is stupid.'

'I know what I see. No matter what Uncle says about

50

you, you don't belong among us safe folk. So you can go and with our blessing but you'll take none of our young men as guides. And there's an end on it.'

'You're a selfish old woman,' said Alicia. 'You don't care what happens to anyone who doesn't belong to you. You don't care about the sisters and what they do and what misery they cause. You just want to be safe.'

'Is that so terrible?'

'It's wrong. Places like this . . . '

Both women sat still, stiff, tense, their words snapped back and forth, duelling. The rattle and spark of swords clashing and at the end there would be blood on the blade and no victors. They should be allies not enemies.

'If there are other places like this,' interrupted Ida.

Alicia ignored her. ' . . . won't last. The sisters will take their time but this will go. They'll make everywhere the same. Someone like you,' she said flatly, 'can't stop them.'

He must stop them, thought Abe.

'And you can?'

'I can at least try,' said Alicia icily.

Abe saw his opportunity. 'She has a track record,' he said.

Ida's hawklike face turned to him.

'Look,' he said, indicating Stokely, 'your very own dear brother, Miss Stokely, brought back to you across the great chasm of time.' That did sound good, he thought: 'chasm of time' would even impress Alicia.

'So you say, but what's that to me? What proof is that of anything but trickery and magic? And where do you stand in all this, you who sit there and give us hardly a whisper and then say this thing? What kind of a puzzle are you, boy?'

'I merely say,' said Abe, 'that Miss Dunne can do much good.'

'And that is not worth half a reckoning in my mind. Perhaps she brought him back, for sure that is what he thinks happened. I don't know the half ways of magic and

I don't want to but if she did do that, then maybe she has some accounting for him being the way he is now.'

'And how is he?' said Alicia. 'He looks as he has always looked to me. He is as he was.'

'That's it,' said Ida. 'He's not changed a whisker.'

'But he's old.'

'Of course he is old. I am old. I am old on the outside and I am old on the inside.'

'I understand,' said Abe. 'It is important not to pretend.'

'You don't understand at all,' she said curtly. 'He hasn't grown up. He's trapped. He's never grown up. He's a simpleton. Aren't you, Uncle? Soft in the head.'

'If you say so, old fish,' and he gave Abe a knowing wink, 'but I'm blinking good at horses, footer . . . '

'That'll do, Uncle.' She pointed a bony finger at Alicia.

'No,' said Abe alarmed. 'Don't do that. Don't point! Alicia doesn't like . . . '

'Nasfali, be quiet.'

Ida ignored the interruptions. 'And it seems you did that to him. Now do you understand, young miss? You do what you think is a good thing and then something bad comes along with it—everything has its shadow, then half the good is gone.' She sounded a little like his father.

'Better half the good, than no good at all.'

The two women held each other's gaze for a long moment and Abe held his breath. And then it was as if there was a silent sheathing of swords and Ida's stern expression relaxed slightly. She nodded. 'That's worth a maybe,' she said. 'But I still won't have you taking my Ralph and others of the young men out beyond the bounds. They that go beyond do not come back.'

'You still won't help us?'

Ida chose not to answer that. 'Why do those women you call sisters and I call foul she-things scour up-dale and down for boys and ship them off to sea, and they have no eyes for you?'

'They don't like boys,' said Abe. He held out his hands apologetically. 'This is it.'

'It's because he was a mistake,' said Alicia impatiently. 'The sisters don't have boy children; they just don't. Not until Nasfali broke the mould. It rattled my mother. She couldn't stand him. Even your own mother couldn't bear you, could she, Nasfali?'

It was no time to be sensitive. Nasfali sat up straight on the old sofa. 'I am half Egyptian,' he said. 'It is true, I am very different to Alicia. My father is a man, I think, of some power, but if it is me that they seek, I don't know why.'

'Mayhap you're the one who is going to rattle their cage,' said Ida thoughtfully.

'I am good at plans,' he agreed. 'I have great schemes.' He hesitated. 'I don't think I am very good at cages.' She continued to fix him with her eagle eyes and he had the horrible feeling that had she an eagle's beak and an eagle's talons she could sweep him away; she could snatch him up and hurl him down from a great height. This is what it is to be a rabbit, he thought.

'You aren't,' hissed Alicia.

It was so very late and they had walked from Worthing to the high Downs, they had been chased and set on by out-folk who would have left them for dead, and now his head was swimming. But no, no he wasn't a rabbit. 'I came back,' he said. 'And I didn't have to. I came back because Alicia asked me. Because there is so much to do to get things back the way they were.'

'Were things better?'

'Not for him,' said Alicia, 'he was always being punished. Weren't you, Nasfali?'

'It is true,' said Abe. 'School was a prison for me, and running away was an adventure. And Cairo I now know is my home. Not here. But I am glad for everything we did because when we ran we were free. And the team won their great game.'

'Yes, we bally well did!' exclaimed Stokely.

'But you came back.'

'Of course,' said Abe. 'I told you: because Alicia asked me. But there is another reason,' he said, remembering the terrible twilight world into which his mother had thrown him, where he would still be if Alicia hadn't rescued him. 'I know what these sisters will make of this world; they will make it a place without hope, without colour, without beginning and without end; it will stretch away in dirt, and rubbish, and terrible, terrible sadness. And this is what they do. This is what they will do to this place; they will make it all their prison.' He thought of the decayed streets of Worthing, the shadowy children flitting through the husks of vandalized stores and derelict houses. 'Indeed, they have already begun to do so.'

Alicia sniffed. 'Unlike a lot of boys,' she said, 'Nasfali is not stupid.'

High praise!

'This is a fact,' said Ida and then for the first time since they had come into the room, she turned to Stokely. 'What do you think, Uncle? Do you know how we can help them without jeopardizing the safety of all our folk?'

He gave a contented chuckle, as if he had known all along that this was where the meeting would end. 'I'd say I do, old thing. And I'll take them to Brighton, because I know the way and nothing happens to me when I go outside the bounds.'

'Is this true?' asked Alicia.

Ida nodded. 'Yes. It is one of the ways that things are. Uncle always goes with the riders and no harm ever comes to him. He goes off on his own too, on what he calls "his holidays" and he sometimes goes to the coast, don't you, Uncle, for your secret.'

'You know about my secret?' Stokely's weather-beaten face flushed a darker shade. 'Who told you?'

'It's all right,' said Ida softly. 'Don't fret . . .'

'But you'll stop me. My one thing. You'll stop me and take it from me!'

'No.' Ida's voice was firm. 'I will take nothing from you.' She patted his hand. 'For as long as I run this safe home, you can do as you always have done, just so long as you come home to me, Uncle, that you must promise.'

'So I can take them?'

She hesitated and then said: 'I am not sure that it would be wise.'

'But you know what I have told you is right and true,' said Abe. 'We will bring him back to you.'

'He only has to guide us to the way into Brighton. He won't actually come in with us,' added Alicia.

'And,' said Abe, keenly studying the expression on Ida's face and trying to judge how much he needed to haggle, 'once we have found out if there are other safe houses, we'll help you to get in touch with them, won't we, Alicia?'

'Of course.'

'This would be good,' Ida nodded.

'And,' said Abe, his eyes moving from one picture to the next, 'I will bring you such succulent oranges as you have never dreamed of.'

'Ah,' she said, 'you like to barter.'

'He calls it haggling,' said Alicia. 'It's not a word I like.'

'You know,' said Ida, 'I haven't seen an orange for more than fifty years. Just after the war, there were a few, and then that was it. I suppose you always long for what you cannot have.'

'We have oranges in Egypt,' said Abe. 'Oranges that I could pile higher than the pyramids of Giza . . . '

'Don't overdo it, Nasfali.'

'I will agree,' said Ida. 'But you come home, Uncle. Do you hear?'

'Of course, old thing.'

NINE

They rode through the wooden gates of the safe house just before first light. Ida didn't come out to see them; they left her sitting in her high-backed chair in the meeting hall. 'Bring my brother home safe,' is all she said. 'I'd not forgive you for losing him.'

'Of course,' Alicia said, but once they were outside the door, she gripped Abe's elbow. 'How dare she talk to me like that! Who does she think she is? Doesn't she know who I am?'

'One should make allowances,' he said, 'for one's elders. Respect is a good thing, Alicia.'

For a moment she looked as though she would shrivel him into charred mouse meat and then with a half sniff, half laugh, she said, 'Like the respect you gave my mother?'

'Your mother was a witch.'

'Yes, well, I think Stokely's sister is the next best thing. She had better mind how she speaks to me when we next meet.'

The three horses were waiting for them in the wide courtyard; Stokely was already mounted. Ralph was holding their horses. Another couple of men were standing by, torches in their hands to give them light. 'You all right to ride on your own, missy?' Ralph said to Alicia.

'I don't mind horses at all,' said Alicia, staring her horse in the eyes, until it ducked its head submissively. 'Just give me a leg up, would you?' And then once mounted, she looked like a queen. 'Hurry up, Nasfali,' she said, 'we want to be off.'

'The camels of the desert kneel,' said Abe, struggling to get even his first foot in the stirrup.

'You have never ridden a camel,' said Alicia.

'Some things,' said Abe stiffly, 'are in the blood.'

Then with a grunt and an ungainly slither Abe was in the saddle. His horse turned its head and eyed Abe's leg doubtfully as if considering whether it was worth a bite, but Abe gave its neck a pat and murmured to it that it was the most wondrous of beasts and he was honoured to be riding it and this seemed to satisfy the animal.

'Nasfali!' said Alicia. 'Sometimes you are just so embarrassing.'

'Why?'

'Using flattery on a horse, how feeble is that!' And then with a quick jab of her heel she moved her horse forward so that she was beside Stokely.

'Politeness never hurt anyone,' muttered Abe. Then remembered his mother using that expression and laughing so much the tears ran down her face. It was the only time he could ever remember her laughing. It had sounded like breaking glass.

The gates were pulled back, and with Stokely in the lead, they filed through. Almost within ten yards of the stockaded outer wall of the house, Abe saw figures running back from the palisade to the thick black line of a hedgerow, and glimpsed a pale moonlike face peering out at him as they rode by. It didn't matter how many times they were chased back beyond the bounds, Ralph had said, out-folk were always sneaking right up to the house, would break in if they could, steal supplies.

It wasn't the out-folk who bothered Abe, however, but Alicia. The closer they came to their destination the more bad-tempered she became. Everything he said was wrong or stupid or foreign until he was so fed up with her that he pulled his horse right back, happy to trail behind keeping them in sight but out of earshot. At one point Stokely reined back to have a word with him.

'Tail-gunner Charlie, eh, skipper? Keeping a lookout for the enemy?'

'Oh yes.'

Alicia's distant back radiated ill temper.

'Be careful, eh? Eyes peeled, that sort of thing. Odd people about.'

'Out-folk,' said Abe.

'Absolutely. Bit rough some of them. Never bothered me but Ralph says they get so hungry they'd eat the horse from under you.' He paused. 'And then when they had finished the horse, they would start on the rider.'

'Thank you for telling me that,' said Abe.

Stokely winked, tapped his nose, then wheeled his horse about and cantered ahead to catch up Alicia. Reluctantly, Abe urged his horse to do the same: better Alicia's sharp tongue than some ragged outlaw's teeth.

'Oh, it's the sheikh of Araby,' sniffed Alicia. 'Are you sure we're good enough company for you?'

'Why are you cross with me?'

'Don't be so stupid, Nasfali. Why should I be cross?' She looked down at her hand and started to bite her finger nails.

And why, thought Abe, are you behaving so oddly?

'I just wish we could get there, get this journey over with. All this mist.' She shivered. 'What happened to the summer?'

Abe shivered too. In Cairo the air had been thick and warm and the sun had rolled slowly across a blue sky, a great gold disc. Perhaps he should have stayed there. It was too late to think that now, but had he known how snappy Alicia was to become . . .

'It's always thicker as you go east,' said Stokely, almost as if he were apologizing for the conditions. 'Closer to them, you see. We're not far now.'

They pressed on, and two hours later, cold, saddle sore, and damp, they came to a crossing of paths and a cairn of stones.

'This is it,' Stokely said, dismounting and pulling off one of the saddlebags. 'Time for tucker, eh?'

'I don't want lunch,' snapped Alicia. 'I want to get there. You're as bad as Nasfali.'

'But we are here, Miss Dunne.' Stokely seemed unbothered by her and calmly laid out bread, cheese, and three shiny apples. 'I get tired if I don't eat regularly.'

'Oh, all right.'

So they dismounted and had their lunch. Then when they had finished, Stokely eyed the sky. 'Not long,' he said. 'You'll see it soon enough now.'

The horses shifted and snorted, impatient to be moving.

'Are you sure, Stokely?'

'Oh yes, Miss Dunne. Just wait till the mist clears and then you'll see it all right. Shouldn't be long; the sun'll burn it off. It usually does round midday, even here.'

'Is it like this because of them?'

Stokely sat easily on his horse; he seemed almost a part of it; his hooded head sunk almost below his shoulders, his eyes half closed, his right hand absently stroking the side of his horse's neck. 'Oh yes, everything's because of them: days are shorter, darker, even in midsummer like now. But you know that, don't you? Don't need to tell you anything, do I, Miss Dunne?'

Alicia didn't answer. She held herself stiffly erect, her expression serious, staring in the direction Stokely had pointed, in the direction of Brighton, stronghold of the sisters, and their destination.

Abe kept quiet. Though the sun was now warm on his neck his stomach felt as if he'd swallowed a frozen pizza, whole, and in its cardboard box. They were going to find their way to Prackton Hall, his old school. This, Alicia was certain, would be the sisters' main base. The book would be there. His job was to distract them; and while they were capturing Abe, she would enter the building, find the book, rescue him, and then they would return to the safe house. Easy, she had said.

He loosened his grip on the reins and his horse ducked its head and chomped easily at the grass. The mist was thinning all the time, shredding and retreating, melting away. And when it was clear, they would go down. 'It is never a good thing,' he told himself, 'to put one's head inside the mouth of the desert lion.'

'You're muttering, Nasfali,' said Alicia.

'I am grateful that I can mutter,' said Abe, still holding the unpleasant thought of the inside of a lion's mouth. 'Without my head this would not be possible.'

'Don't be such a fusser; they are not going to burn you at the stake,' and she gave a snort of laughter. It sounded, thought Abe, quite similar to the sound the horse made.

At that moment the last of the mist dissolved and there was Brighton. What a bad name for such a dark and ugly sprawl: a black smear of smoke and ruin, caught between the sharp blue of the sea and the green of the surrounding country.

And so here they were, high up above the coast looking down at a place that Stokely said was called Lancing, which made Abe momentarily think of King Arthur and his knights and then wonder why that thought had come to him.

'Lancelot, of course,' said Alicia.

Abe wondered if he would ever get used to her suddenly picking up his thoughts. He rubbed his stomach and wished his mouth wasn't so dry and the hard tight feeling in his tummy would go away.

'It looks completely horrible, doesn't it?' Alicia sounded pleased, as if she were relieved in some way. He looked at her in astonishment; where had all the black mood gone? 'And sunshine, too. You know, I almost think this should be fun. What do you think, Nasfali? Ready for some action?'

No he wasn't.

'You know, I was worried on the way over here, but seeing what it's like I'm not worried at all now. Isn't that great?' When Abe didn't answer, she shrugged and turned to Stokely. 'What is the best way for us to get into the town, Stokely?'

'That road. You see all the carts making their way towards the city. Farmers taking in their produce. I expect you'll think of a way of getting by the guards, Miss Dunne.'

'Yes, of course I shall. Now, when I have the book,' she said, completely her business-like self once again, 'I shall come back up here. Where will you leave my horse, Stokely?'

'I thought the plan was that we would both be coming back,' said Abe stiffly.

'Oh, don't be so sniffy, Nasfali. Just a slip of the tongue. Course we're coming back together. Couldn't do without you, could I? You're the one with the brilliant schemes.'

It was true; he was better at planning than she was. He'd rescued the team; he'd got them to Cairo and away from Alicia's mother; and it had been his idea to find Stokely. What worried him now was that going into the sisters' stronghold and pinching this great book of knowledge was Alicia's idea; and it was an idea with no edge or sides or end to it as far as Abe could see. It was an idea that left him, Ebrahim Nasfahl Ma'halli, abandoned, as helpless as a duck in the desert.

She was eying him thoughtfully. 'Stop looking so suspicious, Nasfali. I haven't changed, you know. I am still completely on the outside.' This was her way of saying that she wasn't like her mother. 'So buck up. You're just going to have to be very clever. You're good at that; that's why my mother never liked you, and,' she added, touching the place where her eyebrow ring had been, 'why I do.'

'I thought you had changed,' said Abe.

'Sorry,' she said. 'I was poison, wasn't I. Bit worried that coming to Brighton might be a temptation. Only a witch could be tempted by that dump. Look at it!'

He didn't need to. 'You won't be tempted to use your power then?'

'Oh no,' she said airily, 'except in a dire emergency, of course.'

Hadn't she tried it on at the safe house though, on Ralph? Miss Ida had thought so, and so had he. And then the way she had managed the horse . . . Perhaps she was beginning to change and she didn't even know. He would have to watch her, keenly, like a hawk, he thought.

'I'll have the horses ready for you and the skipper, Miss Dunne.'

They agreed that Stokely would wait at the cairn for two days, and no longer. If they came later than that they would have to walk back to the safe house: it would be a long and hungry walk.

They dismounted. 'Buck up, skipper, you'll be all right.'

'If they don't kill me,' Abe said glumly.

'I'll look out for you, old chap,' said Stokely as he took the reins of Abe's horse from him. 'Can you swim?'

The question took Abe by surprise. 'In the desert,' he said, 'water is for drinking not swimming in.'

'Well, let's hope they don't decide to duck you in the old briny.'

What was old briny? wondered Abe, as he hurried down the hill after Alicia. And why should they want to duck him in it? Ducking. That was what had happened to witches in the olden days, wasn't it? If the poor victim drowned she or he was innocent; if they survived, which they tended not to, they were guilty and were burned. He shuddered. So was this what the sisters had re-introduced, ducking their prisoners until they drowned. He turned back and glimpsed the hooded figure of Stokely standing up on the rim of the Downs holding the three horses, watching them, and then he turned and disappeared from view.

If only I had time to ask him, thought Abe.

'Nasfali, for goodness' sake, get out of sight. There's a cart coming.' She dragged him down behind a broken flint wall. 'I'll talk to them and you scramble into the back, get in under the vegetables.'

'Why can't I sit at the front with you?'

'Don't be ridiculous. They are not going to give you a lift, are they. Remember? Thirteen-year-old boys, darkish skin. Think, Nasfali! You get in the back, and be nippy.'

He would be very nippy, but he did hope that the cart was not carrying cabbages.

TEN

Musty, sickly green, and lumpy. Abe wriggled and burrowed his way into the hard mound of cabbages. It had to be cabbages, of course. School food in the earthy stage before it was school food was still repellent. 'It is,' he decided, his nose bent sideways by a coarse cabbage stalk, 'abhorrent to me.' He wasn't quite sure where that word had come from but it sounded satisfyingly disgusted. Had she done it on purpose, selected this cart because she knew how much he hated this English vegetable? No, she would never do such a thing. That would be mean and spiteful. It would be the action of a witch, of her mother, the hateful Mrs Dunne, and Alicia for all her spiky moods was not, nor ever could be, like her mother.

He eased his way down another layer and wiggled his foot. Was it covered? He had no desire to bump his way down to Brighton with one foot sticking out like a flag for the nearest Lakin to spot. The cart rattled and lurched along the pot-holed road. Up above him, Alicia was sitting comfortably with the farmer and his wife, and Abe strained to hear what she might be telling them, but he could only make out the odd word and the occasional bark of laughter from Alicia. What would they make of her strangeness? Perhaps, in these odd times, she was no stranger than anyone else?

After what seemed like a lifetime, the cart jolted to a stop. 'Wazzat in 'ere?' The slurred spitty question sounded as if it had come rumbling out of a vast belly. Abe scrunched his eyes tight. Lakin. One of them, anyway. And close. He sensed the round sweaty face with its pig-black eyes peering over the side of the cart, the fat stubby fingers shovelling at the cargo of cabbages.

The cart gave a sudden lurch to one side and Abe felt everything shift above him. There was a grunt and more scrabbling. He held his breath.

'You know very well what this is.' He could hear Alicia's sharp voice clearly now but what was worse was that with his right eye he could see upwards. Light. Grey sky. Blunt fingers poised to hoik out one more cabbage.

Abe braced himself. He would move on three. He would just have to chance it, spring up and hope that he'd give the Lakin such a shock that he would be able to spin past him and make off down a side street and Alicia would just have to use some magic. It was an emergency. In fact, why hadn't she done so already? Did she really want to see him grabbed by this monster?

There was a long bubbly sniff and a throaty mutter: 'Is it a jamboy? Is it . . . ?'

'That's enough.'

The Lakin grunted and the cart swayed.

'There's nothing there, is there? Well? Is there?'

Oh, thought Abe, you are still magnificent, more bossy than a hundred thousand matrons. He began to relax. She'd have the Lakin backed up against a wall and whimpering in a moment.

'No.' The Lakin sounded puzzled. 'Thought I could smell 'im.'

'Smell who?'

'Jamboy, miss.'

'Don't know what you mean.' There was a different quality to Alicia's voice, slightly wheedling. 'What is a jamboy?'

Another grunt. 'Boy,' breathed the Lakin. 'All lookin' for this boy, all boys no good but this one's special, see. They want 'im more. Bad as sour rat meat, miss. Big reward if one of us find 'im. They'll give 'im to us to deal with.' The Lakin grunted and Abe could hear his horrible spitty breathing; and then a little slowly and with an edge of suspicion the Lakin said: ''Ere, you should know all about the boy, if you's one of them, shouldn't you?'

'I am one of me,' said Alicia briskly, 'so stand back.' There was a moment of silence and Abe held his breath. 'You'll find yourself turned into boiled broth if you don't stand back from this cart instantly.'

'Yes, miss,' said the Lakin.

The farmer rapped his stick against the side of the cart and urged the horse to walk on.

Abe waited for a few minutes, then he wriggled his right arm free and shifted the cabbages from his face. He could see nothing, apart from a dark, overcast sky. He could hear people calling, though, and the sound of other carts, crates being dragged and dropped, the stamp of feet, and the harsh crying of gulls. Their cart stopped again and a moment later he felt a hand tugging his ankle.

'Come on, Nasfali, quickly, get out.' He pushed aside the last covering of cabbage and sat up. 'Now, quick,' she said, 'while the farmer's busy.'

Aching and stiff, Abe hauled himself over the side and dropped heavily to the ground. 'Here, take this, it'll make you look less obvious.' She gave him a sack, scooped a few cabbages into it and then made him sling it over his shoulders. 'Duck your head down, Nasfali, and pretend that the sack is heavy. That's it. You look wicked, a real scruff and you smell positively disgusting.' She sounded pleased.

'Thank you,' said Abe with as much dignity as he could muster. 'I did not choose to lie among cabbages.'

She rubbed her nose ring and gave one of her odd barking laughs.

'I do not think I am funny.'

'No, you don't, do you?' She sniffed and pulled a face. 'Did you know witches don't mind any kind of smell?'

'And you do?'

'Seem to, don't I?' And she gave a discreet thumbs up.

Was she still worrying about being like her mother?

After everything she had done? He was about to reassure her when she said, 'Put your head down and don't speak to me. We're being watched. The farmer's talking to someone. Follow closely, Nasfali, but don't open your mouth.' And she set off. How she knew which way to go Abe hadn't a clue but he kept his head down and shadowed her, keeping just a couple of paces behind. They cut through the large open market to which the farmer had brought them; through the carts and stalls and stacks of produce, mostly vegetables of one sort or another, nothing exotic, of course, just greens and onions. They skirted pens with pigs and cattle, and in all that filth and noise and activity no one paid them any attention. If the farmer had suspected something and was intending to betray Alicia he would have said something at the gate into the city. Abe relaxed a little, lifted his head, and looked around.

There seemed to be three types of people there: farmers, buyers, and slaves. The farmers' faces were ruddy from outdoor work but anxious looking. The buyers were hard-faced middle-aged women in brown cloaks who marched purposefully about with lists which they ticked. They didn't seem to be witches. The sisters would never have anything to do with something so plain as a market. They liked boardrooms and smart suits, Gucci shoes and blood-red lipstick. This was all too earthy and smelly for them. These women, then, were servants of some sort, a step up the ladder from their attendants: raggedy men, hooped over under heavy sacks or hauling hand-carts piled with produce, their faces grey with exhaustion, their feet bare and their legs streaked with filth. Abe realized that this was what he was meant to be: one of the slaves. He thought of his father and that trick he had of being able to change his appearance just so slightly, just enough to deceive a casual watcher, and almost without thinking, Abe stooped his shoulders and imagined himself with grey streaks in his jet black hair.

In five minutes they were through the last of the stalls and into a side street. Alicia pressed on, winding her way up through the town and then down towards the shore. They passed blackened buildings that had been gutted by fire and then a band of Lakins marching big-bellied down the middle of the road. Everywhere there were slaves carrying and hauling and hammering and digging. Everywhere there was activity but with no sense of rhyme or reason to it. Tall chimneys belched black smoke and the streets were strewn with filth and covered in ash.

They passed one work-gang smashing all the windows in an old church and another collecting the shards piece by piece in their bare hands and then feeding them into a huge iron cauldron. There were rats and scraggy cats picking through the rubbish. There were Lakins with ladles stirring greasy stew over open fires and serving it out to lines of grey-faced workers. There were Lakins with whips and Lakins armed to the teeth with pikes and spikes and stubby meat cleavers. There were sour-faced women and threadbare men snarling and snapping at each other. There wasn't a single face with a smile; there wasn't sight nor sound of a child.

Abe kept his head down and thought old thoughts. He didn't want to end up being chased by Lakins and then served up as stew. He kept close to Alicia. Eventually they emerged onto an open space which in another life might have been a park or a public gardens but which was now bare but for a single leafless tree and a huge raised stage. Perhaps they had rock concerts there, thought Abe, though that did not seem a very witch-like thing to have. Alicia muttered: 'Gallows, Nasfali, gallows. There's no such thing as Glastonbury any more.'

Gallows! That meant there were executions. Who? Who did the witches want to hang? They had all the power, what did they need to go round executing people for?

'They don't,' muttered Alicia. 'It keeps everyone nice

and frightened though. Not a bad idea when you think of it.'

What was she talking about? Everything about the place was a bad idea and, as they cut across the space and headed through a maze of lanes, Abe decided that the positively worst idea of all was coming into Brighton in the first place.

They rounded a corner into a rubbish strewn alley and, not really looking where he was going, Abe almost bumped smack into a very cross Alicia. 'What do you mean? Are you going to give up, Nasfali? Are you going to be a rat?'

'I don't know what you mean.'

'Oh yes, you do.' Her eyes were blazing. 'You've gone all weak and I never thought you would,' she said disgustedly. 'I thought you were the one I could rely on.'

'I never said anything.'

'You don't have to.'

No, he didn't. She read his thoughts. Instinctively Abe took a step back from her. 'I wish you wouldn't do that. I don't do it to you.'

'You can't. And, anyway, it's not what you think. I don't spy, Nasfali. How many times do I have to tell you I'm not like them. I can just hear you sometimes, that's all.' She suddenly cocked her head on one side. 'How did you do that?'

'What?'

'You look different. No, no, don't change.' Abe didn't know that he was changing. 'Stay old like that, it's good. Clever, Nasfali. How did you do it?'

'My father could make himself look different.' He shrugged. 'I was just thinking about him, trying to do the same.'

'It's rubbed off, hasn't it?'

'I don't know what you mean.'

'I think you do,' she said. 'And you know what? I

think they are looking for you because for the very first time ever they're frightened there might be a boy witch.' She looked at him coolly as if curious to see how he would react to this.

He shuddered. 'Not possible.'

'You were a mistake, Nasfali, my mother said so. Witches don't have boys. They just don't. But here you are. And now they're so rattled they're sending every boy they can find out of the country. It's brilliant!'

Abe couldn't see what was so brilliant about it.

'You're our secret weapon.'

There was an old potato by his toe. He gave it a kick and it disintegrated. 'I don't feel like a secret weapon.'

'Does that mean you're going to run off then? Off back to your precious Cairo?'

'I just don't see how we can change all this. There are too many of them, and everything is so different from how it was.' He threw out his hands palm upwards. 'And I don't see the point.'

'Point!' She snorted derisively. 'The point is to stop them. The point is to get everything back to how it was. I would have thought that was pretty obvious. I think,' she said, 'you just don't see what you'll get out of it.'

He hadn't meant that but it was a bit true. He shrugged. 'I am good at schemes and this isn't a scheme; it's dangerous.'

'It's fun, Nasfali. It's an adventure. What's happened to you. Don't you trust me?'

'You're different.'

'Oh, of course I'm different!' she said crossly. 'But don't you see that I'm also the same?'

At that moment a work patrol hauling a hand-cart piled with broken crates and sacks spilling over with tins and bones and the thick reek of fish turned into the alley.

Instinctively Abe let his shoulders sag and his back stoop. Alicia stepped back and put her hands on her hips.

'Pick that up and carry it out of here at once,' she snapped loudly.

The work party paused. The guards coming up behind their charges looked their way. Abe scoured the ground wondering what on earth he was meant to pick up.

'That! That! That!' she snapped.

Abe spotted a long bone that looked as if at one time it might have belonged to some unfortunate cow and picked it up.

'Exactly! Now follow me.' And she turned on her heel and stalked towards the guards and the work gang, who were all staring at her and Abe as if they had dropped down from another planet; which in a sense, thought Abe, they had. Except he couldn't help noticing how like the sisters Alicia suddenly seemed.

She stopped in front of the guards and immediately started to snap at them. What were they doing? This was where she kept her materials. She indicated the bone Abe was holding. She would report them. She would dissolve them. She would reduce them to rats, to woodlice, and then pick off their legs one by one. Abe shuddered. Where did she get these horrible ideas from?

The work gang, not knowing whether they were going to have to dump their evil smelling sacks here or take them away again, stood around uncertainly. One by one they lowered whatever they had been shouldering down to the ground and Abe suddenly noticed that each one of them was murmuring something to himself. It sounded like the same thing over and over again.

Abe sidled up to the nearest slave. 'Are you all right?'

The man looked at him blankly, his lips moving all the time. He looked so old and grey. His face was stretched, the veins knotted in his scrawny neck and bare dirt-streaked scrawny arms.

'What is it? What are you saying?' And then he caught the hoarse barely audible mutter.

'I hurt,' the man was saying. 'I hurt. I hurt. I hurt.'

Abe looked at them all in horror. All of them were saying the same thing, over and over again. 'I hurt. I hurt.'

He stepped back and Alicia beckoned him. 'Hurry up, slave,' she snapped. 'Remember what I said,' she said to the guards. 'This lot is to go on the beach and never, never, dare to cross my path again.' And she stalked out into the road with Abe keeping close behind her.

'I was magnificent, wasn't I?' said Alicia. 'What was I like, Nasfali? Give me one of your compliments.'

'You were like a desert lion.'

'Good.'

'Among jackals.'

'Very good, Nasfali.'

'We have to free them, Alicia.'

'It's not far now, about twenty minutes if we walk quickly.' She seemed to have forgotten their argument in the alley, forgotten or dismissed it as unimportant. And maybe it was unimportant because Abe realized that there was no real choice. They had to go on and, until he could come up with a better plan, he would have to follow Alicia. 'What did you say?'

'We have to free them. That is what we have to do.'

'Who?'

'The slaves, of course. Did you hear what they were saying?'

'Oh yes, yes, I was a bit busy terrifying mother's little helpers. I rather wish she had been around to see. It might have given her a nasty shock. Don't worry, Nasfali, we'll get rid of all this,' she said making a sweeping gesture with her hand that appeared to encompass the whole of Brighton. 'Trust me.'

Why, thought Abe, does she keep saying that?

ELEVEN

'Tea time,' said Alicia. 'Just the time to call on mother.'

The sky was dull and grey, the air was still and heavy, like it is just before a storm breaks. There was no way of knowing whether there was even a sun lurking somewhere behind the thick cloud, let alone whether it was late afternoon or not, except that Abe's stomach told him that he hadn't eaten for quite a long while. Food, however, was not what was on Abe's mind.

'I thought your mother was dead,' he said, keeping his voice low. 'And I saw the two of you fall.'

'You thought I was dead too, didn't you, and I wasn't. Witches don't die very easily, Nasfali; they just disappear for a bit and then they come back.'

'You now think that's what happened to your mother, then?'

'Well, look at all this.' Alicia waved her hand at what had once been Prackton Hall, Abe's school, and its extraordinary grounds into which they had just sneaked. In fact it was only Abe who had done the sneaking, Alicia had simply stalked through the open front gate and now stood in full view of the building. Abe sheltered behind the first of a line of palm trees which edged the drive up to the front door of the witches' stronghold, their palace, the seat of their power. 'Don't you think all this looks like mother? None of the others could do this on their own. I bet she's back.'

Prackton Hall was transformed utterly from the tall, gaunt school where Abe had spent almost six years of his life, into a gleaming, ivory-pale building with high pitched roofs and thin rounded turrets. Almost like a fairy castle, Abe thought, except that the windows seemed to be made of that black glass used in limousines driven by pop stars. The grounds that had once been thickly edged with trees enclosing cricket pitches, playing fields, and a newly planted rose garden that Abe had attempted to dig up, had now become a dazzling and very odd formal garden of exact geometric patterning. Gravel paths criss-crossed triangular beds of poppies. Apart from the palm trees, the whole garden was red. 'It makes me feel dizzy,' murmured Abe.

'Yes,' said Alicia. Abe wished she would keep her voice down. 'But it's all on the outside, of course. Disgusting, isn't it?'

'Where are the guards?' He couldn't believe that there weren't Lakins stacked shoulder to shoulder round the building.

'No need. Who'd be daft enough to come here?' She giggled. Abe had never heard Alicia giggling before. Her laugh was bad enough; this sounded something between a gulp and a hiccup—unnerving. 'Sorry,' she said, giving her nose a rub and then beckoning Abe to stand beside her. 'Off you go then. As soon as they see you, there'll be a proper stir and I'll slip into the building from the other side.'

'And you'll rescue me?'

She wasn't looking at him but towards the Hall. 'You will be rescued.'

'How?'

'Don't be silly. How can I know until we find out what they're going to do with you.'

This was hardly very encouraging. 'Supposing something goes wrong and we get split up, we'll meet up on the Downs, where we left Stokely.'

'Yes, yes, of course. Now get on with it, the sooner I can nick this book from under their stupid noses, the sooner we can start getting things sorted.' She gave him a push.

Abe took a deep breath and set off up the drive. The families of blood-red poppies seemed to be staring at him as did the blackened windows of the ghost-pale building. He felt small and Ebrahim Nasfahl Ma'halli did not enjoy feeling small. He didn't particularly like being told what to do, even by Alicia Dunne. He lifted his chin, avoided looking at all the dizzy-making symmetry of the gardens, puffed out his chest, and quickened his step.

There was no knocker or bell pull, so he just banged with his fist, three times. Instantly the door swung wide open and there in front of him was a tall, slim woman with jet-black hair, thin black eyebrows, and lips the colour of the blood-red poppies. She was dressed, as the sisters always seemed to be, in a beautifully tailored trouser suit. The moment she saw him, her eyes widened in horror, her hands flew to her face, and she emitted a loud hiss.

'Hello,' said Abe, 'is Mrs Dunne inside?'

The sister, her hands still over her mouth, nodded. 'Boy!' She finally managed to utter the word, spitting it out as if it were a disgusting food.

'Yes, of course,' said Abe, for a moment forgetting the terrible danger he was in and simply enjoying this witch's huge discomfort at seeing him standing on the doorstep. Perhaps they would all be equally astonished and he would be able to walk away as easily as he had arrived. But first, he thought, I shall do some stirring up, because that is what Alicia needed me to do. 'Aren't you going to invite me in?'

'Oh yes.' Suddenly there was a second figure in the doorway. 'Nasfali,' the voice was thick and warm and, as always, it reminded Abe of faintly rotten fruit, 'you disgusting foreign boy, how delicious of you to save us the trouble of scouring the country. Do come in.'

The first sister, now fully composed, stood to one side, while Mrs Dunne, the foremost witch in Britain, the eldest and most powerful of all the sisters, and, in what now seemed like another lifetime, the controlling wife of Abe's hopeless headmaster, came to the door.

'Mrs Dunne. How are you? I rather hoped that that fall you had would have flattened you like an omelette.' Abe just managed to keep his voice steady. The confidence of one moment before had evaporated. He curled his fingers into a fist to stop them trembling.

'Very good, Nasfali. Now be quiet and step inside my palace so that we can deal with you satisfactorily.' She held out her hands almost as if she were about to embrace him. Abe found his eyes fixed on the ring she wore on the fat white finger of her right hand and suddenly it was as if his head were fixed in a rigid clamp. He was yanked towards the doorway and his feet stumbled, trying to keep up with the pressure.

'Oh, having trouble walking?' said Mrs Dunne. 'What a useless creature you are, Nasfali.'

He heard a brittle laugh that must have come from the sister who had opened the door. She was slightly behind him now but, unable to turn his head, he could no longer see her. Gripped by whatever force Mrs Dunne was exerting on him, Abe stumbled clumsily through the front hall after her. Of course, Alicia had been right. Though Mrs Dunne's palace looked so elegant from the outside, behind the door it was just like his own mother's secret bedroom had been. He felt the icy cold air and he glimpsed filthy, peeling wallpaper, runnels of damp, and long hairy strands of cobwebs across the doorways.

Helplessly he followed her into a large room, as derelict and dismal as the hallway. She stood him at one end, the blackened glass of the windows behind him. Then she tilted back her head and let out a single piercing howl that shivered the air and made everything blur in front of Abe's eyes. A moment later the room was a neat conference chamber, carpeted in blue and grey. 'Hey presto,' murmured Mrs Dunne. 'Never trust your eyes, Nasfali,' she said.

Then in filed the sisters, gliding silently to their seats

where they sat all in the same way, leaning slightly forward, hands on knees.

'Well,' said Mrs Dunne brightly, 'and what do we have here?'

'A boy,' they hissed and there was a moment of silence. Then pandemonium broke loose.

Abe felt himself shaken by icy blasts of wind that howled round him and within this funnel of wind he heard their screeching and hissing voices. He hoped Alicia had stolen away that precious book she needed so much but how, he thought despairingly, could she ever rescue him from this?

'It's him! It's him!'

'Don't bring him in here.'

'Burn him!'

'Boil him!'

'We can't let him live, he'll ruin everything . . . '

Abe felt himself being yanked and pulled one way and then another. He tumbled into darkness, and then he was suddenly in a familiar setting: a vast, ruined underground station. Behind and in front of him dusty brick walls curved up high overhead; to left and right stretched a long, grey, rubble-strewn desert that disappeared into a horizonless distance. He felt small hands plucking his sleeve and a terrible aching sadness pressing in on him. This was his mother's special prison. She had trapped him there once before and he would have been lost for ever if Alicia had not found him. Oh, where was she now . . . ?

Suddenly he was in another place, a damp cave, with moss-covered walls and scuttling rat shapes flickering through the half darkness. And then another and another . . . Hurtled from one witch prison to the next, as each sister instinctively, in her horror and rage, tried to shut the boy away in a place where he could be forgotten about for ever.

Finally, through the chaos, Abe heard Mrs Dunne's

unmistakable fruity voice. 'Sisters,' she called. 'Sisters, please be calm.'

The voices fell silent, the room settled back before Abe's eyes into the conference chamber that Mrs Dunne had conjured up. He still couldn't move but even so, he felt a moment's relief; almost anything had to be better than finding himself in an endless series of hell-dungeons, each one more terrible than the one before. He scanned the faces before him, looking for his mother. She had to be there, didn't she? And she was: third row, in the middle, looking at him with exactly the same expression of cold dislike as all the other sisters in the room. For a moment their eyes locked and then she shifted slightly as Mrs Dunne spoke.

'We don't want him here, anywhere here. None of your own private storage places, your little prisons, your quaint dungeons, are suitable for this boy, for this is the one we have been looking for.'

They nodded. They knew. They too had sensed that the one called Nasfali had somehow walked right in among them.

'Imprisonment is not good enough for him, but we do not want even a shadow of a shadow of this one lingering among us. He ruins,' she stretched out the word ruins as if it were a particularly long strand of weed, 'everything. But we don't want his death on our hands; he is,' she shuddered, 'our sister's child. So we shall do what we had already begun to do with all the other boys who might have been him: expel him.'

They nodded but without great enthusiasm. They wanted something more, something a little more refined, a little more unpleasant.

Mrs Dunne smiled and adjusted the red scarf round her throat. 'The sea shall have him. SWSP.' She clapped her hands together with pleasure. 'The acronym for the day, sisters.'

'SWSP,' they all said and all gave their hands a single clap.

What did it mean? thought Abe. Meaningless, like everything else about them.

Mrs Dunne turned to him. 'Oh, there is plenty of meaning,' she said. 'Salt waves solve problems. You will be going to sea in a boat, Nasfali; or rather you will be going to sea in a sieve and you will, eventually, dissolve on the ocean floor and then you will never do us, or anyone else, any harm, ever again.' She turned to the sisters. 'We'll have a celebration,' she said, 'a rest day for the workers. They can watch the boy being launched into oblivion. It will do them good. Now, take him away,' she said, her voice suddenly turning harsh. 'He sickens me.'

A boat then, thought Abe. Better than he had expected. There was at least a chance in a boat. The bit about the sieve didn't sound so good though. However, there was that rhyme, wasn't there, about creatures called Jumblies going to sea in a sieve and everyone had said that they would all be drowned but, of course, they weren't. There was some comfort in that, perhaps.

Abe found himself hustled out of the room, through the hallway, and onto the drive. A cart, with a sister sitting up at the front and four miserable looking slaves harnessed to the yokes, wheeled up and Abe was hauled up onto the back where he was fastened to the rail with a strap, presumably so that he wouldn't fall over. He would not make a very impressive spectacle sprawled flat on his face; they wanted everyone to see him.

Then, with the sisters stalking behind, they trundled off, down the long drive and out into the town. There weren't many people to see them, not until they approached the seaside where there was a vast crowd that parted wordlessly to allow the cart and the parade of sisters to pass through.

Old, stoop shouldered, blank faced, the witches' slaves

watched. They didn't applaud or cheer, they didn't clap or spit. They just stood in silence. In amongst them, Abe could see the towering bulky shapes of Lakins, also watching, but their eyes were not on him or the cart but on the crowd, and that struck Abe, even in his present state, as curious. Could these hollow-faced people ever cause any trouble? It didn't seem possible.

And could he? He could move his legs, that was something, and, with difficulty, he could clench and unclench his fingers, but how would he be able to manage an engine, or sail, or oars or whatever it was that they were going to provide him with, unless he could move his head and arms?

The cart trundled onto the shingle and then stopped. Below them, hauled up just above the tideline, was the boat. A small, clinker-built wooden dinghy, battered and rotten, but still intact. If he could stay afloat long enough there might be a passing ship or the spell might ease and then he would at least be able to swim. There might even be a chance for Alicia to come and get him. Perhaps she was here already, hidden in the crowd. He couldn't see, though, because he couldn't turn his head. Before him there was just the shore, the boat, the grey expanse of the English Channel and, to the left, the stark wooden piles of what had once been the Palace Pier sticking up from the water like a prehistoric forest, or the skeleton of some gigantic creature.

Mrs Dunne stood in front of him and looked at him intently. He knew what she was doing, he could feel it: probing his thoughts. It was disgusting, like dirty fingers in his skull. He would have shaken his head had he been able to move, not that that would have helped. All he could do was instantly to clear his mind of everything apart from the image of himself adrift in the boat.

'Haven't seen my daughter, have you, Nasfali, mm? No, of course not. She only used you, didn't she, used you to defy me. She'll come back.' She smiled. 'Back into the fold; but you won't. You won't stay afloat very long, Nasfali. Don't fool yourself. The sea will swallow you up.' She shuddered. 'And that will be it. Goodbye.'

Abe was half walked, half dragged down to the dinghy and placed in the stern. No oars, no sail, no engine, just the hull and single thwart to sit on.

There was the lonely sound of a gull crying and then Mrs Dunne's voice floated over the beach: 'This is the one we were looking for. This is the boy who defied me. Witness and be sure you avoid his fate.'

He heard a lone voice breaking the silence: 'Good luck, sonny!' Then there was the snap of a whip and silence again apart from the rattling 'shush' as the dinghy was slid down the few yards of the beach and into the sea.

Now there was only the gentle slapping of the water against the rotten hull of the dinghy. He couldn't look back but he could tell he was moving, forging away from the shore. How far could Mrs Dunne's magic propel the boat? he wondered. How far over sea water did her power extend? Already he had left the last of the wooden piles of the pier behind him. Ahead was just the open sea and the grey sky, thickening and darkening. He heard the low rumble of distant thunder; the sea shifting, tilting, moving, and a slow swell building.

TWELVE

All alone on a wide sea, Abe drifted. The air was still and heavy; the waves oily smooth. Thunder rumbled again but further away, it seemed. Perhaps the storm would pass him by. He flexed his fingers and tried to move his arms but they were still rigid as iron, which wasn't so good, but at least he was away from Mrs Dunne. That was something, he thought, attempting to make up a list of all the positive elements in his present situation: alive, yes; away from Brighton, yes; able to move fingers, yes, and legs and feet, yes; but what was that sploshing sound and why were his feet so cold . . . and wet?

He looked down and saw that the bottom of the dinghy was rapidly filling with water which had begun to stream through the jointing of the planks. The level was rising rapidly; the dinghy was sinking.

Don't panic!

He didn't.

Think!

He thought. He thought hard and fast but no brilliant schemes bloomed in his mind.

The water was over his ankles and then up to the thwart he was sitting on. This, he told himself, is very bad indeed. A breeze began to pick up and the dinghy wallowed sluggishly; another few inches and she would disappear.

'But I shall float!' he suddenly exclaimed and just as he did so, he thought he heard far away in the distance a voice calling: 'That's the ticket, skipper.'

Of course he had imagined it. There wasn't another boat to be seen anywhere on the horizon. He eased off his shoes but even that slight movement made the dinghy tilt very slightly. The left side slipped under the surface and then that was it: the dinghy just slid down into the cold sea.

Instantly Abe let go his hold of the sides and began to kick and he did float—on his back. With any luck, he thought, if my head is pointing in the direction of England, and I keep kicking I shall end up back on shore. Ebrahim Nasfahl Ma'halli, first boy to cross the English Channel floating on his back, would that bring fame and fortune?

And what would Alicia say? 'Don't be so silly, Nasfali. You can't possibly swim to France.'

No. He would probably just paddle around in circles. He needed something more than luck.

Where was she? Hadn't she promised? She said she kept her word but he was here in the middle of the English Channel. He mustn't think like this.

He closed his eyes and tried to do Alicia's trick of picturing where he wanted to be. That had worked brilliantly when she had rescued him from his mother's underground prison; perhaps it might work now. So he concentrated and tried not to think about being wet and cold but, even so, at first all that came into his mind were images of a blazing wood fire and slices of warm, steamy buttered toast. That was no good. He needed a shoreline, a beach; but the only shore he could imagine was the one with Mrs Dunne standing on it. That wouldn't do either. If they caught him wandering through Brighton a second time they would certainly think of something even worse to do to him than sending him to sea in a leaky boat. What he needed was another boat, one with a sail perhaps. He thought of his old bedroom with its walls plastered with pictures of Cairo, the Pyramids, and the Nile and those little sailing boats the fishermen used, with their long sloping gaffs and scoopy sails: *felouka*. No, no good, not here. Then, uninvited, another image sailed into his mind: a small grey boat with a dirty grey sail and single figure in the stern. It was quite far off but bearing in his direction. Beggars, thought Abe, cannot be choosers.

'Hold on, old chap!'

Is this me, Ebrahim Nasfahl Ma'halli, talking to myself? he wondered. Am I in a delirium? I am certainly in a pickle. Pickle and cold meat and yogurt make a good breakfast. I shall, of course, hold on but the water is very cold. He could feel the side of his face becoming numb and his fingers too, though he could move his arms a bit now. It is strange, though, that I should call myself 'old chap'. I do not ever do this but then these days have been nothing but strange. It is the way it is.

'There you are! Lost sight of you for a while.'

The voice was familiar and seemed to be coming from somewhere behind him; and it was most definitely not his. Instinctively, he tried to turn his head and, as a result, swallowed a sloshing mouthful of water which made him splutter and spit and curse himself. Alicia was right: he was silly. He was stupid. He needed to save his energy, not flail around like a mad monkfish.

Flail around? Move his head? Had dreadful Mrs Dunne's spell worn off? He opened his eyes and found that he was able to tread water, which meant he could turn around and see the shore, just, a long, long way off. He was so tired, though. For how long could he go on? The paths of the sea are as long, and as hard to follow, as those of the great desert . . .

'Skipper!'

He turned again and there was the grey boat with the grey sail and an anxious grey-haired Stokely sitting in the stern.

This is indeed timely, Abe registered before slipping under the surface. There was a roaring in his ears and a pounding in his chest and he had a momentary impression of a sleek shape passing overhead. A whale, he thought. Perhaps, like Jonah, I shall be swallowed. Then he was up on the surface, spluttering, and there was a hand gripping his right arm, pulling him up, and the sail flapping and snapping above him. His face touched the smooth side of the boat, then his fingers found an edge to grip on and he held tight.

'Here we go, old chap.' Stokely caught hold of him with both hands and with a fierce grunt hauled him straight upwards and Abe tumbled in over the side.

He was vaguely aware of being wrapped in a rough blanket, of Stokely rubbing his hands and feet to get the warmth back into them and being given a drink of pure spring water. He gulped and gulped at the bottle, vaguely surprised that he could even swallow a mouthful of the very thing which had been on the point of swallowing him.

'Some clothes behind you, in that bundle under the foredeck, skipper.' Stokely was busy at the helm, tightening up the main sheet, glancing up at the sail, bringing the boat back on to course. 'Might not fit you too well, but they'll keep you warm. Nothing hot to drink on board; you'll have to hang on till we get ashore.'

'Thank you,' said Abe. 'I shall hang on with pleasure.' Then: 'You saved my life, Stokely. Thank you.'

'Yes, I did, didn't I? Only fair though, one good turn deserves another, doesn't it? You were the chappie who got us out of the photograph and whisked us off to Egypt away from . . . '

'From Mrs . . . '

'From Mrs She-who-shall-be-nameless, if you don't mind. Gives me the colly-wobbles every time I have to think of her. Have some chocolate.' He handed Abe a bar. 'Keep a little store that Ida doesn't know about.' He chuckled. 'Have to keep a few secrets from the old girl because she's a great one for wanting us to share everything.'

'You're sharing your chocolate with me.'

'Special occasion, skipper. Special occasion. A half drowned chap needs a bit of tucker.'

Water and chocolate, thought Abe, tucker of the gods.

Revived now, Abe struggled out of his wet things and put on the clothes that Stokely had for him: baggy woollen trousers that he had to fold over at the waist and hold up with a length of rope, a clean but well-worn collarless shirt, soft cow-hide boots, and a sleeveless sheepskin jerkin that still had a sour sheepy smell to it but which kept him deliciously warm. 'I thought Alicia had perhaps forgotten about me,' he said, once he was clothed and seated facing Stokely. 'Either that or she'd got caught herself, though I didn't believe that was very likely. I think she is a match for Mrs D—for her mother. Though maybe not if they all ganged up on her at the same time.'

'Miss Dunne could knock 'em all for six, I reckon.'

'Yes. So she told you to get a sailing boat and be ready to pick me up. Quite astonishing,' said Abe. 'How could she know what her mother would do, or where I would end up? Did she say exactly where you had to sail to?'

Stokely looked up at the sail and trimmed his course slightly. 'She didn't tell me anything.'

'She didn't arrange my rescue?'

'She might have tried to arrange something but not through me, skipper. But then I never told her I had the dear old *Grey Whisper* . . . '

'The what?'

'This boat—hidden away down on the marshes at Shoreham. You're the only one that knows, skipper. Be grateful if you keep it hush.'

'Of course,' said Abe. 'Hush will certainly be kept.' But what he was actually thinking was why hadn't Alicia helped to rescue him? Was this book, stolen from his father's care by the witches of Britain, more important than everything, more important than friendship? Perhaps it was; but could he really say that Alicia was a friend? He liked her: she had a ring in her nose and she did not do what she was told. He had hoped she would come to

Egypt with him, and she had come, but only to rescue the team. She was magnificent, a vision, a partner but he did not really know her, did he? She was too full of secrets.

That made him wonder why Stokely felt the need to keep secrets from his sister and the rest of his household. They seemed good, kind people and, most importantly, they were determined to keep away from having anything to do with the witches.

'Don't know really, skipper,' he said when Abe asked him. 'Feel different from the others. I sometimes wonder if the other chaps in the team, you know, feel like me. Can't really fit in at all. Have to pretend, you know. Bit of a game, pretending, but sometimes I feel as if I'll explode if I don't get away, so I sneak off for a bit of a ramble or a sail in this old thing. That does the ticket.'

Abe smiled. He found it hard to imagine Stokely with his quiet chuckle and secret bars of chocolate ever exploding. 'And this does the ticket very well for me,' Abe said, patting the boat's deck. He watched the wake creaming and bubbling from the bow and then asked: 'How did you know how to find me, Stokely? If Alicia said nothing what made you sail out here?'

'Took a chance. Those sisters have been piling boys into boats and sending them off to sea for some months now. Fruitcakes the lot of them. I took a chance they'd do the same to you. You see I've always wanted to do a sea rescue. Thought it would be topping.' He chuckled. 'It was too.'

'I see.' He remembered how it had been Stokely up on the Downs who had asked him whether he could swim or not. There was much more to him than he'd first thought; he was no longer just one of the team of irresponsible boys trapped in the bodies of old age pensioners. No, he was more than that, and Abe wondered about the rest of the team, whether they too had changed and yet were, as Stokely suggested, different to other folk. 'We'll find them all,' he said finally.

Stokely looked at him oddly.

'The rest of the team. What do you think? Get you together.'

'For a game of football?'

'I don't know, probably not,' Abe admitted. 'I just think it might be a good thing.'

'You're worrying about Miss Dunne, aren't you, skipper? I wouldn't. She said we'd all meet up on the high point of the Downs. No point in fretting; she'll be there.'

'Yes,' said Abe.

They slipped into the little estuary at Shoreham, and keeping to the edge of the current, they made their way upstream to a wide area of reedy marsh cut through by a tangle of channels. Still catching the sea breeze, Stokely skilfully weaved his way between the reed banks until they drew up alongside a wooden landing stage and a little boathouse, thatched in reed. 'Best hiding place in the world, this,' said Stokely with undisguised pride. 'Invisible, even from the air; not that I've seen a plane for years and years.'

They packed away the boat and then Stokely led Abe along a raised, narrow path through the marsh till they reached a wooded stretch of dry land. Here he gave a long low whistle and was answered by a soft whinny and a moment later his horse trotted out towards them. 'He'll manage us both, won't you, boy,' said Stokely, rubbing the horse's nose affectionately. The horse ducked his head and butted Stokely in the chest; almost, Abe thought, knocking him over.

'Are you sure he won't mind?'

'The only thing he minds is if he gets his supper. It will be a late one tonight though.'

The sun was low when they started the climb up the Downs and was right down on the horizon by the time they reached their meeting place. There they found Abe's horse but not Alicia.

They scoured the surrounding area, looked for signs of a scuffle, or marks of more riders but there were none. 'She's hoofed it, I'd say,' said Stokely at last.

'Hoofed it?'

'Yes, hoofed it. Not to the safe house; rather had the feeling that she and Ida didn't see eye to eye . . . '

'If she has gone anywhere at all,' said Abe suddenly, but with absolute certainty, 'it's to Oxford. It would be a perfect place for her to study the book she's stolen, and it's safe too, isn't it, you said so.'

'Safe as houses,' said Stokely. 'Not a witch for miles, so I believe. Or that was the case.'

And if she's not there, thought Abe, it means she's still in Brighton and has joined her mother. He didn't say this to Stokely, though. Instead, he stood a little apart from his companion, looking down towards Brighton. It was an ugly smear of grey mist, derelict buildings, and sullen orange fires and as he stood there the full darkness of the evening drew down on the city of witches.

'Time to get cracking,' said Stokely, having saddled up Abe's horse for him.

'Yes,' agreed Abe. Alicia would never stay in Brighton, not in a million years—not her style. Whatever it was that she really wanted it wasn't all this ruin and misery. He remembered the single voice calling out good luck to him just as he was launched into the sea. If there was one, then there would be others who would defy the witches; the beginning of an army, perhaps. The team, if they were all like Stokely, and if he could find them all, would be the core and then they would draw in others: the ragged out-people, escaped slaves . . . They would flock to his standard: Ebrahim Ma'halli, hounder of witches, war-lord of Britain. 'Yes,' he repeated, 'let us hoof it to Oxford and there we shall find Alicia.'

THIRTEEN

Of course they didn't ride straight for Oxford. 'Home first,' insisted Stokely, and though Abe argued that time was precious, he wouldn't listen. They would have to see Ida, he said, and anyway they would need supplies. 'She won't like it,' he chuckled, 'won't like it at all, but the old girl has to know.'

Abe called him stubborn and threw up his hands in despair. He saw a dark horde of witches and Lakins sweeping the country, closing in on Alicia, hunting her down while he and Stokely plodded around Sussex. It made no sense, he said, it made no sense at all. But eventually Abe had no choice but to give way; Stokely was the guide, he would be lost without him. So, a little sulkily, he followed Stokely through the darkness, down across the River Adur and then, skirting woods and copses, they made their way up to higher land, cutting past Chanctonbury Ring and then, with no misadventure, across into the high-hedged fields of Ida's safe house.

Ida did not like their plan at all. 'I never trusted that young She and you know that well, so bad riddance to her. Your friend here can stay or go,' she said to Stokely, 'but you stay back here and none of your roaming, Uncle. Keep quiet and keep safe.' Her eyes glinted fiercely but Stokely was as quietly stubborn with her as he had been with Abe. He just nodded and chuckled and called her a dear old thing and told her that she should stop being an ostrich and that they would be leaving at first light. And then he went out, leaving Abe and a very cross Ida alone.

After a moment's silence she suddenly said, 'That She is one of they-people and they do nothing but harm. Why did you bring her here? Maybe you're like her, are you? Maybe with your dark skin and foreign way of speaking, maybe you are as much one of thcy-people as that twisty honey-tongued She.' She glared at him and he knew that there was little he could say to calm her down; she feared losing her brother for a second time, and that was it.

'No one is safe, while Mrs Dunne and the sisters have all the power,' said Abe. 'But Alicia will stand up to them and we'll help her.'

'And when you fail?' she said, gripping the arms of her great wooden chair, and glaring at him. 'And when they gut you and skewer you over their black cauldrons or whatever foulness they do and when they take my poor brother and all the other fools who you'll steal away into danger, what then, what is left? You tell me. Now at least there are safe houses, and they leave us be. What blight is going to fall when you start meddling with the way of things?'

Abe stood up. 'We shall not fail,' he said to Stokely's sister. Then he turned on his heel and walked out, wishing that he felt as convinced as he sounded.

They bedded down in the stables, snatching the few hours that were left before sunrise. Abe fell asleep almost immediately, aware that Stokely was still sitting up, a blanket round his shoulders, watching the candle burn down.

Abe was woken by the murmur of voices. The candle had burnt out, but there was light coming from a lamp over the stall. Stokely was already up and talking to Ralph. Abe suspected that Stokely hadn't slept at all. Ralph handed Abe a heather-coloured hooded cape and told him to wear it. 'Folk'll be suspicious of strangers and more so of a boy riding open when they-sisters are rounding up all the boys they can find, so keep your head covered.' He also gave them leather satchels packed with supplies, which they slung behind the saddles and then they led the horses out into the yard. There was no group of well-wishers this time, just Ralph.

'Good luck to you both,' he said and then to Abe's surprise, coming up close to the horses and lowering his voice, he added: 'Know this, Uncle, if it comes to a fight, you can count on me and maybe others here too. I won't gainsay Aunt Ida, but I fear me, sometimes, how long we can keep safe up here, ducking out of sight of they-people. You been down to the coast and seen what they do. Maybe they have all the country in their power, maybe not, but if you find some fashion of sweeping them away, you call on me, do you hear?'

And so they rode out, for the second time, through the gates of the safe house, but this time they turned west. They followed the River Rother on their long route to Petworth, a ghost town, and then towards Winchester, where Stokely had an idea they might find shelter.

'The word is that it's one of the towns that's stayed clean,' he said. 'But they keep to themselves. Don't expect a red carpet rolled out, skipper.'

'How do you know so much, Stokely?'

'Me? Oh, I don't know much, skipper, just knocked around a bit and got big ears, you know. I hear things.' He chuckled and rode on ahead. Abe pulled a face and then nudged his horse to catch up. It would be nice, he couldn't help thinking, to get simple answers to simple questions.

They passed through rough land tangled with briar and gorse and hamlets where shadowy people scuttled out of sight and then peered at them from behind half closed doors. They kept a sharp lookout but saw no sign of witches or Lakins hunting for them. Still, they were careful. They kept away from shady places, dark valleys with twisting streams, and all woods, no matter how small. 'All bad news,' said Stokely, 'sour with old magic. Don't know what you'll meet.'

'You mean the magic is in the air itself?'

'Couldn't tell you, skipper. Just know they're dodgy, like those battlefields of the First World War, all the craters and holes filled up with gas and bad air; except now, thanks to Mrs D and her crew, it's not mustard gas but half-spent spells.' Passing by one such wood, the silence was suddenly broken by a wild cacophony of howling and sobbing and they glimpsed shapes crashing through the undergrowth and then some creature bolted out into the open. It looked like a pig but was as big as a horse and when it saw them it barked and snarled and bared its teeth before wheeling back and out of sight.

That night they took turns to keep watch but nothing troubled them and the next morning they reached Winchester. Though it was early, there was a hive of activity around the edge of the city: men, women, and even children were bustling to and fro, carrying buckets and baskets, wheeling barrows and leading carts. The city's perimeter was marked by a wide ditch, on the inner side of which was a raised bank and it was along this bank that the people toiled. It suddenly dawned on Abe what they were doing: they were building a wall, a city wall! 'Like the middle ages!' he exclaimed.

Stokely shook his head. 'They hope stone walls will keep out the sisters and their magic but I bet all it will do is keep away travellers like ourselves. Well, let's see how friendly they are, skipper.' And he spurred his horse forward.

They followed the dirt road down to the ditch and crossed a crude wooden bridge. They had been seen approaching and a band of men armed with heavy looking cudgels and staves stood waiting for them. Those working on the early stages of the wall nearby downed tools to watch.

'That's far enough.'

Both Stokely and Abe reined in their horses.

'What do you want here?'

Stokely did not seem in the least put out by their

reception. 'Looking for a night's shelter, old boy, and a bit of tucker would be spiffing . . . '

'What do you mean: "boy", and what in the devil's name is "tucker"?'

The men, unlike those working on the first stage of the city wall, wore heavy beards which made Abe think of the seven dwarfs in 'Snow White' though they were neither friendly nor small. They were dressed in much the same way too: baggy brown jumpers that flopped loosely at the sleeves, and trousers tucked into riding boots. The jumpers had a red circular patch sewn on the right shoulder. It was a uniform of sorts, which meant, Abe realized, that there had to be someone in charge. He edged his horse up beside Stokely. 'Food,' he said. 'He means food.'

'Then why can't he talk properly?' The men began to move in around them.

'I think we should ride on,' said Abe quietly.

'But I'm starving.'

Abe glanced up at the people working; their faces were impassive. One of the women turned away and picked up her basket as if she didn't want to be party to whatever was going to happen. A boy of about his own age stared down at him and then he too turned away. They all did, one by one, and carried on with their work, or moved away from the wall, down towards the first houses of the city. It was odd, unsettling, but the fact there were boys there was a good sign, Abe decided. It did mean the city was safe from the sisters.

'Down from your horses!' barked the leader. 'And pull back them hoods.'

Stokely dismounted and Abe lifted the cowl off his head and was about to follow suit, when the leader suddenly shouted: 'Grab them; that one's a boy,' and in two seconds Abe was tumbled from his horse and had a bearded giant on either side of him.

Stokely, always so quiet and mild mannered, suddenly

straightened; his face sharpened in anger. 'What do you think you're doing! I have never been treated like this before.' There was a thin fleck of foam at the edge of his mouth and his eyes were grey shards of flint. 'You will take me straight to your council and if you don't move right now I promise you you will burn on a slow fire!'

The leader took a step backwards, blinking stupidly. One of the other men raised his staff, but then hesitated, uncertain what to do in the face of this old, thin man who half a minute ago they could have cudgelled and tossed into the city ditch without a second thought. The others looked equally bewildered.

'Worms!' snapped Stokely. 'Who's in charge here? You!' He rounded on the men holding Abe. 'Let go that young man before I fry you in boiling oil.' They did so and very quickly, too, almost pushing Abe away from them, as if his arms were red hot. Then, to the leader Stokely said, 'Out of the way, you slack-jawed, black-bearded maggot, I need to speak to the mayor of this dung-heap of a city.' And with that, he snatched the reins of his horse from the man who'd been holding it, and swung back up into the saddle. Abe instantly followed suit and the two of them put their heels to the horses' flanks and set out for the centre of Winchester at a smart trot, the humiliated city guards in their baggy jumpers running along after them.

'Magnificent!' said Abe. 'Magnificently waxy.'

'Eh? Was a bit, wasn't I?' And Stokely chuckled. 'He-he. Found out ages ago that nobody liked me shouting. Don't do it often. Bad form. Are they still following, skipper?'

Abe looked back. 'Yes, but they can't keep up.'

'Good. Good. This way.' And without hesitation, he led the way straight to the centre of the city. Rather oddly, there were still one or two signs of the old world that had existed before Abe's trip to Egypt: cars painted in bright greens and yellows that had been turned into horse-drawn carriages. Abe also noticed a rusting Belisha beacon and telephone booths which seemed to be used as shelters, perhaps for the baggy-jumpered guards, a number of whom Abe saw patrolling the streets in ones and twos. The houses were shabby, but for the most part they were occupied and the streets they rode down were free of rubbish; there were shops and stalls open for business though there wasn't anyone to do business with. Most people must have been out working on the walls.

'How do you know which way to go?' said Abe as they cut through a narrow street and came out in front of a large square building with wide steps leading up to a double-fronted door, in front of which stood two more bearded guards.

'You'll see,' and he chuckled again but his expression was uncharacteristically serious.

'What's going on here, Stokely? You said the town was safe but those guards with their patches—did you see?—and these ones are the same.' Abe lowered his voice. 'Red is Mrs Dunne's favourite colour.'

'I know.' He slipped down from his horse. 'Come on, skipper. Bit of a surprise for you coming up.' He looped their reins round a railing, 'And for an old friend who should know better.'

Abe was surprised. 'So, you've been here before?'

'Oh yes,' said Stokely absently, 'I've been everywhere before.' And before Abe could question him further he was striding up the steps. He barked at the guards to stand aside, which they did, though sullenly enough, and he and Abe entered the building.

Inside there were more men and women than they had seen in their whole ride through the town but none of them paid any attention to the two cloaked strangers. They were all busy rushing upstairs and in and out of different rooms, carrying piles of papers and stuffed briefcases, scribbling notes and looking busier than ants in an ant hill.

Stokely threaded his way through the bustle, and with

Abe following close on his heels, made his way up the main staircase, through a series of small rooms where people were working, heads down at their desks, and then finally burst into a large imposing chamber with a polished wooden floor and huge windows that looked out onto the cathedral. Sitting behind a splendid desk at the far end of this grand room was a rather small, but very round elderly man; a man whom Abe recognized instantly.

'Goodness me!' he exclaimed.

The little man got to his feet. 'Stokely, old bean, how spiffing.' And then he saw Abe. 'I say! The skipper!' He hesitated slightly. 'What larks, eh! Come in. Come in.'

Stokely shut the door firmly behind them and turned the key in the lock. 'Roberts, you stuffed prune,' he said coldly, 'what have you been doing?'

FOURTEEN

'This and that, don't you know. Pull up a pew, chaps.' Roberts, ignoring his friend's cool tone, beamed and bobbed and rubbed his hands together, but he did not come round from behind his huge desk to greet them.

'What are you now?' asked Stokely.

'Mayor,' said Roberts. 'Lord bloomin' Mayor. Good, don't you think? Doing splendid things. Absolutely tip-top, Stokely, no, really, you'll be impressed. You too, skipper, I expect, though you're a bit of a sprog now, compared with us chaps. Ha! Ha! Still, that's all past, isn't it? Onward and upward, that's my motto . . . '

His forehead gleamed with perspiration and he spoke more and more quickly as if he were terrified of allowing a gap in which Stokely might ask more questions.

'Probably passing through are you, chaps? Shame, terrible shame. Still, I can sort out plenty of tucker for your journey. Probably want to go right now. Won't hold you up . . . '

Roberts, one time forward in Abe's football team, didn't want them there; that was obvious. He was frightened, that was obvious too. He avoided looking at either of them directly and was behaving, Abe thought, very much like a dog who knows it has done something very wrong, like being sick in the middle of the carpet. And Roberts had done something wrong before.

As a thirteen year old, Roberts had made cruel fun of a gangly little girl called Delia Dunne. That was before either he or his team mates had realized that Delia was not an ordinary little girl at all but a girl on the edge of becoming a witch—the most powerful witch in Britain, as it happened; Mrs Dunne, mother of Alicia. Because of

Roberts, this gangly girl cast her first spell and the whole team were, as a result, trapped in a photograph. And that, until Abe came along, was that.

It is not wise to make fun of anyone, thought Abe. But then Roberts, despite becoming mayor of Winchester, seemed far from wise.

'Won't hold us up?' There was that steely quality in Stokely's voice again. 'You're a rum one, Roberts, aren't you? Been doing a little business with the sisters? Been picking up a few tips from "Her" have you, old chap?' He advanced on the desk and towered over Roberts. 'What are all these thugs you've got? And how did you manage to make all those families slave away humping huge stones about? Explanations, you fat weasel, and right now.'

Roberts slumped into his grand chair where he looked even smaller. 'Well, the city needed walls. Keep all the riff-raff out. Bit of protection. It's the way things are, Stokely. Living in the real world, you know. Everyone agreed, or most of them did, you know, and it was all for the best. This city is going to be the absolute tops, Stokely, safe as houses. I mean absolutely . . . ' His explanation tailed away and he sat there rather miserably twiddling his thumbs. 'I did do a deal,' he admitted. 'They said they wouldn't come for the boys, if I agreed to something and they said they would help me get things done and, don't you see, they promised that Winchester would be safe . . . '

'You let them in?'

He nodded.

'You clot, Roberts! The place was safe until you let them in!'

'It didn't feel safe,' he said miserably. 'She said she would do terrible things.'

Abe gave a loud involuntary sniff and then looked around. Was it safe now? Those guards, why did they all look the same, just like the Lakins? The sisters could do that: pick a willing slave and multiply it into an army. Surely it could mean only one thing: there was a witch in the city. He went to the window and scanned the street. No sign of anything wrong but they should leave all the same.

'I think we'd better go now,' he said.

'Yes. Yes,' said Roberts. 'It's not safe. You really should go, Stokely. I have made a bit of a bosh of it.'

'Is that it?' said Stokely. 'Are you positive you haven't left anything out, anything you'd rather get off your chest?'

'It was the deal,' said Roberts miserably. 'It seemed harmless at the time, specially the bit about you, skipper. Awfully sorry.'

'Me?' said Abe.

'Yes. They were to give me all this help and in return all I had to do was to hand over a few people from time to time. Didn't think that was so bad. We've had to lock up the odd outlaw for pinching things. Serve them right, I thought, to pitch them over to the witches. It was the other thing that'll make you miffed, I'm afraid.' He took a deep breath: 'I said I would give you to them, skipper, if you ever turned up. But we'd left you behind all that long time ago, back in Egypt. I never thought we would see you again.' He stared at his thumbs as if they were somehow to blame. 'Told you I'd made a bosh of it.'

Abe sniffed again. 'That is not everything, is it? They are here in the city! Why didn't you tell us straight away?'

Roberts shook his head miserably but as he opened his mouth to speak there was a thundering bang at the door and then an icy cold voice called out, 'Why is this door locked? Let me in instantly.'

Roberts shook himself. 'In a meeting,' he shouted. 'Come back later.' Then he said to Abe. 'Don't have any tricks or schemes up your sleeve, do you, skipper?'

Another bang and furious screeching from the other side of the door.

Abe closed his eyes and concentrated; they needed to be somewhere else. Anywhere would do—but all he could picture was the room they were in. It would even help if he could disguise himself; if he could do what his father managed so well and make himself look a little different but there was no time for experimenting now. He pulled the cowl of his cloak low over his head.

'Hang on a jiffy,' shouted Roberts. Then to the other two, he said, 'Bluff it out, or a barge through?'

There was a crackle and a sharp stink, the door suddenly disappeared, and in stalked an angry white-faced sister. 'We're looking for the girl, Mrs Dunne's daughter.' She stopped in the middle of the room and slowly looked around. 'Has she been here?'

Abe held his breath. The hunt was on for Alicia, of course, not for him. As far as they were concerned he was fish food now.

'Girl?' said Roberts. 'No, absolutely not.'

The sister made no sign of having heard him speak. She stood very still for a moment and then stared at each of them in turn. Stokely gave his sheepish smile, Roberts ducked his head, but Abe felt as if he were gripped in an ice storm. He felt the sudden cold suck the air from his lungs and he gave a slight gasp from the shock and then it was over. She turned her attention back to Roberts.

'Who are they?'

'Friends.'

'Friends! How very human.' Then, her cold voice sinking into permafrost, she said, 'If we ever find out that Miss Dunne has been here, we will turn your precious "safe" city into the rat-ridden refuse dump that it really is, and you,' she poked her long sharp finger into Roberts's large soft stomach, 'will just be another rat, but fatter. Guards!' she called, and two of the bearded militia appeared in the doorway. 'We'll take these two "friends" back to Brighton. And another thing, old man, never keep me waiting.'

Come on, Nasfali, wake up! Abe's brain rattled like a

train. Where was Plan A? Plan B? Then he had it! 'Six!' he shouted.

Instantly both Roberts and Stokely shot their right arms up in the air, screamed: 'Warra hot tub!' and then winked at the startled witch.

'Five!' yelled Roberts. They spun round and wagged their bottoms.

It was genius. It was the team's secret weapon.

'Eleven!' yelled Roberts again.

Abe remembered eleven. He hurled himself into a forward roll, as did the other two, and kept spinning straight past the straight black legs of Mrs Dunne's minion and the slack-jawed guards through into the outer office. Then without a word to each other they were up on their feet, barging dizzily down the main stairs, shoving aside all the bustling self-important assistants, managers, under secretaries, and consultants. There was a screech from behind and above and then a hissing crackle and snap as the witch hurled a bolt of power snapping after them. It missed; searing along the ceiling and then smashing through one of the hall's big windows. The two guards stepped in through the front door to see what all the commotion was about and were belly-charged by Roberts and Stokely.

'Oof!' they exclaimed in unison.

Once outside, the three of them mounted, Roberts scrambling up behind Abe, and then they set off at a gallop across the slippery cobbles as guards came streaming out of the main entrance, and more converged on the square from the high street.

There was the clatter of hoof on stone and then the snake-whispering hiss of witch's magic rippling across the cobbles towards them.

'Don't look back!' shouted Stokely.

Abe gritted his teeth, expecting the magic to burn, bite, or freeze them but nothing happened and there was not even any time to wonder why.

'Left!' shouted Roberts in Abe's ear and he yanked the reins, bringing his horse into a skidding turn, and they were galloping across the green down one side of the cathedral and in seconds all the commotion was behind them. There was a series of rights and lefts as Roberts guided them away from the main thoroughfare, down a twisty little street, and then they forded the shallow, chalk-clear River Itchen and so out of the city.

They rode hard and fast and only stopped when they reached high ground and could look back to see whether they were being followed. There seemed to be streams of people running to and fro and parties of riders setting off at the gallop up the London road and down to the coast but for the moment at least no one had picked up their trail.

They pressed on, kept to rough ground and away from the old roads; and that night they camped on the edge of Micheldever Forest. When Abe wondered whether this was safe, Stokely chuckled. 'Oh no, but that nasty piece of mischief that Roberts has been doing business with is too stupid to think that we might take a risk and come this way. She'll just have her guards rattling up and down the roads till their feet are blistered and she herself is so mad she'll burn half the city down.'

Roberts, who had been staring disconsolately at the little portion of biscuit and dried meat that they were sharing for supper, looked up, horrified, and then pulled out his handkerchief.

Stokely broke his biscuit in two, selected the smaller portion and began to eat it. Roberts dabbed his face with his handkerchief. 'It's all my fault, isn't it? My fault again.'

Abe felt sorry for him. 'You led us out of the city.'

'Yes, but it was your idea to use Griffin's tricks.'

'That's the skipper's job,' said Stokely.

'This is true,' said Abe, though without much conviction. 'I have ideas. I have schemes.' In truth, he felt particularly bereft of any schemes at all. Here they were, the three of them, huddled against the creeping darkness, the looming presence of Micheldever Forest hanging over them, and yet they had escaped, and it wasn't the first time they had managed to do so. Was this something that he, Ebrahim Nasfahl Ma'halli, was particularly good at or was it because he and Alicia and Stokely and perhaps all the other members of the team were bound together in some way that made them stronger or slippier than the witches? That was a comforting thought.

We are like the silver links in chain mail, he thought. Then he looked at gangly Stokely and the profoundly round Roberts and frowned. They didn't look much like gleaming chain mail, and that was a pity. But it seemed true that on their own they could be captured or tricked or terrorized but together, they were . . . what? They were . . . like the arms of the mighty octopus! Yes, thought Abe, this is what they were, and with their weaving arms they would indeed unravel Mrs Dunne's misery making, her malice, her endless spells. 'Octopus!' he exclaimed, much cheered by the direction his tired thoughts had led him.

'Where?' Roberts, who, despite his expansive mayor's waist could move with surprising agility, was up on his feet and facing the forest.

'No, no, I was just thinking,' said Abe. 'We are all different, you see.'

Roberts nodded, looking around him and not seeing very much.

'We do different things but it is when we are together that we are at our best.'

'Like at the match at the pyramid place,' said Stokely.

'Yes,' said Abe, 'and we won there, didn't we?'

'You think that with the team together, we can beat her?'

'With Alicia too,' said Abe, 'no problem.'

'Wizard,' said Roberts, folding himself down into a

sitting position again and resting his hands on his comfortable stomach.

And with that the tension eased and they talked quietly over their meal. 'How did you know I had made such a bish,' said Roberts. 'Was it really the wall?'

'No, you said you always say "onward and upward" and you never do,' remarked Stokely.

'No, I don't, do I? I panicked a bit. Sorry.' And then, after a moment's silence, 'I didn't really like being in charge, you know. I don't think I am very good at it; but you know what I think I should do?'

'What's that, Roberts, you veritable prune,' said Stokely.

'I should like to help you bring everyone back together again, Stokely.'

'You will,' said Abe, but he was only half listening and didn't register that Roberts had been addressing Stokely and not him. What Abe was wondering was whether Alicia felt the same way about the team as he did or whether she felt she could manage all on her own. He wondered why that witch in Winchester hadn't managed to stop them or stun them with her bolt of magic.

Roberts unfolded himself and lay flat on his back and began to snore. Stokely, like Abe, remained sitting staring into the dying embers of their tiny fire. Abe studied him and wondered how different he was from other people, and whether Roberts was different too. Was it only coincidence that they both happened to live in places that were, or should have been, outside Mrs Dunne's sphere of control; though she had wheedled her way round poor Roberts, hadn't she? Tricked him or frightened him into becoming her agent almost.

He shook his head. He was rambling. Was it wishful thinking to believe that these two had special powers? If only he could talk to Alicia. He hoped she really would be in Oxford. She had to be. She just had to be.

Part Two
The Gathering

FIFTEEN

That night, camped on the edge of Micheldever Forest, they had all been racked with nightmares. The next morning, they had stirred early, pale and exhausted, and immediately set off. The day had been dull, heavy with mist, and Stokely, the only one of them to have made the journey before, found it hard to keep his bearings. It was eerie: shapes loomed at them out of the grey. They heard creatures grunting and howling and they were chased not once but twice by packs of lean, long-toothed hunting dogs. The first time they escaped by fording a river and though the pack bayed and howled, none were bold enough it seemed to plunge into the water after them; the second time, they took refuge in a ruined and roofless cottage. The dogs hurled themselves at the rotten door and bounded at the gaping windows. Armed with anything that could be used as a club—Abe found a rusty poker, Roberts, the leg of a chair, and Stokely a blackened frying pan—they clouted the nose of any beast that appeared snarling and yellow-eyed at the window.

After an hour of these sudden attacks, the three of them despaired of ever being able to escape from their siege. Stokely managed to light a small fire and they were contemplating making a dash for it on horseback, each of them wielding a burning torch. 'It will be heroic,' Abe had said hoping to encourage them, and himself, but they could not manage to make the wood do more than sputter and glow. Roberts complained that it wouldn't frighten a fish or even a poodle, and Abe was forced to concede that maybe it wasn't such a good idea. Then when they had almost given up, they heard thin, high whistling, first from one direction and then from another. There was a renewed frenzy of barking from the dogs and then, quite suddenly, the barking was further away and then muffled by the mist, and then silence. They never heard the whistling again.

They waited for a good twenty minutes and then cautiously led the horses out into the open. Above them the day seemed to lighten a little. For the first time the sun was visible, a sick, hazy yellow blur low in the afternoon sky, and they moved through a kind of twilight world of patchy haze, dull light, and lengthening shadow. But even that small sight of the sun cheered them.

Although they were in better spirits all of them were conscious of being watched. 'Out-people,' murmured Stokely, 'just keep going.' Abe saw them on a number of occasions. At least he thought it was them, shadowy figures who slipped back into the grey whenever he glimpsed them.

'Why did they whistle off the dogs, do you think?' asked Abe.

'Just be jolly pleased they did,' puffed Roberts. 'Not much rhyme or reason about anything, if you ask me.'

Abe had felt better. 'I was asking Stokely,' he said bluntly.

'They're not all so bad.' Stokely gave a chuckle. 'Or so I'm told.'

'Who told you?'

'Oh, you know. Friends in the right places and that sort of thing.' Clearly the thought pleased him for he chuckled again.

'Like me then,' said Roberts.

'Oh no, not like you,' replied Stokely, nudging his horse ahead. 'Not like you at all, old prune.'

'Well, how different?' asked Roberts.

'Clever,' came the distant reply.

Abe wasn't paying attention to this last exchange but remembering the band who'd attacked him and Alicia up on the Downs. Frightening though they had been, they were no friends of Mrs Dunne and the sisters. Supposing there was a way of making an alliance with them; there had to be thousands of them, scattered through the countryside, scavenging a living, but determined to stay free. Could they ever be a force, he, Alicia, and the team could use? He would ask her, he thought, when they reached Oxford. How he longed for the end of this slow journey. He pulled his cloak tight round him. Not much comfort in this freedom—what was it to be cold, hungry, and living all the time with the danger of what Stokely called the old sour magic.

Another day had passed and the mist finally drifted away. The world felt as if it had stuck somewhere on its orbit and they lived in a perpetual half light; but at least they could see, though what they could see provided little comfort. Groups of Lakins, some in fours and fives, and some in great columns, slouched purposefully along the roads, all heading north. Outside Newbury, tucked out of sight on the edge of a cutting, the three travellers watched a long ramshackle train silently gliding along the track; like a snake, thought Abe. He turned to Stokely who was crouched down beside him. 'I thought the trains didn't work. I thought they just used slaves to pull them.'

'See. At the front,' he said, ' "they" are doing it.'

He was right: there was no engine hauling the carriages, but at the very front, on an open car, stood four of the sisters, legs slightly apart to balance, hands gripping the rail, their hair streaming behind them, their blood-red lips moving, as if they were chanting, driving the train silently on in a rush of air. As carriage after carriage streamed by below them, Abe saw hundreds and hundreds of Lakins, stonily sitting, never looking out, their sweat-fat faces blankly staring forward.

'And they are going the same way as us,' said Stokely. 'I only hope they are not heading where I think they're heading.'

'You don't really think they're going to Oxford, do you?' said Abe.

'If they're on the hunt for Miss Dunne,' said Stokely, 'I think I'd say it was a distinct possibility, old chap.'

It wasn't just possible, it was fact. On the third day of their journey, they found their way blocked. Looking down on the Oxford plain from the Berkshire Downs, they saw a scattering of fires, right and left, stretching for miles. Roberts volunteered to go down and spy. Returning several hours later and completely out of breath from the climb back up the hill, he told them that what they could see was a sprawling camp, without any kind of centre or limit, a confusion of patched tents, old caravans, and shanty shelters knocked together with bits of tin and old boxes. There was nothing to indicate that this was a military camp but that was exactly what it was; Mrs Dunne's army of monstrous, greasy, barrel-chested chefs, her Lakins, armed with meat cleavers and clubs and then, in amongst them, thousands of slaves.

'They looked awful,' Roberts said. 'I didn't realize. Didn't want to know what happened to all those out-people we sent to the witches. Shouldn't have done it, skipper.' He mopped his red face with a handkerchief. 'They've had all the stuffing knocked out of them. Never seen anything so wretched. You know, they don't talk to each other but they mutter all the time. And you know what they say?'

Abe knew.

Roberts's usual self-satisfied plump face had a genuinely upset expression.

'They say: "I hurt", don't they?'

'Awful,' said Roberts. 'Bally awful.'

Abe thought of those slaves he'd seen in Brighton, dulled by drudgery, devoid of will power, capable only of obeying. They were hardly people any more; just husks. But there had been that one voice calling out to him before they'd shoved him into that rotten boat. Perhaps there was always hope.

'They've got hangers-on too,' continued Roberts, 'Johnny no-goods, weasel faces looking for some pickings. Heard them talking about what a whopping shopping trip binge they were going to have when they finally got into Oxford and that would just be the first.'

'There are a few free towns,' said Stokely to Abe, 'like Winchester and Oxford.'

'Where the other members of the team live?'

Stokely nodded. 'Perhaps.'

'And London?'

'London,' said Stokely, and then started to hum 'London Bridge is falling down'. 'London is full of tricks and surprises,' he added and nodded contentedly.

'Well, it may be,' said Roberts, 'but I think we are well and truly stumped. Either we find our way round that lot or we might as well pack up and go home.' Then he suddenly bit his lip.

'We do not go round,' said Abe. 'There are many paths through the desert but the wise and the brave choose the one that is straight.'

Stokely stopped his nodding and gave Abe a keen look. 'Sounding pretty Egyptian today, skipper.' He arched one of his tangled wiry eyebrows.

'Is this a good sign, Stokely?'

The old man tapped his nose. 'I'd say so.'

'But how are we going to barrel our way through that lot?' complained Roberts, clearly unimpressed by oriental wisdom. 'It's one thing sneaking about on the edge but we show our faces in there and we'll be pea soup!'

'They won't notice us,' said Abe. 'We shall wear disguise.'

'Bravo, skipper,' said Stokely. 'What disguise?'

Abe showed them. He padded up Stokely and himself so that they had the bulk of a Lakin.

'Why not me?' said Roberts and then looked down at

his tummy. Stokely chuckled and Roberts, catching his eye, gave his portly belly an affectionate pat, and chuckled too. 'All right, all right, but what about the rest of the disguise?'

'Wait.'

Abe vigorously rubbed dirt and grease into their sparse hair, and into his own. Finally he rummaged in their supply satchels, triumphantly holding up a couple of small apples.

'Cut them in half, and when we get to the camp slip them into your cheeks, it'll puff them out. Look.' Abe demonstrated what he meant and the two men nodded.

'I see.'

'Mmm, clever.'

But when Abe turned back to his horse to get an apple for himself, he was sure he heard a very clear 'Not' though he didn't know who said it. And then one of them muttered 'Lakins' and sputtered and the other murmured, 'Look more like muffins, if you ask me.'

'Muggins.'

More sputtering.

Abe pretended not to hear but the funny thing was that it cheered him up. They had no choice but try to go straight through. If the sisters caught Alicia and sacked Oxford, there was nothing else. As for their chances of getting through without being spotted, Abe had to admit that they were not wonderfully good, but it was better to face the danger with a laugh, even if, he decided, it was at his expense.

They waited till half-day turned into half-night, for there was hardly a difference between the two. Could these witches truly have the power to stop the turning world? And if they could do that, what was happening in far off places: would it always be mid-day in Cairo? Nobody could survive that, the Nile would evaporate, all the green lands would turn to dust; the people would shrivel, become as dry as husks; the children would die.

Not if he could stop them, they wouldn't. He kicked his heels against the flank of his horse and led the way down the hill and towards the fires. Roberts followed on foot, leading Stokely's horse.

And no one minded them: not a single guard, not on this side of the encampment, anyway.

Once inside the camp, Abe's confidence faltered. With neither stars nor sun visible, he no longer knew which way to go. Stokely, seeing him hesitate, drew his horse up beside Abe. 'Won't find your way without this little chap,' he murmured. 'Hold out your mitt, skipper.'

Abe was puzzled. 'I don't have one.'

'Your hand.'

Abe did so and Stokely slipped a tiny compass from a thong around his neck and passed it over. 'Fantastic,' murmured Abe. He clicked it open with his finger and then nudged his mount forward, following the needle north.

They wound their way past tents that were swollen with the snores of the monstrous Lakins; and gave as wide a berth as they could to the fires that had men grouped around them, muttering hoarsely, passing jugs to each other, swilling whatever brew it was they drank. They kept their cowls low on their foreheads and let their mounts pick their way slowly through the rubbish of the witches' army.

As they moved further north, they began to see signs of the sisters: silken pavilions billowed blackly up amongst the pinprick of fires. The Lakins they now passed were uniformed and they eyed the trio narrowly but still let them go by. Then, with half the night gone, the road ahead was suddenly clear.

They weren't more than a couple of paces beyond the Lakin front line before Roberts gave a great sigh of relief and exclaimed loudly: 'Blinking bravo! My feet are boiled with blisters. Haven't walked so far—'

'Shush!' hissed Stokely.

But it was too late.

'Oi! You! Watcher doin', fat guts? Come back 'ere.'

Abe reacted instantly, pulling up on his reins and leaning down to grab Roberts by the shoulder. 'Quick, up behind me again.' He shifted his grip to the fat forward's wrist and with a deal of kicking and 'oofing' Roberts struggled up.

'Oi!' shouted the guard again, starting to run towards them. Behind him there was more yelling and figures lumbering from the tents and shelters.

'Go!' Abe shouted. 'Ride like the wind!'

Stokely spurred his horse and streaked down the road ahead of them. Abe's horse, more heavily weighed down, could only manage a trot to start with. 'Come on! Come on!' urged Abe. 'You have to do better than that.' The patient horse pricked its ears and bent its neck; it was clearly trying. Close behind Abe could hear the pounding of heavy feet and the Lakins' laboured breathing. They were almost on them!

'Smash 'em and pulp 'em!' The voice that lobbed this unhappy suggestion to Abe's pursuers seemed to have been strained through thick gravy. 'Boil 'em and mash 'em!' it spittled and then the first Lakin was beside them, his great forearm reaching up, his stubby hand clamping like a lobster onto Roberts's leg.

'No, you jolly well don't!' snapped Roberts. There was a thwack and a sharp yelp, the Lakin snatched away his hand and then their horse finally picked up speed and they began to put some distance between themselves and their pursuers.

But the Lakins didn't give up. Over the sound of their horse's hoofs, Abe had heard the harsh clatter and boom of the giant dustbins they used as drums calling the alarm. Then, when he glanced back and got Roberts to duck, he could see more and more figures streaming out on to the road, spreading towards them like a thickening storm cloud.

'They'll tire soon,' he shouted back to Roberts, though he was not wholly convinced that they would.

'I'm jolly tired now. If I hold tight do you think I could grab forty winks while we ride, skipper?'

Abe didn't get the chance to reply because the air shuddered as a splinter-high piercing screech ripped through the banging and hoarse yelling of the pursuit.

Witches!

Overhead, flipping and twisting like bats, suddenly swooping, white faces distorted as they screamed their rage at him. He felt battered and buffeted. 'Nasfali!' they screamed. 'The boy, Nasfali!'

From down the road behind them, hundreds of Lakins suddenly roared: 'Jamboy!' Abe's eyes watered, his head rang, his hands began to lose their grip on the reins. The horse faltered. And then he felt Roberts's hand gripping his shoulder. 'Steady on, skipper. Don't mind them. Just keep going. Just keep going. Here's the Thames now . . . '

There was Stokely on the bridge, waiting for them. 'No,' Abe wanted to shout at him. 'Go. Don't wait.' The sisters would have them all, swoop down and snatch them with talon-like nails and scraw out their eyes. They were so close! He flinched as a sister hissed by, her black-heeled shoes catching the side of his head with a nasty crack. His exhausted horse, its eyes rolling with terror, its mouth flecked with foam, stumbled and stopped. Abe was aware of Roberts tumbling down and then grabbing the reins.

'Come on, come on,' he urged. The sister swooped again. Roberts somehow got the horse to move and half-pulling, half-cajoling the terrified beast, they too crossed onto the bridge.

'That's the ticket,' Stokely said, 'thought this might do the trick.'

Abe lifted his head and with some effort looked back. What trick?

'Thames,' said Stokely with a pleased chuckle, 'edge of their power for the moment. Safe as houses now.'

I do not feel safe as houses, thought Abe.

But Stokely was right.

As if they had run into an invisible barrier, the flying sisters zigged and zagged like flies at a window and then with a final stinging scream turned away and disappeared back towards the camp; while on the ground the bulging crowd of Lakins were wedged up to the beginning of the bridge, faces dripping, barrel chests heaving; the stink of their sweat wafted towards the three cloaked travellers. 'Come 'ere, jamboy,' they shouted. 'Come 'ere and we'll make yer into stew!'

Stokely, holding a handkerchief to his nose, beckoned Abe and Roberts to follow him, which they did; and so, at a slow walk, ignoring the fading shouts, they completed the final stage of their journey.

A soft, drifting rain had begun to fall as they reached the edge of the city. It seemed to wash away some of the fear and smell of their journey and Abe began to feel his spirits rise. It was as if they were entering a different country. Some houses were deserted but more were not. There were lights at windows, gardens that were tended, foxgloves drooping under the weight of their heavy heads. Figures they passed on the road even nodded greetings to them. They crossed the Folly Bridge and as they did so, the day had begun to lighten and the sun appeared. It was hazy, and a sickly yellow, but that didn't matter, in fact it cheered them further. The sisters didn't control everything. They couldn't stop the world turning; they couldn't stop night becoming day. They could just make it seem so.

'It's on the outside only,' said Abe happily. 'It's just pretend,' he added when he saw Roberts pulling a face.

'If you say so, skipper,' said Stokely.

'I jolly well do,' said Abe and gave Stokely the good

old thumbs up. Stokely chuckled and nodded and returned the gesture.

Intent on seeing the state the city was in, they hurried up to Carfax, passing more and more people as they did so. There were no cars, of course, but horses and carts and folk on foot, no thronging crowds, but busy enough. Almost normal, thought Abe, except perhaps for the slogans up on the walls. He'd seen the first on the Folly: 'Magic is tragic' and then more on Christ Church: 'Women against Witches!', 'Spells Smell', 'Watch out! Witch out!' and more and more that said the same thing: 'Keep this City Free'.

They left Roberts to find food in the market and Stokely led the way to Jonson's college, Greyfriars. They banged on the gates and a monk-like porter let them in. Jonson, the dean of the college, came to greet them, and nearly fell over himself with delight, particularly at seeing Abe whom he immediately recognized. 'Skipper,' he kept saying, 'Skipper! My blessed aunt! Skipper! And you're no older than you were! What a thing!' And there was much back slapping and hand shaking. Pleased as Abe was to see Jonson, he was more anxious to find out about Alicia.

'Of course! Of course! She is here. Miss Dunne is here, indeed she is. And you want to see her, of course, of course.'

'Yes!' Abe felt so happy, he punched the air. 'Yes! Yes!' he exclaimed. 'I knew she would be here. I knew it.' Which wasn't strictly true but joy sometimes makes exact memory a little dodgy.

'But she's terribly busy,' continued Jonson, 'won't see anyone at the moment. Won't see me. Doesn't even want to eat. Hasn't eaten since she pitched up two days ago.'

'She'll see me,' said Abe firmly. 'I have to tell her about what's been happening, she probably doesn't know. And she'll be anxious to know I'm all right.'

'Yes, of course.' But Jonson sounded doubtful. 'Thing is, skipper, she's upstairs in the college library and we can't actually, um, get up there.'

'It is not a problem,' said Abe, 'take us to the library of your college.'

Jonson led the way out into the fellows' garden, and then through a doorway overhung with the tangled stems of an ancient wisteria. 'This,' he said, 'is the library.' There was no one in the long room, no one studying at the tables, no sign of her. A little flight of stairs was visible at the far end. 'Up there,' said Jonson, 'but there is a problem, skipper, if you . . . '

But Abe didn't wait to listen. Though tired and lightheaded from lack of sleep and food, he ran down the central aisle. 'Alicia,' he shouted, 'I'm here!' and he would have bounded up the stairs except he couldn't. The air suddenly thickened and made a barrier; it was like pushing into sponge. 'Alicia! What are you doing!'

She was using magic, that was what she was doing, and she shouldn't have been.

'Alicia!'

Eventually Abe heard her voice. 'Nasfali, is that really you?' and with that the way suddenly became free. He went up the stairs, but not bounding two at a time, the excitement replaced by concern.

She didn't even look up from her book when he came into the reading room. 'Oh, Nasfali,' she said, eyes on the opened page. 'I knew mother wouldn't be clever enough to get rid of you. What did she do, put you to sea in a boat?' Abe couldn't believe it. No apology for abandoning him, none for failing to meet up on the Downs as they had arranged to do. No explanations, and no interest in their escape, their two escapes, or that terrible last part of their journey, and the terrifying things they had seen and of the imminence of their danger.

'What has been interesting you so much, then?'

'Power, of course. What else is there?'

He couldn't believe what he was hearing. 'What do you mean?'

'Are you deaf, Nasfali? Did my mother do something to your hearing or are you just being stupid. I do hate it when you're stupid. You are meant to be the clever one, you know.'

'But that's all they're interested in! I thought you weren't going to be like them.' He threw his hands up in the air in a gesture of despair and then quickly folded his arms before she criticized him for being so Egyptian. He had to be calm for if he was not disaster would overwhelm them all.

'Of course I'm like them. What did you think? I am what I am, Nasfali. My mother's a witch, and so is yours. We're different, that's it. I am just more different than you are.' She plucked a short black hair from her head and laid it carefully down the centre of the page she had been studying. 'And when I have finished studying this book I shall become more different still, and then we shall see what we shall see.' She slowly turned the page, smoothed it down and began to read, tracing the words and symbols slowly with her forefinger, pursing her lips slightly as she concentrated. A moment later, she said: 'You're still there, Nasfali. Have all those years of being made to stand out in the corridor of Prackton Hall done something to your legs?' He felt a firm pressure on his chest forcing him to take one and then another step backwards, until once more he was standing at the top of the stairs. 'Off you go,' she said. 'I have to concentrate. There must be something useful you can do.'

Useful! She had no idea. And she simply would not listen to him. 'They are coming and they are coming for you!' he said with suitable drama and arm waving. 'A huge army. We barely made it here with our lives.'

'You mean, you barely made it here alive.'

'This is what I have said.'

'But you are alive, which is,' she paused, 'wicked and of course they are coming for me, what did you expect? So can you go now so that I can get on with my work and then I'll be ready for them. See?' The gentle pressure on his chest turned into a poke, as if from one of Alicia's sharp fingers.

'All right,' he said, with as much dignity as he could muster, 'I shall go and be useful,' and he turned to go down.

He muttered crossly to himself as he descended. 'Be useful? Why should I be useful? I have been useful. She has her book because of me; that is useful. I have told her of the army; that is useful. Why should I be more useful?'

The air closed behind him, thickening with a faint 'glop' as Alicia once more sealed herself away.

'Something up, skipper?' Jonson and Stokely were waiting for him outside in the garden.

'Something is most definitely up,' said Abe. 'And "up" is not a good thing.'

Sixteen

Jonson's room looked down onto the garden and the library. Abe could even make out Alicia's desklight and her unmoving hunched outline. Behind him, Jonson, Stokely, and Roberts were holding what Roberts insisted on calling a 'council of war', but Abe ignored the sensible murmur of Jonson's voice, the clink of cup against saucer, and the louder, more excitable suggestions made by Roberts: 'Like to stuff thirty pairs of smelly socks up her nose! That would stop her sniffing after us. What do you reckon, Stoker?' Abe ignored them because he wanted to think and when he wanted to think he liked to make lists, numbering the points to himself. It made him feel he was being organized, decisive, and one step ahead of everyone else, except, at the moment, he didn't feel one step ahead of anyone. Shoved down the staircase like that, he just felt distinctly unwanted.

'More ignored,' he decided, 'than the most flea-ridden cur dog in the dirtiest back alley.' And that rather satisfyingly dismal picture made him think about Cairo. A dusty grey pigeon landed on the windowsill, eyed the glass and puffed up its chest, stepped jerkily to the other end of the ledge and then, startled by some movement, it exploded upwards in a sudden burst of feathery energy.

One, thought Abe. Why am I here, in this town, which is even now under threat of attack by Mrs Dunne and all the sisters of Britain? All my schemes, all my most cunning ways of raising money were devised with one single purpose: to get me to Egypt. He felt like smacking himself on the forehead. He was so stupid. I was in Egypt. I found my father. My father says, Ebrahim, come with me, and what do I do? I let myself come back here! And I do this because of 'she'. He couldn't bring himself to say her name. She had said come back. There was much to be done, much to be put right. She had not said that he would be hunted and used as a decoy. She had not said these things, so why should he help now? He nodded to himself. Why should he? Why should he not go back to Egypt? It was most tempting and he would find that most strange man, his father, again. But then he thought of a second point.

Two. It is not possible to go back. There are no planes and, unlike that pigeon or Mrs Dunne, I cannot fly. Yet he knew that there were other, more important reasons, and hearing Roberts burbling on to Jonson and Stokely reminded him.

'Build a bally great elephant trap,' he was saying.

'Why?' said Stokely. 'Why should we trap elephants? Elephants are already in the zoo, aren't they, Jonno. They always were.'

'Crikey, Stoker, how've you survived?' And then with elaborate emphasis, as if poor Stokely was the dimmest light bulb in the pack, he explained: 'We make the trap for them, and they all fall in and we have something really disgusting in the bottom of it, so that they get thoroughly bogged down.' He snickered and the others joined in.

Three, thought Abe. The most important reason was the team. He couldn't possibly leave them. What would it have all been for, if he walked away now? Nothing, it would have been for nothing.

And four. Four could not be omitted. Mrs Dunne was four, a poisonously pointy four. Everything she did was wrong; everything she did was bad. She would turn England, and the whole world, if she could, into a stinking, rat-ridden rubbish dump. She would make ordinary mothers and fathers into skeleton-skinny, empty-eyed slaves and their children would disappear into witch prisons. He remembered that grey, rubble-strewn underworld into which his own mother had thrown him; that terrible feeling of sadness, the faint touch of small hands, the voiceless pleading and he remembered the hurting slaves. Of course it was right to stop her and her kind. It was right to be a warrior. He saw himself caught in the glare of the desert sun, cloaked in black, no, no, midnight blue, his curved sword, his scimitar held high . . . and he would lead all those enslaved out from their wilderness . . .

He pulled a face. But was there mileage in doing so? All plans and schemes should have mileage. He was not sure why, but they should. Over in the library he saw Alicia close the book and stand up.

And there was a five, was there not? Alicia, the 'she'. Alicia was a serious problem because he didn't know what she was going to do next. He didn't know what she was going to learn, and, what was worse, she seemed to have forgotten that by using magic she was putting herself, and all of them, in danger.

Her silhouette slipped across first one and then the next library window.

What was she doing? he wondered. Was she stuck? Clever as the vision was, could she really manage to read a book that was perhaps hundreds, even thousands of years old? Neither Mrs Dunne, nor his mother, nor the whole gang of sisters had been able to make use of it. Of course, they were stupid and she wasn't but even so . . . But if she was stuck how would they be able to defeat Mrs Dunne? They would have to rely on themselves, wouldn't they, on being cunning, on clever schemes, on the team . . .

He saw Alicia at the window, like him, looking down, lost in thought. If she looked up, she would see him. She didn't, but abruptly turned away and went back to her desk. Would she really change because if she . . .

'Skipper?'

'Sorry?'

Abe turned back to the room, his train of thought interrupted. Roberts stood up, and rather bossily said, 'Skipper, Stoker and Jonson want to hear your plans. I've told them what I think. I think we should jolly well leave it up to Miss Dunne. She's up to some whatnotery or other and we know she can deal with her mum. Did it before, didn't she? You remember, chaps, don't you?' They nodded; they remembered the escape and the terrifying fight when Mrs Dunne had swollen into an octopus-armed monster and Alicia had battled with her, flashing wild blue magic. 'And so, I reckon that we shouldn't really stick our necks out if we don't need to, so I said to the others . . . '

'You mean you want to run away,' said Abe. Round Roberts was not brave. Abe didn't blame him for this. To run away is not a bad thing necessarily. People are what they are.

Roberts dabbed his brow with his handkerchief. 'Retreat,' he said fussily. 'Strategic whatnot. Desert campaign. Regroup. El Alamein. You know the sort of thing . . . '

Abe held up his hand to stop him. 'Please.' He would start talking about Spitfires in a minute. 'Is this what you all think?' he said, addressing Jonson and Stokely.

Stokely hunched his shoulders and pressed his knobbly hands between his knees. 'I do think Miss Dunne probably knows best but I don't know about leaving her on her own. I don't know that that would be right . . . '

Roberts, clearly thinking that he was still Mayor of Winchester, puffed up his chest and opened his mouth ready, no doubt, to put Stokely back in his box. But Abe gave him a stern look, which made him snap his mouth shut and sit down with a plomp.

Jonson leaned forward. 'I agree with Stokely, you know.' He spoke slowly, almost as if he were thinking out loud. 'Miss Dunne will need our help, I am sure of that. At the very least she has to eat sometime. We all have to eat, don't we.'

'It's only human,' agreed Roberts.

'And if she wants to study here,' continued Jonson, 'I am sure it is for a good purpose. I trust Miss Dunne to do what is right. She got us home, didn't she? It would be wrong not to help her now. And I think it wouldn't be at all decent to leave her here with Mrs You-know-who wanting to hunt her down. Wouldn't be right at all.'

The tips of Roberts's ears burned crimson. 'Wouldn't leave anyone in the lurch,' he huffed. 'Jolly well wouldn't. Skipper knows that, don't you? Got you both out of Winchester, jiggety jig, didn't I?'

'That is true,' said Abe.

'What do you think, skipper?' said Stokely. 'I'm sure you know what Miss Dunne is trying to do with that book she's got in there, don't you, and now you've told her about what happened to us and Mrs . . . ' he cleared his throat, 'and all that. Miss Dunne is bound to want to sort it out, isn't she?'

Sort it out! Stokely had such a simple way of putting it, as if someone had made a mistake over the laundry rather than the whole country becoming wrapped up in a sticky web of bad magic and misery.

'I'm not sure,' Abe said carefully, 'that this is something that can be just "sorted out" by leaving it all to Alicia. Though,' he continued, seeing the worried expressions around him, 'I think we should, of course, see how Alicia gets on.'

They nodded. Miss Dunne would 'get on'; they had little doubt of that.

'I also think,' continued Abe, 'that we should do two other things: we should get the team together again. I have a feeling that would be a good idea.'

This pleased Jonson. 'Yes. Yes. Had a hunch for long time now that we should be together. Already done a bit of tracing and you've kept in touch here and there, Stokely, haven't you?'

'Oh, yes,' said Stokely with his quiet little chuckle, 'here and there. I'm looking forward to seeing Thomas again. You remember, Jonno . . . '

Jonson smiled. 'I think that can be arranged.'

'Yes,' said Roberts importantly. 'This is what I've always said. We're at our best as a team and this is what I meant by going off, you see. I meant going off to get everyone together.' He looked around for support and when the other two politely nodded, he seemed to unwind a little, lose a bit of the pompous mayor and gain a little bit of the old eager schoolboy. 'We could have a game of footer again, couldn't we? Kick Mrs Thing over the goalpost. Hey? What do you think Jack would say?'

'Probably ask for a free kick!' said Stokely.

Roberts snorted and the rest of them laughed, Jonson included, at the thought of Jack booting Mrs Dunne down a football pitch. Wiping the tears from his eyes, Stokely said, 'But that wouldn't be a very monk sort of thing, would it, Jonno?'

'Well,' Jonson began.

'Oh, Jonno,' said Roberts, slapping his knee delightedly, 'you really are a bit of a shepherdy monk type of chap, aren't you? Still, it is a good wheeze, I must say.'

It was a good wheeze. Particularly good because the idea itself seemed to lift a shadow from the old men, and for a moment they sparkled as if they didn't have a care, almost as if they were thirteen again. However, there needed to be a practical side to any plan they made now. Mrs Dunne hadn't gathered that huge army just to sit around camp fires and sing songs; there was a war coming. He let them get over their giggles and then he said, 'We also need to plan the defence of this city. Is it possible, Jonson? The sisters didn't want to cross the Thames. Something was holding them back. Did you know about this?'

'Oh yes, sort of,' said Jonson. 'All the country round the city has been good for years. I mean safe. Farmers able to do their work. But we have been getting more refugees coming in. More in the last few weeks. Families having to leave their homes, because of horrible things happening: plagues of worms in their cereal at breakfast, horrible bright lights and screams all the way through the night. Those that tried to brave it out and lock themselves into their houses have disappeared. It's not been good news. But you're right; it's only been those families the other side of the Thames who seem to have been affected.'

'They don't like water,' said Abe. 'This is a certain fact. Could we ring the city in some way? It might act as a wall.'

'Oh yes,' agreed Roberts, 'that would be a proper job, better than the silly bit of building I tried to organize.'

'Perhaps we can. I know just the person we can ask.' Jonson walked over to the corner table by the fireplace where there was a black box with a winding handle on one side. He busily cranked the handle and then lifted up an old-fashioned telephone receiver. 'It's me,' he said. 'Can you come up. Some friends I want you to meet . . . Yes, yes, fine.' He put down the receiver.

'Are you really a monk?' said Roberts. 'I mean I know you've got the rig and all that . . . ?'

'Franciscan. Well, Capuchin, really, see, we've got hoods.'

'Is that to cover up the bald bits?'

'Course it is, Stokely. Don't you know anything . . . '

Cappuccino, thought Abe, watching the three men chatting, Roberts giving Stokely pokes in the ribs every so often and Stokely not minding, just leaning away from him and chuckling all the time. If we can defeat Mrs Dunne, it would be a great thing, greater than the match at the pyramids. In such an achievement there would surely be mileage. However, once they had defeated her, there would still be one more task that he would undertake; one that he wouldn't tell either Alicia or the team about. He turned back to the window. There she was still, hunched over, poring over the pages. The book could not stay in her keeping; it must go back to its true keeper, his father, and that would mean removing it from Alicia. He bit his lip. She wouldn't be at all happy about that. She would blaze and crackle like summer lightning and frizzle him up like a kebab. There was only one thing he could do: not mention it, not even think about it because of her way of knowing. So he shoved this long-term plan way down into a corner of his mind and turned back away from the window.

There was a sharp knock at the door.

'In you come,' called Jonson. In walked a short, thick-set elderly man, dressed in blue overalls and working boots. He had a snowy square beard and a rusty out-door face.

'Oh, my goodness me,' said the man in a soft sing-song voice, 'what are you boyos doing here? It's a flippin' miracle, Jonson. Been at the old prayer wheel, have you?'

'Thomas!'

Roberts, Stokely, and Thomas crowded together, shook hands and thumped shoulders, harder than they needed to, of course. At last Thomas broke away from his two old friends: 'Skipper,' he said coming up to Abe, and vigorously shaking his hand. 'You're part of all this bloomin' miracle business, aren't you, eh? And here you are, all this time and not hardly a whisker on your face! Well, now, if there's anything we can do for you, you just say the word.'

So Abe told him and Thomas listened closely.

'There's already the canal and the rivers,' he said. 'They make a kind of a horseshoe. Now, if we closed that off, you would have your ring all right. You'd be leaving everything but the old city on the outside, but we could do it. A bit of digging, mind, but a bit of digging did no one any harm, I'd say. A bit of a ditch.'

'A ditch a day, keeps the witch away,' chuckled Stokely.

'That's more words from you, laddy,' said Thomas giving Stokely an affectionate pat on the shoulder, 'than we had all the time on the farm. Well, boys, we had better get started. You'll authorize this, will you, Jonno? The whole city will have to pitch in, you know.'

'I shall call the assembly,' said Jonson.

At that moment there was a loud explosion, the sound of glass shattering, and a scream of rage.

SEVENTEEN

'What was that!'

Stokely paled. 'A bomb? They're dropping bombs.'

'No, the war's over, old chap,' said Jonson, giving his friend a pat on the arm, but he looked worried too.

'Dynamite,' said Thomas. 'Must be dynamite, but I wouldn't have thought there was any of that in the city. Somebody's gone and blown himself to pieces.' He gave his beard a tug. 'That would be a pity, wouldn't it?'

Abe wasn't paying attention. His eyes were fixed on the window where a wisp of blue-black smoke had suddenly drifted into view.

'Oh no,' said Roberts, scrunching himself into the corner of the sofa and jamming a pillow over his head. 'The witches are attacking.' His voice was muffled by the pillow. 'We'll all end up back in that beastly photograph!'

The smoke had thickened and was behaving in a very odd fashion. It was winding itself into a coil and, as Abe watched, the centre of the coil lifted and curved into a snake's head, with wide gaping mouth, and blind white eyes. The head slowly, lazily almost, turned and moved towards the window, staring in, as Abe, horrified now, stared out.

Sands of the desert! What did it want? The head swayed to the right. Was this the work of Alicia or of Mrs Dunne? What did it want?

'Skipper, you look as if you've seen a ghost.'

'Don't you see it?' he said, pointing, but even as he did so the smoke snake pressed itself horribly against the glass, flattening and spreading its head into a face from some black nightmare, and then dissolved into a wispy cloud.

'Fire!' they shouted.

'No, it wasn't that . . . ' but there wasn't any point in trying to explain. He ran to the window with the others crowding around behind him and they stared down at the library where blue smoke, threaded with veins of flickering light, was pouring from the shattered upstairs windows.

'Oh my,' murmured Stokely, 'I hope Miss Dunne is all right.'

'Alicia!' Abe hared out of the room, down the bare stone stairway. Poor Alicia. Was she dead? Blown into a thousand pieces?

His feet skidded as he pelted full tilt out into the garden. Dead? Lost? And what had she done? What had she released from that wretched book? 'Oh! Curse the book,' he muttered as he ran, 'and curse mother for having stolen it. A hundred million curses . . . '

He reached the library door at the same time as Alicia, her hands black, her face smudged, stumbled out into the garden.

He stopped in his tracks. 'Alicia! You're not dead! You're all right!'

'Of course I am not all right.' She rubbed her face, smearing the smoke stain into savage streaks and then she looked at her hands, turning them this way and that, as if she barely recognized them as her own.

'Are you hurt?' Something prevented him from stepping closer to her, as if she had a barrier round her. 'Did the book do this to you?'

'No! I did this. I did it. See? Books don't do things, you should know that.'

She was cross, in fact she was sounding as if she was cross with him, which was hardly fair.

'This book you wanted so much is not like other books,' he said solemnly.

'Oh, Nasfali, don't be so pompous. I know that perfectly well. I'm just tired, that's all.'

He wanted to tell her she looked as if she had been in a Tom and Jerry cartoon—was Tom the one who usually got blown up? But he didn't think it would be wise to say anything like that. Alicia liked to look different; she didn't like to look funny. Behind him, he was aware of Jonson, Stokely, and Thomas standing at the end of the corridor, not quite sure whether they should come out or not. Roberts, presumably, was still under a cushion up in the room.

'Should I get you a glass of water?'

Her voice softened. 'No, don't bother.' And the barrier which had seemed to surround her was suddenly no longer there. 'Here. Come here.' He stepped towards her and she caught hold of his wrist. 'Come and see this, Nasfali,' she said, pulling him into the smoke-filled library. He coughed. His eyes stung and began to stream with tears, so he shut them and let her tug him along, up the stairs where the air was now clearer, and to her desk. 'Look at it,' she said, indicating the book which lay open and undamaged by either smoke, fire, explosion, or anything else.

What was so special about it? He wiped the wet from his eyes. It was neither gold, nor on papyrus, nor illuminated; it was rather small, and its pages were creamy with unending lines of tiny cramped script, hand-written, of course. It lay open at the page which she had presumably been reading and looked as innocent as any open book might.

'See!' she said. 'It's not my fault, is it?'

He had never, as far as he could remember, ever said that anything was her fault. He shrugged. 'No.'

'Well?' her voice quavered. 'Look at it. How can I work out what to do when it's written like that?'

'What do you mean?'

'Look!' She gave her nose a sharp rub with the back of her dirty fingers. 'What's the matter with you? Can't you see?'

He looked. He said, 'May I?' and turned the page carefully. The paper was thick, a little shiny. Perhaps it wasn't paper at all. The writing itself was Arabic, some of it unfamiliar but clear. The characters, though small, were perfectly legible. What was the fuss for?

'Oh, Nasfali, you don't have to make a meal of it.'

'I am not making a meal.' Why did she say these peculiar things?

'I can't read it, can I?'

He stared at her blankly and then suddenly realized the problem. How stupid he was.

'I can only guess.' She gestured towards the shattered windows. 'And this is what happens when I guess.' She slumped down into the chair. 'I'm so tired, I could sleep for a hundred years.'

'You mustn't say things like that,' said Abe, alarmed.

'Why not? Oh why not . . . I'm knackered.'

'Because, if you say things, they can happen. Your mother . . . '

'My mother couldn't read Arabic either. The only difference is that she's happy just to have something important like this, have it in her power, even if it does her no good. She'll sit on it like a fat spider. That's no good to me.' She sighed. 'And the truth is, if I can't learn all the big stuff, Nasfali, we're sunk.' She closed the book slowly. 'We might as well give up. What would you say about that?'

He didn't immediately know what to say at all. If she couldn't read it then it would be a lot easier to smuggle it away from her and back to Cairo—but she was, he knew, right that unless she could unlock the book's knowledge she wouldn't be able to defeat her mother. And unless she defeated her mother, she would never be able to put things right.

'I thought you would be able to read anything,' he said. 'How did you think it would be written? No, no, all right,' he said quickly, holding up his hands when he saw

135

her darkening expression. 'I am not making a meal. It is just that this is the sort of thing that I thought you . . . ' he hesitated, 'your people were used to. You know, books of knowledge and ancient mysteries and so on.'

'Give me a break. My mother and her sisters! They're too lazy to do any serious study. They know what they know because it's been passed on to them. The most radical bit of research in the last thousand years was them finding out about the existence of this book and nicking it from your dad.' She paused. 'Oh well, maybe it's not such a terrible thing that I can't read it. It was just making me bad-tempered and . . . '

'And?'

'Well, if you must know it made me feel weird.'

Abe looked down at his feet and then, rather carefully, said, 'You're never weird, Alicia.'

That cheered her up. 'I know,' she said. 'I am as magnificent as the great Nile.'

'Indeed, and as splendid as the sphinx.'

She gave a short laugh, more like a snort than a laugh. 'I'd rather go clubbing than be a sphinx.' She closed the book. 'OK, Nasfali, you're the smart schemer, what's next?'

'I can read it,' he said simply.

'What did you say?'

'I can read it. Mostly, anyway. I can read it. What did you think? I am half Egyptian. How could I go back to Egypt and not speak some Arabic?'

'Nasfali,' she said slowly, 'I am deeply impressed.'

'I didn't say I could understand what was written.'

'That doesn't matter.' She leaned forward, all the tiredness gone, her eyes sparkling in her blackened face. 'You translate and I'll make sense of it. We'll work together.'

'A team?' said Abe.

'Exactly,' said Alicia.

The last puffs of smoke, still flickering faintly, coiled together and then streamed upwards past the library's broken windows. Abe wondered if it would join together with that smoky serpent. He imagined it winding itself through the blue sky, swallowing clouds, becoming more and more monstrous, until it settled above the camp of Lakins.

He didn't want to say it and Alicia wouldn't want to hear it but this was the last chance. 'All that magic,' he began.

'Yes.' She gave him a cool look.

'Have you thought what it's already doing to you?'

'Will you forget about that, Nasfali. Just think what mother will do to us, if I don't.'

Overhead, the heavy iron bell of Greyfriars college began to toll. Then, one by one, further off around the city the inhabited colleges picked up the call. Alicia and Abe made their way downstairs where they found Thomas and Stokely coming to get them.

'Jonno's called a meeting, you see,' said Thomas in his serious singsong voice. 'Jonno wants you there, so if you follow us, we'll show you the way. He likes this sort of thing,' he said as they went along, 'big meetings and all that, calls it assembly. Very clever he is, you know, though you wouldn't think it to look at him, of course, all that monkish stuff he wears. But it's the fact he's bald. Bald people are often clever. You'll probably grow bald, skipper.'

'I don't think I should like you, Nasfali,' said Alicia, 'if you went bald.'

The thought offended him. 'Egyptians do not go bald,' he said haughtily.

'You're only half Egyptian, you could go half bald.'

'Don't you like Jonno, then?' Thomas sounded shocked. Alicia didn't reply, perhaps because she didn't hear him. Stokely gave Thomas a jab in the ribs and told him not to be a nosy windbag. 'I'm sorry, Miss Dunne, I am a bit of a nosy windbag, as Stoker says, and Stoker doesn't say very much but he is often quite right in what he does say, you know.'

'Don't be silly.'

'Sorry, Miss Dunne.'

Alicia washed the soot from her face and they crossed a small stone-flagged quadrangle and then joined a stream of citizens making their way into the great chapel that formed one of the sides. It wasn't really like the inside of any church that Abe remembered. Rosy light filtered in through the long, skinny, pointed windows above the nave and dimly lit a raised dais on which stood a large round table where Jonson and three other monks of his order, all dressed in their plain, brown, hooded habits, were sitting. There were six other seats at this table and these were, one by one, taken by individuals coming in from the main entrance: three men and three women. They all acknowledged each other with a nodded greeting or handshake.

The rest of the citizens took their seats on heavy wooden benches that were banked up in rows on either side of the building. It was a rather odd arrangement, Abe thought, having all those people seated like that, their heads tilted one way. Thomas and Stokely tried to urge Alicia to join the town's leaders down at the table, but she shook her head and sat on the end of the lowest bench on the right. Her face was pale and there were dark rings of tiredness under her eyes, but she sat stiffly upright, proudly. A queen in the crowd, thought Abe, slipping in beside her. Stokely and Thomas shuffled into the row behind and were joined a few minutes later by Roberts.

Abe studied the nine people around the table. 'They are all elected,' said Thomas, leaning forward so that his beard tickled Abe's ear. 'Very democratic. Is my beard itching you, skipper? They represent different bits of the town. Jonno organized it years ago. He could have run the whole bang-shoot, if you ask me, but he didn't want to. In my view everybody just likes to talk at these things, talk and talk . . . ' He leaned back. 'Bit like me, I suppose. Hold in your stomach, Roberts, you're squashing me.'

The leaders were talking earnestly. One of the women was jabbing the table with her forefinger as if she were hammering each point she was making down into the hard surface. She was a solid looking woman, with big bare arms and a wild mop of black hair, and when she had had her say, she leaned back, nodded, and folded her arms. It seemed to Abe that whatever it was that she had been saying met with approval from most of the others, apart from those on either side of her: one of them a young man and the other a pencil-thin woman. Abe's nose twitched and he gave an involuntary sniff.

The man, the youngest by far of those sitting at the table, was elegantly dressed in a pale grey two-piece suit, which was odd given that most people, as far as Abe could see, wore rather rough homespun clothes, tunics, breeches, cloaks, old stuff. This young man looked as if he had a personal tailor. He sat studying his sleeves, occasionally picking at an invisible thread.

Jonson leaned forward and addressed the young man directly but the man in grey acted as if Jonson didn't exist. He put his hands to his mouth, yawned, and then looked out towards the people still spilling in through the entrance. Then he began to look, almost carelessly, towards their side of the church. Jonson mopped his shiny domed head and sat back in his chair. Abe continued to study the man, whose eye was drifting along the rows of Oxford citizens, a faint expression of scorn on his face, but he seemed to start slightly when looking directly their way. He stared for a moment and then turned back towards the table and the other committee members. Someone to avoid, Abe decided.

The thin woman sat straight-backed and never once took part in the discussion. Even in that softening rosy glow of light from the window, she looked hard; everything was buttoned up tight, her hair close cropped, her neck sinewy, her lips pursed. Flinty. Abe shifted uncomfortably. She didn't look anything like Mrs Dunne or any other of the sisters, but for some reason they came to Abe's mind as he sat there staring at her, and the man too.

He felt Alicia shift beside him. He glanced at her. She seemed to have shrunk, become ordinary somehow, her expression blank. 'Don't look at me,' she muttered.

'What's the matter?'

'Why didn't you make me sit in the back row?'

'You wanted to sit here!'

'I don't want that woman to see me.'

'Which?'

'Don't be stupid, Nasfali, the one you've been staring at.'

'Who is she?'

'Can't you tell?' And she was just about to say something else when Jonson stood up, and the noisy chatter died away.

Eighteen

The hall resonated like a bass drum. 'Out. Out. Out . . . ' And with each 'Out!' feet stomped on the wooden floor.

Jonson had spoken first and everyone in the hall had listened quietly. He was so reasonable and just so nice that it was impossible not to like him. Good old Jonson, thought Abe, giving him a discreet thumbs up. Everyone sitting around Abe had nodded in agreement, everyone apart from Alicia, that is, but that was just Alicia and so it didn't count. 'You see, they are all around the city,' he had said, 'and they just don't want us here any more, it seems, so we have no choice but to keep them out, wouldn't you say.'

Alicia snorted impatiently. 'Couldn't talk his way out of a paper bag.'

Abe found himself trying to imagine this. It would have to be a large paper bag, in order to be inside it in the first place . . . He leaned towards her. 'We are not in any bag,' he whispered to her.

'Don't be dense. Of course we are.'

Then Jonson outlined the plan.

'But they got an army, don't they,' muttered a man sitting in the row behind Abe. 'That's what we need. Army. Guns and stuff like that. Can't see water doing much good.'

They had become restless. Thomas's great engineering work, linking the moat that would circle the city and keep Mrs Dunne, her sisters, and all the sweating Lakins well away from their doors, didn't impress them. It was not what they wanted to hear.

'Got better things to do than go diggin', tha's for sure. Diggin' holes? What's he on about?'

The pale languid man in the pale languid suit leaned back in his chair and stretched out his legs, and smiled. The pencil-thin woman, who hadn't moved or looked at anyone other than Jonson while he had been speaking, now turned her head towards the young man, catching his eye for an instant.

'Well, if we are all agreed,' Jonson said finally, seemingly unaware of the bubbling discontent in his audience, 'I think we should take a vote and then all these good representatives here can go back to their districts and begin to get organized. I don't think we have much time, you see. So what do you say?'

Uproar.

Everyone round the table wanted to talk. They stood. They banged their fists. They leaned forward and shouted. And, of course, everyone in the hall pitched in. Thomas was furious. 'Lazy idle loafers!' he bellowed. 'Frightened by a bit of honest work, are you!' Stokely tugged at him to make him sit down while, up on the rostrum, Jonson, dressed in his long brown monk's habit, flapped his hands like an agitated owl.

'Why did he do that?' mouthed Alicia through the din. 'Why didn't he just order them to do what was needed?'

'Democracy,' Abe mouthed back to her.

She rolled her eyes. 'What a pain!' and got up to go.

At that moment there was a crack and shiver of breaking glass and a hole appeared in the rose-coloured high window. The lizard-like young man suddenly swooped forward, scooped up the missile that had been hurled into the hall and flung up his hand for silence. The noise died away. Alicia frowned and sat down again.

'A message,' he said. 'No name. Just a message but one I think we should do well to attend to. It says here . . . ' He paused and raised an eyebrow as if he were puzzling over the message that he had written in front of him.

It's a set-up, thought Abe. Pre-arranged. He was about to whisper this to Alicia when she gripped his wrist.

142

'It says that there are witches in the hall.' He pulled a face.

There was a stunned silence. The young man slowly crumpled up the paper. Then Miss Flint, the pencil-woman, snapped to her feet and shrieked, 'I know! It's her!' But just as she was about jab her stick-like arm in what was certainly going to be Alicia's direction, she was somehow jostled by Jonson and the large woman in black, and that was when the chanting started.

'Out! Out! Out! Out!'

Alicia sat very still, her face sheet-white. The young man pushed past Jonson and the other councillors and was scanning the rows again. Abe was certain he was looking for them, or rather looking for Alicia.

He felt Alicia's tight grip around his wrist. 'I've got to get out of here.'

Abe shook his head. These men and women of Oxford had turned into a mob. If Alicia ran out of the hall now they would tear after her like a pack of hounds, convinced they had found their witch. And, of course, if it was Alicia they were chasing, they would be right. He looked back and caught Thomas's eye, who nudged Stokely, who gave such a jab to Roberts that he nearly fell off the end of his bench.

'Distraction,' mouthed Abe. 'Anything.'

Thomas frowned, then nodded and pulled Stokely close so that he could speak right into his ear, and then Stokely nodded and repeated the process with Roberts, who shook his head and stubbornly folded his arms across his round stomach. Stokely gave him another jab, said something else into his ear, at which Roberts jumped to his feet, waited for a second for the other two elderly team members to slide out beside him and then, as if they were a train, one hand on each other's shoulder, the other making little locomotion circles, they chuffed out into the middle of the thundering hall. Abe remembered how the eleven of them had done exactly the same thing when Alicia had taken them to the club. Three old men pretending to be a steam train? Well, it was certainly distracting.

One or two wide-faced women on the far bench pointed and laughed. Then someone close to Abe shouted: 'Give us a dance, why don't you?'

Whether they heard above the din or not, it seemed to be a cue, for that was exactly what the three did. Out shot their arms and more people laughed and pointed, and the chanting, though noisy, had lost its hard rhythm. Then down the three old men squatted. Abe was sure they intended to spring up into the air in a great big rabbit leap, but they didn't quite manage it.

Roberts plomped down so heavily his large bottom banged against the floor and somehow catapulted him backwards leaving him flat on his back, his stumpy legs poked up in a V and an expression of surprise on his face. Long-legged Stokely dropped straight down and simply stuck, his bony knees poking up beside his shoulders so that he looked rather like a stick insect. Thomas, the fittest of the three, gave a loud 'Hup!' and shot out one leg like a Cossack dancer, except that was all he managed to do. Unable to retrieve the leg and shoot out the other, he simply, and rather slowly, toppled sideways.

The hall suddenly erupted with applause and cheers and laughter. Clearly, thought Abe, there was little fun to be had in the city. Little fun to be had anywhere with Mrs Dunne and her sisters spreading across the whole country like a stain.

Alicia tugged his wrist and they slipped out of their row, who had just stood up to get a better view of the three old men. And then they were out through the door before the noise died away. The last thing they heard was Jonson appealing for everyone to be reasonable and that now was the time to take a vote and not for them to be witch-hunting.

★   ★   ★

'Where are you going?'

'Library.'

'What are you going to do?'

'Work.'

'The book?'

It wasn't easy talking to Alicia when she was cross. It certainly wasn't easy talking to her back as she marched through the college, across the quadrangle, and down the master's passage that led to the back garden. At the door to the library, she stopped and faced Abe. 'Are you sure you want to come in, Nasfali?'

'Don't you need me?'

She considered this for a moment. 'Yes, but you realize this is witch business.'

He realized. He realized that what Alicia was saying was that she might not remain Alicia but become someone who cared little for anyone but herself; not for Stokely, Jonson, or the others, and not for him either. But surely, Abe told himself, their only hope was to stick together. 'We're a team,' he said.

'Yes. I keep forgetting.' She pushed open the door and went into the dusky gloom of the library. 'You know, until you and the boys came along, I was only ever in a team of one. Just me against everyone.'

'One is not a team.'

'No, it isn't, is it?'

He followed behind and the door whispered shut behind them. 'We might be too late, Nasfali. It's a miracle that she hasn't swamped the whole country yet. A miracle that there are still towns like this one. But not for long. She's already here.'

Abe felt the back of his neck prickle. 'What do you mean?' He glanced over his shoulder, half expecting to see Mrs Dunne, the blood-red scarf floating around her plump neck, standing in the shadowy space between the book stacks.

Far away, as if from another world, came a faint,

muffled roar from the hall. It made Abe think of the distant sound of waves rolling onto a beach.

'Whatever they manage to agree in there will change nothing,' said Alicia. 'She's here. Couldn't you feel her in there, in the hall, talking through that woman? She can do that, ooze her way into a weak mind. She doesn't need an army. She'll turn the town rotten and maggoty with spies and traitors, then she'll just come squelching in and that will be that.' She sat down at the desk, clenched and unclenched her fingers, and then delicately opened the book. 'Aren't you going to sit down?' He sat beside her. 'You translate and I listen and we will just have to hope I manage to do better than that horrible smoke snake.'

'Hope is a good thing,' said Abe. 'It is like a jewel in the darkness.'

'Not bad, Nasfali. Not bad at all. Let's start.'

NINETEEN

'Yes,' said Alicia. 'Yes, yes, yes.'

The tiny Arabic script wriggled across the page. It danced and weaved beneath Abe's shadow-ringed eyes. He was exhausted. His shoulders ached from being hunched over the desk; his eyes stung.

'Go on, Nasfali.'

All night they had worked and still she urged him on. He struggled to focus on the next line. 'And the darkness . . . will something stronger, no, no, will tighten into a . . . great fist and hammer . . . Alicia, I must stop, I'm so . . . '

'No, no, Nasfali, go on, this is very good; this is totally the thing. A hammer, I just have to have this.'

He didn't look at her but he knew she would have that tight expression on her face: concentration pinching her mouth together, her breath coming heavily through her nose, and her eyes narrowed. He'd never noticed before but there were tiny flecks of red right in the darkness of her pupils, as if they were flames deep in space, burning. Excitement. Not fun like rebelling against her mother. No, it wasn't that. This was a deeper excitement that burned in her and each word that he translated for her was like a coal being shovelled into the furnace; and the furnace was power.

'Come on. You said hammer. You can't stop now.' Her fingers drummed on the edge of the desk. How strange. They were not long and fine, not the hands of a princess, but thick, strong, and grubby; the nails bitten to the quick. Tough hands.

'We're a team,' he said. 'And I need a break.'

'What? Yes, of course. In a minute, though. All right? Now just finish this bit, Nasfali.'

And he felt a firm grip round the back of his neck, tilting him forward, making his eyes lock onto the dancing dots and curves of the Arabic script.

'Alicia!'

'What?'

'Don't do that!'

'What?' She wasn't really paying attention. Her lips were moving, shifting the words he had given her round and round in her mouth, jostling them into place in her mind, locking them in to be used later.

'You don't have to force me.' He closed his stinging eyes. 'We're on the same side, aren't we?'

She blinked. 'Was I? Sorry, Nasfali.' She didn't sound that sorry. 'It's just I'm close, you know. Very. It's all beginning to make sense. So do the next bit, can you? Please?'

The pressure on the back of his neck lightened, but it didn't disappear altogether, as if the tips of her fingers were still resting there. Like a hand on a shoulder, he thought, a pat on the back. They were comrades. Brothers in arms . . . Except Alicia wasn't his brother, nor his sister for that matter.

He rubbed his eyes with the back of his hand and then concentrated on the writing scratched across the yellowing paper in front of him. 'And the darkness will become a fist, a hammer to drive all other shadows back into the cracks of the earth . . . or something like that,' he said, and finding himself free to move pushed his chair back, stretched out his arms, and rolled his head to ease his neck.

'Yes, yes, I see,' said Alicia. 'Look, like this, I think,' and she began to mutter to herself.

'Are you sure you know what you're doing?' She didn't answer.

Outside the college bell tolled four times. Four o'clock in the morning; they had been working all through the night. He rubbed the pins and needles out of his legs and then stood up.

Her muttering stopped. Then she jerked her head back and her eyes flicked open. For a second they looked terrifyingly blank as if somehow she had emptied herself out of her body, but then she blinked and with a cry of triumph exclaimed: 'See! That's it!'

There was a sharp, sour smell and above the desk at which they had both been working, right in the centre of the pool of light from their desk lamps, hung a thick clutch of darkness. So thick and dense and gleaming it looked like stone, or that polished wood, ebony. 'That's it! That's the hammer, Nasfali. Oh, she won't like that at all. Not at all. Do you see it? It's like a fist, isn't it?'

Startled, he took a step and the darkness rolled a little and seemed to bunch and knuckle and quiver slightly, as if angry. 'It wants to smash something,' said Abe a little croakily, half fearing that it, this bit of conjured darkness, might be able to hear him.

'Yes,' said a pleased Alicia, 'shall we try it?'

As she spoke, the fist moved, swooping suddenly towards the door and then, equally suddenly, soaring back straight for Abe's face. It was all so quick that Abe didn't have time to think. Instinctively he jerked his head back, lost his balance, and ended up sprawling on the floor.

'Why did it do that?' he said outraged, but warily looking around to see if it was going to come swooping back at him. 'Was that you?'

'Sorry!' sang Alicia. 'It's a bit hard to steer. There we are now.' And the fist quivered back over the desk.

'Please,' said Abe. 'Remove this thing; you don't know what it can do.'

Alicia, still sitting hunched and concentrating at the desk, began to mutter again, a stream of words which Abe could only half recognize. Slowly the fist began to shrink, but it didn't just smoothly become smaller, it was more as if it were being squeezed, squeezed smaller and smaller, and it gleamed blackly, and there was that faint splintering sound. Like the crunching of small bones, thought Abe, and shuddered. And then it was gone, leaving behind nothing except a sudden whiff of sourness. Like bad breath. Then that too was gone.

'There,' said Alicia. 'What do you think, Nasfali? Bit of practice and we'll soon give mother a wake-up call.'

'I have no wish to wake up your mother.' He got up from the floor. 'Are you sure we are doing the right thing, Alicia? Really? This,' he indicated the book, 'and that, what you called up, it's not like before. It's not like when you just . . . ' At a loss for words, he puffed out his cheeks and stretched out his fingers, remembering how zigzags of blue light had flickered from her fingertips. Such sudden power, such wild magic. That had been wonderful and mysterious while this, this studying and learning, was dark, oily dark and dangerous.

'Oh, I don't do that any more,' she said dismissively. 'This is the business, Nasfali. A few more tricks like this and we'll sort her.'

'Are you sure?'

'Of course, I'm sure. Have a bit of faith, Nasfali, for heaven's sake.' She pulled the book back in front of her and started turning the pages back, looking over what they had done that night. 'Better than being at school, isn't it? And the boys went home, didn't they? I managed that all right.' Her voice dropped into a murmur, almost as if she were talking to herself, not him.

'I'm going to bed,' said Abe. 'You should too. You must be more tired than I am. Too much of this,' he waved his hand towards the book, 'is not so good.'

'All right, all right, no need to lecture. You go on. I'll come down in a minute.'

He left her sitting up there and went down the stairs and through the dark library and out into the garden. Then, wearily, he made his way up to Jonson's room, which was open, but empty. At least there was no sound of snoring so he presumed it was empty. He was too tired to look for a candle and tinder so he felt his way across the room, stood for a moment by the window, and looked down towards the library. Yes, Alicia was still there. Then he made his way back to where he remembered the sofa to be. It smelt old and dusty, but it was soft and the night was not cold so he curled himself up and closed his eyes and then groaned.

Images flickered brightly beneath his eyelids. Alicia. His father. The Lakins chasing them to the bridge. The smoke snake and lines and lines of dancing Arabic script weaving and looping around and around into a massive tangle. He shifted and turned and kicked off his shoes, opened his eyes and then closed them again, and tried to think of only good things: the great pyramid, massive, unmoving, an anchor, and then the team, one by one, calling up their faces, all of them. Only then did peace come, and he slept.

Days followed the same pattern. Abe got up, found Jonson, Stokely, and sometimes Roberts, had breakfast with them, and they reported on the digging of the great canal defence. Who was helping and who wasn't. Thomas grumbled that there were whole districts refusing to volunteer workers and at the rate they were going it would be another fifty years before the city would be safely encircled by the river moat. Jonson refused to be dismayed. 'We must press on,' he said. 'You're really doing a great job, Thomas. Only you could do this,' he said patting his friend on the arm, 'and you'll save the city, you'll see. We'll have to be putting up statues to you: Thomas the Builder. How would you like that, eh?'

Thomas, who didn't hear fat Roberts muttering, 'Thomas the tank engine more like it', glowed pinkly behind his thick square beard. 'Of course I'll do what I can, won't I? It's just there is so much digging, you see. If only we had a few tractors and things, Jonno, like in the olden days. None of this filling baskets, and carts, and what have you.'

'We'll persuade everyone to help. You'll see,' said Jonson.

However, neither Stokely nor Roberts seemed as confident but they said little and, despite the odd muttered jibe from Roberts, did what they could to help.

Alicia, if she slept at all, slept in the library and became paler and paler and skinnier and skinnier. She was cheerful enough as long as Abe did what she wanted him to do, which was to carry on translating the Arabic script for her. This he did day after day, and late into the night, until the words wriggled and swam before his eyes. Exhausted once again, he would stagger down into the garden and gulp down lungfuls of fresh air as if that would cleanse all the horrid mumblings and mutterings that Alicia made as she tried one then another of the book's dark secrets.

He worried.

He worried all the time now, worried that all this business with the book was changing Alicia. When they were working together, he found himself sneaking glances at her out of the corner of his eye, checking whether there was even a hint of her beginning to look like Mrs Dunne. Of course there couldn't be: her mother's chin and cheeks were softly fleshy, her eyebrows arched, and her lips and nails always painted a dark dangerous crimson. Mrs Dunne could smile and ooze charm; Mrs Dunne would look at home in Harrods; Mrs Dunne was as deceptive and as deadly as a quicksand; as soft, stealthy, and pitiless as a predatory big cat.

Alicia wasn't like that at all. Alicia made him think of something thin, like a sliver of energy, like an eagle falling like a bolt from the sky.

'Nice,' murmured Alicia without looking up.

'Sorry?'

'Better than a snake coiled up and ready to strike. I thought you were going to say snake.'

'I didn't say anything,' said Abe. 'Did I? I'd never think of you as a snake, anyway.'

'That's good,' she said.

But he did worry. She looked the same but she definitely was, each day, a little different. It was as if there was an invisible shell thickening around her. And the idea became so strong in his mind, he felt that he could almost click his fingernails against the outer surface. But, of course, he was careful not to do that; in fact, he was careful not even to think about it.

Finally, he reached the last page of the book.

'Thank you, Nasfali,' she said. 'I don't think I need you any more. Do you think you could leave me for a little while?'

'Very well.'

Abe busied himself helping Thomas, and making plans with Jonno, but it didn't stop him worrying. Stokely knew he was worried and so did the others but they all had faith, more faith than he had, that Alicia was all right.

'Miss Dunne knows,' said Stokely coming up beside him very quietly in the garden when Abe was just taking a break.

'Knows what?'

'Oh, what to do.'

'And us?' asked Abe. They were up on the path that ran a bit like a parapet along the back wall of the garden, looking up at the darkening west sky. 'Do we know what we are doing?' There was something odd in the air; a strange taste. He sniffed. That smell? What was it? It wasn't the monks' cooking but it had that greasy kitcheny taste.

'I would say we do, old chap.'

Had Abe been paying more attention to him, he might have noticed that Stokely had been on the point of saying something else, but the smell distracted Abe. It was dark and wicked. He glanced back at the library. No, not quite the smell that sometimes came with Alicia's conjuring, but close to that, just heavier, slimier on the tongue, sour. Sweaty.

'It's coming from there, isn't it?' said Abe, nodding to the west, beyond the river, and Christ Church Meadow; there beyond the furthest edge of the town: Mrs Dunne's camp. 'What is she waiting for?' murmured Abe. 'She could walk in, couldn't she?'

'Oh no. Miss Dunne wouldn't let her, nor would Jonno. Or you, skipper. Once bitten twice shy.'

'She thinks I am drowned.'

'Spies.' Stokely nodded. 'Spies everywhere, skipper. I'd say she knows about you. Probably makes her jolly peeved too.' He chuckled. 'Goes red as a lobster, doesn't she, when she's peevy.'

Abe shook his head. Mrs Dunne was waiting, but not because she was frightened. No, her power was growing, swelling. She would be drawing the sisters from all the corners of England and Scotland and the western reaches of Wales, calling them and their Lakins and their slaves and hangers on. She wanted every single witch here. Then they would cross the Thames and the smaller rivers round Oxford without batting an eyelid. This time she wanted Alicia broken, completely, utterly; she wanted her daughter as her shadow. As for the team and Nasfali, he doubted if they figured at all in her cold, spidery plans.

The smell was the stink of her vast army.

'We need an army too,' said Abe.

'Righto,' said Stokely.

Yes, thought Abe. An army: white cloaks, flashing pennants streaming from spears, tall warriors on stately camels . . . Camels! What was he thinking about camels for? What was he thinking armies and spears for? He'd soon start day-dreaming about King Arthur and the knights of the Round Table, if he wasn't careful. He needed to be clever. He needed to think round corners and see what was coming. That's what he needed to be doing.

He turned around, about to say as much to Stokely, but Stokely was gone. There was something so secret about Stokely. Perhaps there always had been. He wondered what mission Stokely was on. Better keep an eye on him, he told himself. Wouldn't want him disappearing on his own. Far too dangerous now. Except, he seemed to have a knack of not getting caught. That's what his sister implied; the witches left them alone, in their safe havens. Why? Because Stokely was there. And at Winchester, until Roberts lost courage, they had left the city alone too; and up until now, because Jonson and Thomas had been there, they had left Oxford well alone. Was there something a little untouchable about the team?

Perhaps there was, but Mrs Dunne was just getting too strong and when she had all of the sisters gathered Alicia would never hold her, not on her own, not even if Thomas managed to finish his project. But perhaps if all the team were together, would that make a difference?

Abe turned to go back down towards the library. Alicia surely knew what had happened to the team when she had spelled them back into their homes. She must have known all along that they had gained some sort of protection, like a waterproof slick. And if they had, then maybe Alicia would know how to make use of that and protect them all! Wonderful! He slapped his hands together. Mrs Dunne could do what she liked: she could turn herself into a scaly monster as high as the Eiffel Tower but she wouldn't be able to touch them; she wouldn't ever be able to threaten to put them back into the photograph frame. Ha!

He stopped. Except. Except if Alicia had the power to do all this, why hadn't she done so?

Because she didn't want to?

No, it couldn't be that. Because she hadn't thought of it? Unlikely.

Because she had thought of it, but didn't know how to do it. Most probably.

My brilliant scheme, he thought, a mere flash in the pan. Still, he must go back and see Alicia, he decided. At the very least getting the team back together might help them all; that is, if they could ever be found in time. Maybe he and Alicia should have an army led by the team?

He put out his hand to push open the library door but it was as if there were a rubbery barrier in the air which prevented him actually getting his hand on the door knob. He tried again. No good. He tried to bang on the door and his hand simply bounced back at him without even touching the surface of the door. 'Alicia, open up!' he shouted.

But the library remained dark and silent. He stepped back and looked up. Yes, the light was on in the reading room. She was there. He could see her at the broken window. He waved. She ignored him. He jumped up and down and shouted, his voice sounding silly in the evening silence. She turned away from the window.

'Alicia!'

He was locked out.

TWENTY

There is always hope.

Abe thought his father might have said that, but he wasn't sure. He wasn't sure about very much at the moment, except that the end was coming. The smell of Mrs Dunne's army grew thicker and sharper with each day that passed. Surely the time was coming when they would feel strong enough to cross the river. Unless Alicia came out from the library soon so that he could at least talk to her about his plans to gather the team, they would all be swept away.

But she didn't emerge.

Days passed and, unaccountably, everybody became more and more exhausted. In the college, grey-faced monks dragged themselves to and from the chapel, and the refugees who had sought shelter within the college walls sat around listlessly, as if just waiting for their flickering existence to be extinguished. Only the team members appeared untouched, carrying on in the way they always had: Jonson quietly and calmly, with time for everyone; Thomas, busy; Roberts, in the kitchen worrying over the dwindling food supplies; and Stokely . . . Stokely was almost invisible, appearing at Abe's elbow with his secretive chuckle, staying for a few words and then disappearing just as suddenly as he had appeared.

Every day Abe visited the library and every day he found it locked against him. Sometimes he saw Alicia's face at the window, pale as a ghost. Once she looked straight down at him and waved her hand angrily, as if shooing him away. When he waved back, she banged open the window and shouted: 'Clear off. Stop disturbing me!' Not a whisker of the good old thumbs up there. Weren't they meant to be partners?

'Getting on all right, is she?' asked Thomas.

'Oh yes.'

Every day he climbed up to the wall of the college, straining to see through whispering fingers of damp mist whether Mrs Dunne's army had begun its final advance; but there was nothing to see. The smell grew worse, though, thick and sour. How many thousands did she have now?

Thomas decided that a moat round the entire city wasn't practical so instead he drew a line just north of St Giles and with his work parties managed to excavate not so much a moat but a wide ditch. Even that was a struggle as the promised support drained away, workers became resentful, and the other colleges, fearing the attack, closed their gates.

One evening, a rowdy mob with burning torches surged across Magdalen Bridge and up to the gates of Greyfriars shouting and chanting: 'Out with the witch! Out! Out! Out!! Get the witch out!'

They banged and boomed at the gate and the families sheltering inside held their children, and whispered worriedly to each other, glancing back in the direction of the library as if half expecting that the 'witch' the rabble were screaming for would suddenly appear, as if conjured up by all the yelling. They all knew that Greyfriars sheltered a young woman, a strange young woman; but few had thought there was great harm in that. After all, for most citizens, Greyfriars was, because of Abbot Jonson, 'the safe place'.

Abe pulled Jonson to one side. 'We have to get rid of the crowd out there.'

Jonson wiped his bald head. 'The gates are solid enough to keep an army out. No need to worry yet.'

'I think we'll have a panic and that's what Mrs Dunne wants. Then she'll just walk in.'

'All right,' said Jonson. 'I'll tell them to go away.'

'No, I didn't mean that . . . '

But Jonson was already walking swiftly to the porter's lodge and, before Abe could stop him, had opened the small door inset in the gate, stepped outside, and pulled the door closed behind him. There was a sudden lull in the yelling and banging.

Abe took a deep breath and eased open the door an inch so that he could spy through; and there was Jonson watching the crowd slinking back into the shadows. One or two lingered, snarling like hungry dogs, but without the courage to try anything on their own. After a few minutes, they too backed away.

'What did you say?' asked Abe, astonished and relieved in equal measures.

'Oh, just what anyone would say,' replied Jonson modestly. 'Not to frighten the children, and I think that reminded most of them that they had children of their own to look after and so they went away.'

How was it so simple? I have a father and a mother, thought Abe, and would they go off like this just because of what a Jonson might say to them? He did not think so, but then, neither of them, though as different from each other as ice from sand, would go rioting around and banging on gates. Still, if Jonson could do this thing, he thought, there is hope indeed.

There might have been hope, but there were also rumours and fears fluttering through the city like fallen leaves. Packs of dogs had attacked a party of workers; spies had poisoned the water supply; black plague rats had been seen slurrying up from the sewers; the inhabitants of Summertown up on the north side of the city had all gone over to the enemy; and so it went on. Of course, some of the rumours turned out to be true. There were infiltrators and spies. There were fires, at first around the edges of the city, lonely houses suddenly blazing in the middle of the night, and then closer and closer, till even the High Street was scarred with a scorched and blackened ruin; and then another frightened family would come looking for shelter in one of the colleges, until modest Greyfriars was bursting at the seams.

'I say, skipper,' said a gloomy Roberts, as they were queuing up in the hall for their lunchtime bowl of green lentil soup. 'All I dream about now is burger and chips. Wouldn't think you could dream a taste, would you, old chap, but you can. Must be nearly sixty years ago that we went to McDonald's with you and Miss Dunne. The little yellow box and the napkin . . . '

'At least we're not starving,' Abe pointed out.

Roberts nodded doubtfully. 'Trouble is, I'm always starving.' And he wandered off to find a corner of a table where he could eat his soup and dream it was something else.

Later on, Abe met Thomas, shouldering his way in through the gate just before it was closed for the night. 'Miss Dunne's got no message for us, I suppose?' he asked.

'No, no message,' said Abe.

'About time you started thinking clever again, skipper, like you did before. You know, tricks, you were good at tricks. That fellow Moses in the Bible, he had clever tricks, didn't he? Frogs and snakes and that.'

'I'm working on a few ideas.'

'That's good. That's great. With you and Miss Dunne pulling we'll be all right, won't we?'

'Oh yes.'

The next day Roberts disappeared.

It was Stokely who told Abe he'd gone. He didn't seem worried at all. 'Told me he was fearfully sorry but he just needed some decent tucker.'

'He went off for food! Is he mad? And he didn't say where he was going?'

Stokely gave his dry little chuckle. 'Oh no, not Roberts. Probably had some plan, though. Bit like you, eh, skipper? Planning, you know.'

'Would you say he's . . . ' Abe hesitated, 'gone over to Mrs Dunne?'

'Oh, he'd never do that. Knows you'd get in a terrible wax if he did that.'

'He's frightened that I'd be cross?'

But Stokely only chuckled again, pulled his hood up over his ears and, lifting his knobbly hand in a gesture which might have meant goodnight, or don't worry, or goodbye, went off towards the stables, which is where he had taken to sleeping, claiming he liked the warmth and company; and, he said, the horses didn't snore as badly as Thomas.

The next morning there was no sign of Stokely, either.

'Where's he gone?'

Jonson looked up from his work. He was down on his hands and knees in the warden's garden, transforming it into a vegetable patch. He rubbed the black dirt from his hands. 'Oh, don't you worry about Stoker, he hates to be stuck in all the time. You know him.'

Why were the team never worried?

'You don't think,' Abe said, reluctantly repeating the question he had asked of Stokely about Roberts only the day before, 'you don't think he has gone over to her, do you?'

'Good Lord! Stoker's always been a bit of an odd chap, wandering off at the drop of a hat, you know, but he's not bonkers.'

'And Roberts, is he not bonkers either?'

Jonson laughed. 'He's not clever enough to be bonkers.' He stood up and rubbed the edge of his cassock across his damp face. 'Without any sun who can tell if anything will grow. I think she's maybe trying to turn us all to frogs or newts.'

'Water is a blessing in the desert,' said Abe without thinking.

'Are you all right, old chap? You don't look so good.' Jonson cocked his head on one side. 'Do you miss your father?'

'Yes.' Somewhere in Cairo was his father. And what was he? Trickster? Forger? Man of knowledge? Would he ever be able to help Abe again as he had helped him when Jonson had been sickening. 'I can only cheat a little, Ebrahim,' he had said. Perhaps that was all anyone could do.

Abe said: 'Jonson, do you remember anything special happening when Alicia sent you all back in time to your families?'

'No.'

'Did you ever feel wrapped in anything; a cloak, not a real cloak, of course, but something protective?'

Jonson shook his head. 'I have to say, skipper, I never felt there was anything special about me at all.'

'But there is,' insisted Abe.

Jonson's manner changed. 'No,' he said, the tips of his ears beginning to turn red. 'Absolutely not.'

'But don't you see . . . '

'No!' Jonson was as close to being angry as he had possibly ever been. 'Miss Dunne,' he said, 'is one thing. What she does is because of what she is. We are not like that. If we were, we would become like them.' He turned on his heel and walked off, leaving Abe standing in the vegetable patch feeling as if he had just been blasted by a gale-force wind.

Abe looked after him, a little shaken but also rather thoughtful. How did Jonson know what the rest of the team wanted or didn't want? The time has come, he said to himself, to stop waiting and to start doing. The desert is not crossed until the camel takes its first step. It was time to find all the team and bring them together, to bring them here.

Abe made straight for the stables, pushing open the door and taking a deep breath of that rich horse-and-strawy smell. He went up to the stall where the horse he'd ridden up from Sussex was kept and held out his hand with a twist of salt in it, like Stokely had taught him. Then he patted its nose and murmured to it, flatteringly. It was a great desert stallion, a cool shadow from the burning sun, a great heart . . . He lifted down his saddle from its peg and pushed open the stall gate.

'No, she's not a stallion, skipper,' said a familiar voice from the dark corner of the stall.

'Stokely! I thought you had gone. What are you doing in there? The horse will tread on you or kick you, surely.'

Stokely chuckled. 'This mare? She wouldn't kick me, wouldn't kick anyone. And, as it happens, skipper, I was waiting for you.'

'But I only just decided what I was going to do.'

Stokely looked up. 'Couldn't squeeze a pea past Mrs Dunne's camp now. I went out to check because I thought you'd be wanting to leave soon to gather up the others. That is what you want, isn't it?'

'Yes.'

'Only way of getting through is when Mrs Dunne comes calling. We might just get a chance of slipping through the camp in the thick of things, if you see what I mean.'

'You think she'll attack tonight?'

Stokely nodded. 'Just a test, to see how ready we are.'

'Have you told Jonson?'

'Oh, he'll be all right.'

'How can you be so sure?'

Stokely chuckled. 'Miss Dunne's here, isn't she, and Thomas. On the pig's back, safe as houses.'

'How can you be so sure?'

But Stokely didn't or wouldn't answer. His eyes were closed and his chin settled down on to his chest. Abe looked at him for a moment and then softly left the stall. He wasn't going to sleep down there, he wasn't going to sleep at all, if tonight was the night. He would have to tell Alicia—and she would have to listen.

TWENTY-ONE

He found Jonson up in his room, looking out of his window towards the orange glow in the night sky: the fires of Mrs Dunne's camp, miles on miles of fires all the way round them. 'Ah, dear old skipper, have you come to say goodbye?' he said without turning round. He sounded extraordinarily calm, but then he always did. If there had been a Lakin banging at his study door, he probably would have murmured politely: 'Come in.'

Abe straightened his shoulders. 'I shall gather the team,' he said. 'It is time for action. "United we stand . . . "'

'Yes, and divided we fall, I know,' said Jonson, 'I know, I know . . . ' His voice faded into silence for a moment. 'Dear old skipper. You're a bit like a sheepdog Thomas had for a while. You keep wanting to round us up, don't you? Well, well, you might be right. Tried it myself, of course. Stokely, when you can pin him down, is good at that sort of thing, finding where everyone is . . . '

'You got them together! What happened?'

He turned round and Abe was surprised to see how sad he looked. 'Happened? What do you expect happened?'

'Well . . . ' Abe began and then wasn't quite sure what he would expect the team to do when they got together. He hoped there would be a tremendous forging of power; a great shield that would enable them to drive Mrs Dunne and her hordes away from the city, drive them back to the edges of Britain and into the sea. But he couldn't say all that to Jonson, not after the kindly abbot had made it quite clear that he wanted nothing to do with any shreds of Alicia's strange power that might have clung to them after their journey back through time.

'Well?' Jonson raised an eyebrow.

'That, at the very least, you would have agreed on how to deal with Mrs Dunne. To have some plan, some strategy, you know, to stop all this.' He waved his hand towards the window and the distant fires.

Jonson smiled. 'My dear old chap, you forget what we were like. Could we ever agree on anything? We were only any good when we were playing football and Griffin was egging us on. Oh, we were pretty good then.'

'You were exceptional. No one could come near you. Don't you see? You were like that before anything happened and now you could be that and so much more.'

'I don't think so. None of them, except Thomas maybe, will stick at anything.'

'What did you try to get them to do, Jonson?'

'Join my order of monks, of course. This is the way. We are the rock, here. Mrs Dunne may wash through the city but we'll be here after she has gone. All we need do is hold on and keep our faith.'

'Mrs Dunne won't go away. Surely you know that. Witches don't give up. Ever. They go on and on until they have everything. We have to defeat them,' stressed Abe, 'and I think if the team are all together and we have Alicia with us then we might just manage it.'

'Fighting's such a boy's thing, skipper. You forget, I've grown up. I'm in my seventies. Did you know that? And the others too. You think they'll want to go scrapping? They were terrified, we were all terrified, of Mrs Dunne when we were running around in shorts. It won't be different now.'

'I'm going.'

'No. Wait! I think we should wait and see what happens. I am sure Miss Dunne will manage something on her own.'

For the first time since he had arrived in the city, full of hope, and full of delight at seeing Jonson again, he now felt impatient. 'On her own! You expect to leave everything up to her. You wouldn't dream of getting your own hands dirty with magic, you said it yourself, but you'll use Alicia. That doesn't seem fair to me. Don't you remember how much she has already done for you?'

'Miss Dunne is what she is,' said Jonson. 'She is my friend. She has helped us all before and she will again. Don't be sentimental, skipper. I know exactly what is what.'

'And what is what?' said Abe.

'Miss Dunne is her mother's daughter.'

'Well, of course she is!' interrupted Abe. 'And she will do terrible things. She will be magnificent, but in the end there will be too many of them; they will overwhelm her.'

'Perhaps, but remember she is one of them. What is best for all of us is that this tide rolling towards us sweeps her and all her kind away, and just leaves us here. Perhaps clinging to the wreckage, but if we're here we can start again. Is that such a terrible thing?'

Out in the darkness, from the edges of the silent and ruined city, Abe heard the sound of rattling tins and cans, thundering drums, and the wild bellowing of what sounded like a thousand sick cows and then the long howling of a Lakin. It was beginning, and all the tiredness and fugginess of his thinking, all the indecisions, fell away from Abe. He drew himself up straight and addressed the older man firmly. 'I have no time for this, Jonson. All I can say is that it is a terrible thing to use your friends and then abandon them, no matter who they are. Be careful. Be very careful that you don't become as hard as the witches you despise so much.'

Had anyone been watching they would have been surprised at how the venerable, kindly abbot, the protector of the city, the shepherd of all those families sheltering within his college walls, winced at this criticism. Nasfali's eyes blazed fiercely and for a moment he seemed more desert hawk than boy.

Jonson blinked and swallowed as if about to speak again.

'My friends,' said Abe, on full dignity now, 'are sacred to me.' And he turned on his heel and strode out of the room.

Left on his own, Jonson stood, not moving for a moment, and then wearily he lifted the edge of his cassock and wiped his face. Then he went out of the room, closing the door carefully behind him, and made his way swiftly down to the chapel and began to toll the bell.

Abe, standing in front of the library for the hundredth time, wondered quite how sacred his friendship with Alicia was. After all, she was the one who had locked him out; the one who had told him to clear off. That didn't seem so sacred. Then he heard the chapel bell's round sound rolling out into the darkness behind him and the air suddenly felt thick and heavy like it does just before thunder.

'Skipper!' He heard Stokely calling him from the doorway to the main building. 'Time to be off, eh?'

'I will be a minute. I'll meet you at the gate.' Then he took a deep breath and shouted, 'Alicia!'

Behind the banging and howling of Mrs Dunne's army was the rumble of thunder. Abe called again: 'Alicia!' He raised his fist to bang on the door, expecting to feel that rubbery barrier pushing his fist away, but instead his knuckles rapped against wood. She couldn't be sleeping. Where was she? He knew he had to see her. He couldn't go off, not like this. No matter what she had said before. He didn't want her to think he had just run away. She was doing her best, wasn't she? Trying as hard as she could . . . Lightning flashed almost directly overhead, bursting the library with blue-white light, and thunder crashed so loudly it drowned out his third and last shout. Oh, why didn't she come? He raised his fist to bang again and the door was suddenly open and there she was, her face as white as it had ever been but twisted up in a way that he had never seen before, scrunched and smeary, her eyes red. If he hadn't known better he would have thought she had been crying.

'You're going, Nasfali, aren't you?'

How did everyone seem to know exactly what he was going to do? 'Yes.'

'Are you going to hit me?' She wiped her nose with her sleeve and peered over his shoulder into the darkness of the library garden.

'No, of course not,' he said hurriedly lowering his fist. 'I was knocking.'

'You better go then.'

'I'll be back.'

Thunder clapped so loudly overhead that Abe ducked his head. Alicia didn't appear to notice but she looked at him, curiously. 'Will you really? Why? I've been horrid to you.'

Abe shrugged. 'You've been doing difficult things. I know that. I am going to get the team together. I have a theory that when they're together . . .'

'Yes, all right, Nasfali, but I don't think we have time for one of your lectures. Go, and if I were you I would stay away.' She smiled, or tried to, and her voice, usually so cool, wavered a little.

'Why?'

'I am not me any more.'

Abe found himself backing away from her. 'What do you mean? Listen, I can help. I'm sure I can, Alicia.'

'Hurry, Nasfali. You haven't got much time. Hurry. Mother is coming and we wouldn't want her to find you here. She'll be very cross if she catches you again. Very cross.'

Alicia seemed much taller somehow and was not looking towards him but to the college wall, in the direction of the howling and thumping and drumming. He saw her close her eyes and clench her fists and then, to his horror, the darkness thickened in front of her, thickened and hardened, squeezed into a bunched fist.

'Oh, my goodness,' he said, backing into the doorway. 'Not that again.' And he turned and ran towards the main gate. If she let that fist loose, who knew where it would come crashing down. 'Concentrate, Alicia,' he muttered, hunching up his shoulders as he ran, half expecting the fist to coming spinning up behind him. 'Use it outside the college. Outside.'

In the quadrangle, figures were running to and fro. He saw a group of Jonson's brothers armed with an assortment of poles, kitchen implements, and what looked like a cricket bat. Had Jonson changed his mind? There was no time to ask. He cut through the bustling crowd, skirted a bearded citizen hustling his children towards the kitchen cellar, and then spotted Stokely ahead of him, standing by the porter's lodge, holding the bridles of their horses.

'Talking to yourself, skipper, eh?' murmured Stokely handing him the reins of his horse.

The horse whinnied nervously and Abe stroked her muzzle and, without thinking, spoke soothingly to her, as Stokely had taught him. She was a horse of great heart, a horse with wings, a queen of horses. He swung himself up into the saddle, glancing over his shoulder as he did so. Where was that thing—Alicia's clenched fist? If they were lucky maybe it would hammer down on the mob Mrs Dunne had unleashed on the city.

As if in answer to his thoughts, there was a sudden howl from the other side of the gate. Stokely nodded to the gate porter. 'Jiggety jig, skipper? What do you say?'

Abe guided his horse so that he and Stokely jostled knee to knee.

'As soon as the way is clear, skipper, ride like the devil, beside me all the time. All right?'

'Yes.' Abe gritted his teeth and hunched himself up small. Whatever had made him think he wanted adventure? Success, that was the thing. A thriving business. A limousine as long as an ocean liner. Cairo.

There was a roar and a clap of thunder, then the gate swung open and the two riders kicked their mounts and clattered out onto the street.

Mistake.

Serious mistake.

Blocking their way was a wedge of ragged wild men with flea-cropped heads and eyes that were dead; pebbles, like those of a shark. The air stank of sweat and rotten fish. Mrs Dunne's mob: her slaves. At the sight of the two riders the mob yelled and thumped their clubs against the ground. Instinctively, Abe, trying not to gag at the smell, tugged so savagely at his reins his horse reared right up on her hind legs, and then danced back sideways, with Abe clinging tightly to her neck for dear life.

The mob yelled again, stamped their feet in unison, and surged forward two steps and halted. Another bang with their clubs, another two steps. They were like nightmare toys winding themselves up ready to charge, ready to tear down the city stone by stone.

Stokely's horse skittered beside Abe. He leaned over and grabbed Abe's arm. 'London first, skipper, yes?' he yelled.

'Oh, yes.'

Instantly, Stokely banged his heels into his horse's flanks, and spurred straight for the mob, cloak flapping behind him, a raggedy bat into the jaws of death. Abe followed. At least there were no Lakins to deal with. He hunched low, let his eyes close to slits. This would be their magnificent charge. He rather wished Alicia was standing up on the gate tower.

How many seconds before he and Stokely were swallowed up?

Two . . . And . . . One . . . And . . .

Another long loud moan that seemed to swell up from under the ground; blackness thickened into a great gleaming fist, a tight granite-hard shadow that hissed over Abe's head and furrowed through the mob, slamming their bodies left and right, their arms and legs flailing helplessly. And into this gap, this canyon, galloped first Stokely and then, hard behind him, Abe. It was like the parting of the Red Sea! Alicia had done it! She was more than magnificent! She was the wielder of such power that Mrs Dunne would be hammered back into the darkness! 'And I,' exulted Abe, teeth clenched, knees clenched, cheek pressed to his horse's neck, 'I am Ebrahim Nasfahl Ma'halli, schemer of schemes!' which didn't make huge sense but Abe was hardly thinking straight. He was swept along on a great wave of excitement and he gave a yell such as the tribesmen of the desert make, a great piercing yell, as bright and sharp as the flickering of a blade. A yell that he himself had never heard before.

And overhead the thunder clapped and lightning splashed across the sky, and the horses' hoofs thudded on stone and dirt, and ahead they followed the dark hole punched through Mrs Dunne's mob by Alicia's fist.

PART THREE
IN THE JOKER'S DEN

TWENTY-TWO

'Here?' Piccadilly Circus that way. Oxford Circus the other. Regent Street, wide as the Thames, and lined with buildings which, even shabby as they were now, towered grandly above them. London's West End. Abe knew it like the palm of his hand. Nothing had changed . . . apart from the fact that the roads were pitted and pocked with holes, and the houses looked dead and dusty, windows broken or boarded, weeds growing in every crack and crevice. Yes, apart from all that, it was just like it always had been. Empty, of course, emptier than even Worthing had been, everybody washed away, down some huge plug, into the sewers and away off to the sea. There wasn't a car or a cart or a horse or a dog or a child to be seen, not one. But maybe it wasn't quite as empty as it seemed—Abe's neck prickled, a sure sign they were being watched. He could feel eyes on them, had done since they made their way from Shepherd's Bush up through Notting Hill, Marble Arch, right to here.

'Hamleys toyshop?' he said.

'Yes.'

'Are you sure?' Abe looked at his companion in surprise. A toyshop? Theirs was a desperate quest: gather the team and then ride like the wind to save Alicia and what was left of the free city of Oxford.

'Oh yes.' Stokely nodded. He dismounted, stiffly, stretched and then tethered his horse to a lamppost. Abe followed his example. If Stokely said this was where they would find one of the team, then this is where they would. He had led them without flinching straight through Mrs Dunne's rampaging army, never turned a hair, even when Alicia's terrifying shadow fist had fizzled into nothing and Mrs Dunne's rabble had begun to gather their wits and chase after them. Even when the air had whistled around their ears with sticks and stones, he had just kept going and Abe, convinced that this desperate ride would be his very last, had urged his own horse to keep so close to Stokely that they were riding knee to knee. And nothing had harmed them.

And if ever there was a miracle, that was one.

Leaving the outer part of the city behind them, Stokely had threaded his way in the darkness through Mrs Dunne's scattered camp. They kept well away from the fires and the huge clomping clutches of Lakins and other slaves, gathering to launch a second attack, and no one challenged them, no one noticed them. Mrs Dunne and all her sisters must have been staring down on the city, which now prickled here and there with angry flames.

Praying that all those who had taken shelter within college walls remained safe, they turned their back on the plain of Oxford and slipped through the Chiltern Hills. They kept away from the disused motorway during the daytime and camped out west of High Wycombe. Then, the next morning, moving as swiftly as they could push their tired horses, they covered the last leg into the city itself. Now, here they were at what used to be London's finest toy store.

There was no doubt about it, Stokely, who could have passed for anyone's dotty old grandfather, not only knew his way around Mrs Dunne's dark Britain, he knew how to keep out of trouble too. Once past the camp, they hadn't seen a glimpse of witch or smelt a whiff of a Lakin. Then, thought Abe, maybe that's where they all were, at Oxford. Poor Alicia.

Strange, thought Abe, struck by the shop's window display. There was a tangle of punchballs and footballs and hundreds of Action Men, and teddy bears wearing cowboy hats and, most curiously of all, an elaborate train circuit with towns and hills and fields through which the railway ran. But in one place the rail had been ripped up and twisted and all the train engines and carriages were lying higgledypiggledy across the circuit. As if a bomb had hit it, thought Abe.

He was just about to push his way through the double doors when Stokely held him back. 'Don't tread on the mat, skipper,' he warned. 'Hop over it, eh?'

Abe did as he was told and put out his hand to help Stokely, who wasn't up to hopping. 'He-he-he,' chuckled Stokely. 'See.' He pointed to where two large tubs hung directly over the entrance. 'Something nasty in that, I bet. He-he. He loves a practical joke.'

At that moment, as they were facing the glass doorway, their two horses tethered to the lamppost outside, they both saw a sudden flurry of small figures running from different directions but all converging on the shop, or so it seemed. 'Oh no. Oh, dear me, no,' said Stokely. 'We better hurry,' and he started to back away into the store.

'No, wait a minute,' said Abe. 'They're pinching our horses.'

'Yes, yes. Come on, skipper.'

But Abe didn't want to come on. It was bad enough having to rumble around on a horse rather than sitting in a coach, but without the horses, they would be trapped; the quest would be finished before it had properly begun and all their abandoned friends would be lost. 'Oi!' he yelled. 'You leave them alone!'

The figures were children, maybe ten, maybe older, scruffy, dirty-faced, determined. They paid no attention to the frantic shouting and fist waving that was taking place inside the store.

Without thinking, Abe started back. He'd grab them by the scruffs of their necks, the cheeky maggots; he'd get Alicia to turn them into fried green peppers; he'd— His right foot landed with a heavy step in the exact centre of the welcome mat, and the instant it did so, the two suspended buckets jerked upside down. There was a sudden whoosh and a solid glob of goo glooped down on Abe, covering him from head to foot in an evil-smelling slick of yellow.

'Oh no!' He clenched his fists and suddenly it was all too much and he burst out with a shout of: 'I will do such things . . . ' but then some of the goo dribbled into his mouth, the taste was so disgusting he was nearly sick.

Stokely shook his head sympathetically. 'Forgot, eh? Oh, nasty stuff, I'd say. Stinky.'

By the time Abe had smeared the stuff away from his eyes and mouth, the children and their horses had gone. 'See,' he said. 'What are we going to do now?' Anger had drained into irritation and discomfort. Where was he going to get a change of clothes? You can't carry out a dangerous quest looking like a yellow icepop.

'Upstairs,' said Stokely. 'Right as rain, eh, sort you out in a jiffy.'

'Thank you,' said Abe stiffly. Then, as he followed Stokely up the dead escalators, 'Well? Why don't you tell me? Who is it? Who's here?'

'Surprise,' said Stokely. 'You'll see.'

Abe felt that he had had an adequate surprise but he kept his mouth shut.

A voice, which seemed to come from all round them, boomed, 'Ho-ho.'

Abe did not feel full of Christmas cheer either.

In front of them was, according to the large sign painted with wobbly red letters, Santa's Grotto. It wasn't quite like any Santa Grotto that Abe could remember but more like a randomly constructed nomadic dwelling; a roughly circular mound of blankets and bits of carpet and boxes and packing, and glittering paper with an igloo-like tunnel entrance. Who would do this and in August too?

'Ho-ho.'

Someone who liked to joke.

'Is it safe?' said Abe. 'To go in, I mean?'

'Oh yes,' chuckled Stokely, rubbing his hands with pleasure, 'of course. Don't you know who it is, yet?'

Abe knew.

He got down on his hands and knees and crawled in along the tunnel until he could poke his head into the interior. The inside of this ramshackle igloo resembled a nest rather than a home. It was lit with candles and thickly strewn with old cushions and blankets; to Abe's right there was a stool, a packing case, and a large round mirror that reflected the light of the candles, while from the ceiling hung little model aeroplanes, most of them, Abe noticed, rather badly made. To the right of the entrance was a most peculiar tangle of shiny metal pipes, each with a stopper on the end, and there was another twisty tube hanging down from the centre of the rounded roof. Directly facing Abe, and sitting under this last tube, sat a rather ancient man with a stubble of white hair, thick neck, wide shoulders, and a ridiculous fake Santa beard disguising half his face. He was wearing baggy blue shorts and a baggy white T-shirt with a big J on it. He was leaning slightly forward, his hands planted on his bony knees, studying his visitor.

'Ho-ho. What's the Stoker rooted up now? You look a bit like a marmot, old chap. The old yellow stuff got you, did it? Rotten luck.' And he gave another booming laugh and slapped his stomach with delight.

If that was really funny, thought Abe, then I am indeed a marmot, whatever that might be.

'Don't bung up the entrance, crawl in.' Then the old boy pulled the twisty tube until it stretched down to his mouth. 'In you come, Stoker, and explain this marmoty chap to me.'

Abe could hear his words boomily echoing round the store and registered that somehow this old crank had rigged up a loudspeaker system which, Abe had to admit, was clever, very clever since Abe had not been aware of any electricity being in use anywhere since his return to

Britain. He pulled himself free of the tunnel and sat down on one of the stools. 'Hello, Jack,' he said sourly. 'I knew it would be you.'

'Did you, old fish? Did you indeed. You look a bit familiar, you know, but the old lamps are sputtering a bit, don't see quite so well.' There was some heavy grunting and then Stokely heaved himself into the den.

'Stoker! What a rum treat. You'll stay for supper, I hope. Who is this foxy looking marmot you've brought along with you? Seems to know me, of course.' He puffed his chest out when he said this. 'Course everybody knows old Jack. Jack the lad, eh, Stokesy.'

'Oh, yes,' said Stokely nodding happily, and beaming. 'Oh yes, but gone a bit, has it, Jack, the old memory? Bit doddery, are we? Have to put you in a home, old boy, how'd you like that?'

Abe didn't think he had heard Stokely say so much in weeks. He seemed delighted with himself to be here, teasing his old friend, Jack the troublemaker.

'All right. All right. I know what's what and who's who and you better mind your manners if you want your noble steeds back again.'

'You knew about that!' exclaimed Abe. Briefly he entertained the notion of hanging Jack upside down over a tub of his yellow disgusting stuff and dipping him in it every hour on the hour. The thought gave him a degree of comfort.

'Course I did. Poof, you're a bit ripe, aren't you?' He tilted his head, appraising Abe. He clearly still couldn't place him. 'Talking of which, where did you get your tan? Been on the Costa Lotta, have you? Didn't think there were any package trips on offer these days.'

'Jack,' said Abe abruptly, 'we must have those horses back, and unharmed, and right now.'

'Must? Nobody "musts" me, old boy. Who do you think you are? Those horses are mine now. And if you don't watch it, they'll make a fine horse stew. So button up and let your elders and betters . . . '

'It's the skipper, Jack,' said Stokely, nodding still, and looking particularly pleased either with himself or with Jack's pompous display, Abe couldn't tell which.

'What!' Jack jumped up and banged his head on the twisty pipe, then snatched up a candle and peered down into Abe's face. 'Skipper? Not possible. Who are you?'

'Abe Nasfali,' said Abe. 'Stokely seems to be right about your memory, Jack.'

Jack ignored the jibe. 'Skipper!' he shouted. 'Whippersnapperskipper!' He thumped Abe on the shoulder, then pulled a face and wiped his hand on his shorts. 'Stokely, you complete weaselly genius, where did you find the skipper? And . . . hang on. You don't seem to have got any older, skipper, maybe a couple of years. I say . . . I say.' His delight faded and he looked worried. He frowned and rubbed his forehead. 'Bit of a puzzle, eh?'

'Bit of a puzzle,' agreed Stokely.

Abe started to explain but the blank look on Jack's face quickly stopped him. 'Witches,' he said. 'Magic, Mrs Dunne, come on, Jack, cop on.'

'Cop! I say, new word, eh? Cop! By jingo, it's good to see you, skipper. You're jolly jolly welcome. How do you like my city, eh?'

'Your city? All of London?'

'Well, the best bits, anyway. Oxford Street. Loads of shops. All mine.'

'None of Mrs Dunne's sisters?'

'Oh, them,' said Jack dismissively, 'there are a few. Lodged here and there. One of the slimy slugs has got a nest in Buckingham Palace, would you believe it! Nothing sacred, eh? We'll winkle her out of there. You wait. Just a matter of time. They can't handle old Jack, got them skittering about like fleas on a hot pan.' Jack may well have been in his seventies but he still only had the attention span of a first former. 'Want to see one of them on the run? They're skittering all over the place at the moment, got some big witch crisis on, I wouldn't wonder. Still, plenty of fun for us. Sting 'em with our stingers, that's what we do, and they're so dozy they don't hardly ever catch us. Watch this.' He tugged on a cord and part of the fabric wall rolled up, leaving a neat square through which daylight suddenly flooded into the half-light of the den.

'Splendid,' said Abe, 'but your window doesn't open onto anything but the first floor of this store.'

'No, not there, look over there,' said Jack. 'Bittern's cracking wheeze, this was.'

Bittern, thought Abe. Skinny Bittern. They had never found his house; it had been blown up in the Blitz. 'Is he with you?'

'Bittern? Oh yes, key chap in my gang. Absolutely key. Now look here. This is the business. Come on, Stoker, you haven't seen this.' He ushered them both back away from the window and made them stand a little to one side of the mirror so they could see the image reflected there without obscuring it.

Abe took a surprised breath. He could see the street as clear as day.

'Rigged up,' said Jack proudly. 'Different angles can watch different streets. Lines of mirrors tucked away. Look. Watch this. This'll make you chuckle.' And he chuckled in anticipation and Stokely, who mostly chuckled all the time, chuckled too.

Abe wondered if this was also one of the side effects of being zipped back in time. Except, of course, neither Thomas nor Jonson chuckled at all.

'Here she comes,' said Jack, giving himself a good scratch. 'Here comes the blighter. Should know better than to go snooping about in old Jack's territory.'

And there on the shiny surface of the mirror they saw an old double-decker bus, painted a quite shockingly horrible iridescent pink, moving slowly down the street. In front of it were two lines of slaves, nearly a hundred of them, hauling on two long ropes. Perched up on the roof was a huge Lakin dressed in a leather apron, wielding a long whip, which he cracked and flicked round the helpless haulers. The watchers could hear nothing, of course, but Abe imagined the sound of the whip and the grunts of the straining slaves. Through the windows of the bus they could see smartly dressed witches, busily writing and passing each other files. Abe wondered if one of them was his mother but it was too far away to pick out their features.

'Now,' muttered Jack. 'Just about now, I should think. Yes, here we go.'

At first, Abe couldn't quite make out what was happening, except that the slaves seemed to be losing their footing, skidding about, and falling on their backs and the bus, which had been travelling at a smart walking pace, slewed down from the middle of the road and mounted the pavement. Then cracks and holes appeared in the windows.

'Marbles,' shouted Jack. 'Blooming marbles. Marvellous, totally marvellous. Never fails. Has them falling over onto their bums at the drop of a hat. Use 'em in a catapult and they're better than bullets.' In the milling confusion, Abe saw more of the raggedy children speeding out from the doorways and underground pass, flooding round the bus like a sudden grey tide swirling in, and before the witches had gathered their wits, they had punctured the wheels on the bus, and cut through one of the lead lines, before they disappeared as suddenly as they had come. The weary slaves, suddenly finding themselves unattached to the vast bus, tottered around unsteadily on the marble strewn street, until, as it began to dawn on them that they were free, one or two of them broke into a stumbling run. All of this took a matter of seconds and the witches, at first taken off guard, and forced to keep their heads low to avoid being zapped by a marble, now appeared out on the platform at the end of the bus. There was a crack of electric blue lightning flickering like a snake's tongue down to the underpass, another that snaked around one of the unfortunate escaping slaves, and snatched him up into the air where smoke poured from him. Then suddenly he dropped flat onto the road and lay still.

'What's happened to him!' exclaimed Abe. 'Is he killed?'

'Frizzed,' said Jack. 'A bad frizz and you're cooked like a chicken. Oh, chicken and chips, Stoker. Think of it . . . '

'And if you're not too badly frizzed?'

'They dump you back in the slave pit, till you're ready to work for them again. Prefer to be boiled up like a cabbage than work for those horrors, but we've rescued some of their slaves. Part of the campaign, old boy. Part of the campaign. So what do you think? Go out with them sometimes but I'm getting a bit slow on the old pins. Need to be a fast mover if you don't want to get frizzed.'

'Somebody always gets frizzed?' asked Abe.

'It's a war,' said Jack with a shrug. 'Always someone gets frizzed in a war. Not too many. Keep the casualties down, that's my motto. Well now, let's see.' He turned back to Stokely and Abe. 'So you've heard all about Jack's campaign, have you? Stoker, bless him, has been spreading the word. And you've come to join old Jack, have you? Totally wizard. A real cop, eh?'

'Not exactly,' said Abe. And he explained his theory about the power the team would have if only they grouped together again.

'Exactly!' said Jack slapping his hands together. 'What I have been saying all along. I have a few of the chaps here. All the ones who lived in London; they'll be tickled skinny to see you, skipper. We'll hunt down the rest in jig time and then Jack's army will be complete and we'll winkle every last one of those blinking witches out of London.'

Blinking, thought Abe. The team always said blinking when they got excited and he had never known why.

'I need the team in Oxford,' said Abe, 'and I am going to need your help, Jack. But,' he said firmly, 'I am the skipper.'

'Well, of course you are, skipper,' said Jack. 'But do we really have to go to Oxford? That's where snooty old Jonson is. Not having him bossing me around.'

'Miss Dunne needs our help.'

'That's it, then,' said Jack. 'Miss Dunne's number one.'

'She's a mum,' chuckled Stokely.

'There you are, skipper, almost settled. Call a meeting and,' he wrinkled his nose and gave a loud expressive sniff, 'we better hose you down. Got some cracking cowboy suits in the store . . .'

TWENTY-THREE

'What do you think, eh?'

'What do I think!' The wall of noise made it hard to think. Abe felt as if he had been tossed onto the set of a Hollywood epic. 'Flaming pharaohs,' he muttered under his breath. This was indeed unexpected.

There were hundreds of people down in Hamley's cavernous candle-lit basement. Ragged refugees of all shapes and sizes who looked as if they had escaped from some scraggy circus, that's what Abe thought. Shadows flickered and danced; the walls steamed and glistened with damp; and the din was worse than seventeen school dining halls squashed into one. Long trestle tables, packed with eaters shovelling their food, elbow to elbow, filled the central space, while in the far corner was a makeshift kitchen, glowing red like the gate to hell. Sweating cooks tipped the contents of tin after tin into steaming metal buckets hanging over open fires and then carelessly tossed the empties into a glinting heap. And everywhere candles flickered and dribbled wax onto every ledge and inch of spare space on the tables.

Stokely took his arm. 'Do you see them? They haven't spotted you yet, skipper.'

'They're all here?'

'Oh yes, all eight.'

Eight? Of course, no Jonson and Thomas . . .

'Griffin's busy.'

Abe shook his head. 'Jack did all this?' It was astonishing to think that the joker of the team could mastermind anything.

'I found the boys,' said Stokely, 'here and there, round and about. Thought we ought to get together.'

'You? I thought Jonson had tried to and hadn't got anywhere; but you managed.' He was truly a mystery. 'Why didn't you say, Stokely? All the time we were in Oxford, you knew about this. Why didn't you say?'

Stokely avoided answering. 'They're on that table over there.'

And so they were: skinny Bittern, one time full back, in shiny red tracksuit top and a pirate eye patch, all poky elbows and sharp chin and looking more like a stick insect than ever, sat with the other back, Pike, who sported a battered bowler hat. The two of them were huddled together on one bench, heads almost touching. They made Abe think of a pair of conspiring bank managers, but they had been a great defence in the match in Cairo, even if they did cheat a bit—Bittern's long legs had a nifty way of tangling themselves up with those of their opponents. To cheat a little, thought Abe, is not a bad thing. At the same trestle table were also Jissop in threadbare denims and Chivers, the wingers; and, opposite them, Gannet with his shock of grey hair flopping down over one eye, and the tip of his nose as red as a traffic light. Jissop was leaning across the table and talking animatedly to Gannet who was dibbling his finger in a pool of spilt stew and completely ignoring him. While Jack, in his baggy shorts, at the head of the table, was trickling candle grease into Jissop's bowl.

The team! It was hardly possible! Right here, not scattered across the country! It was miraculous! Abe gripped Stokely's hand and shook it vigorously. 'This is a tremendous thing, Stokely. It is wondrous. You,' he said emphatically, 'you are the gatherer.'

'I just potter about, old chap,' muttered Stokely so softly that Abe could hardly hear. 'Just potter about.'

'Maybe you are like the great Merlin.'

'Don't be silly, skipper,' said Stokely extricating his hand, looking Abe, almost for the first time, directly in the eye. 'We don't do magic, you know that.'

'No, of course, I know that.'

Stokely nodded as if reassured but Abe thought, no, the team might not 'do magic' in Mrs Dunne's or Alicia's sense of the word but they would still prove more than a thorn to Mrs Dunne, they would be like a shield perhaps, a shield for Alicia, the great shield of Ajax. What a sadness that the Greek heroes weren't Egyptian. They should have been. And then as Abe continued to scan the tables, he realized that he had forgotten Roberts and felt a tight stab of worry. 'He didn't cross over to Mrs Dunne, did he? He can't have done that . . . '

'No, no. Look. In the kitchen.'

There he was, and in his element, acting as chief cook, surrounded by mounds of empty tins, stirring a vast black pot of steaming stew, his round fat face the picture of bossy contentment. Abe relaxed. It was all well.

'Come and get some tucker, eh.'

'Yes.' Abe followed Stokely across the room to get some of Roberts's stew.

'Skipper!' said Roberts. 'Knew you'd turn up. Here,' he sloshed a generous helping into a bowl for Abe. 'Didn't mind me spinning off, did you? Couldn't take it any more. Food was awful and Jonno was gettin on my wick. There you go. Be over and join you in a jiffy,' and he turned to serve the next person in the snaking queue before Abe could answer.

Abe eyed the sloshy wash of sausage bits and tinned vegetables and wondered whether a diet like this would finish him off, managing to do what Mrs Dunne had so far failed to achieve. But this was tucker, after all, and he was hungry and so he made his way to the table where the team were seated and was greeted with shouts and roars and thunderous table thumping, which Abe slightly suspected was intended, certainly on Jack's part, to make their bowls of stew judder and spill. Then they clambered out of their seats, pushing and shoving each other to get to him so they could pump his hand and bang him on the back and boom in his ear.

'Skipper looks a total gent,' squawked Pike. And indeed, compared to the motley crowd there, Abe supposed he did. While they, like everyone around, wore an assortment of cloaks, rags, battered hats, and combat jackets, Abe, scrubbed reasonably clean after his encounter with Jack's booby trap—'Only for boobies, old boy, not meant for you at all, not in a trillion years'—was dressed in a black pinstripe suit Jack had pillaged from a gentleman's outfitters in Savile Row.

'Jolly nice threads, old boy,' drawled Gannet. 'Not from Boodle and Bumpkin, was it, by any chance? My father was always rigged out there, you know, along with the royals, you know, Prince Thingummy and so on.'

'I don't think so,' said Abe. In fact his suit was not only several sizes too big for him but also had a couple of plate sized moth holes in the back of the jacket. Jack had donated a pair of bright red braces with reindeer on them, pillaged from his Christmas store, which kept the trousers anchored somewhere round his waist and Stokely had then snipped six inches off the legs and sleeves with a pair of scissors.

'Put a sock in it,' shouted Jack. 'Skipper looks like the king of Cairo, if you ask me, and the only royal suit your old man wore was the stripy one for his majesty's prison!'

'Dad did dabble a bit,' admitted Gannet with a sleepy smile. 'Cunning as a fox. Bit like the skipper. Three cheers for our whipper-snapper skipper.'

They cheered. It had never taken much to get them to cheer.

Abe smiled and took his seat at the table. Some things didn't change. He felt a curious glow of pleasure seeing them all but he knew that trying to get them to focus on what had to be done would not be easy.

As he ate his food, Abe learned how Jack, come the rise of the sisters, had done every little thing he could to annoy them. He had sneaked into their dens and stolen anything that he could lay his hands on. 'All rubbish. Everything they have is rubbish. Chucked it all away. Sometimes heard them squealing like stuck bats. Couldn't catch old Jack though, eh, nimble Jack.' He'd set booby traps, too, to tip up their carriages, and did his best to free their slaves. And all the time he had to keep moving, drifting from one deserted shop to another, gradually building up a gang of runaway slaves and parentless children, until finally he laid claim to Hamleys and made that his HQ and from there he had waged his war.

It wasn't long before Stokely pitched up from heaven knows where. Hadn't said much, of course—Stoker always kept a bit mum—and then, one by one, had brought the different members of the team down into London to join Jack. Nobody had asked him to do it. None of the team, apart from Jonson, of course, had thought about coming together, but whatever it was that Stokely said to them, they found that was exactly what they wanted to do. The only sticky part had been that none of them had been too keen to have Jack bossing them around. Even Jack could see that having someone like him telling him what to do every day would drive him bonkers, so instead they each set up their own patch of London and from their hideaways they harassed any witch that came their way. Jack, because he had the biggest gang, was the planner, and when they came together for their 'bean feast', it was always here, in Hamleys.

For all their talk, Abe soon saw that there was no master plan, no worthy scheme. It was more like a game. 'Dunne bashing', they called it. They even had a chant: 'Go, Dunne! Go, Dunne! Godunnego!' They roared it for Abe, all apart from Stokely who just nodded and smiled, and were disappointed that Abe didn't seem more impressed. They would go on like this for ever, he thought, or until they got too rickety and slow on their legs and the witches finally caught up with them; but this they didn't think about. Thinking ahead had never, Abe suspected, been a strong point for any of them, with the exception of Jonson and perhaps Stokely, too. But most of them felt they were doing all right and although life wasn't that comfortable, they were having fun, even managed the odd game of football.

'And then what?' said Abe.

Then what? They didn't worry too much about 'then what'. If the witches left them alone, they would just get on with their lives.

'And when all the tins have gone?'

'Won't be for ages,' they shouted. 'Ages and ages and ages.'

Abe sat back. Jack knew that they had to help Alicia and so did Stokely, so why didn't they say anything? He was baffled by them. He looked at Stokely but his shy and mysterious travelling companion merely ducked his head and avoided saying anything. And Jack, now that he was sitting with the others, was just Jack the lad again. As for the others, he half expected them to start flicking food at each other; they hardly seemed to have grown up at all. And yet they ran their own lives, seemed to look after these wild looking boys and girls and ragged adults, the escaped slaves.

'Well, I need you,' he said at last and as firmly as he could. 'I need you all, the whole team. My scheme will only work if it is the whole team and that is that.'

'That's all very well, skipper-laddy,' said Gannet, 'but if we leave London, the witches will start to take over again and all the work we've done will go down the pan.'

'Hear-hear, Gannet, you're a total bean sprout,' chorused Jissop and Chivers, and they explained to Abe how each of the gangs had a team, but they had to watch out for spies. Nearly got snapped up when they were one goal down in a match they were playing down on Hyde Park—'Got careless,' said Pike, 'Jolly careless. The fat chefs came for us.'

'Lakins,' said Abe.

'That's them. We had to swim across the Serpentine, nearly caught our deaths.'

'What happened?'

'Got stuck in the mud, didn't they? Squelched about like a load of hippos. Witches don't know about swimming and water, can't cope with it. They started their screaming business but we were too far off for it to hurt.'

Abe nodded. They had held back at the bridge outside Oxford, and, in Brighton, when they had set him to sea to drown, they had all held well back from the water's edge. But they could fly; that was the puzzle. They had crossed seas and oceans to get to Egypt. They could go where they liked, couldn't they, so what was it about water that sometimes seemed to hold them back? Perhaps they just didn't like it. Did it wash the magic away from them, like making their batteries run down? It had to be something like that. It was as if there was something in its very nature that they feared. It was one of the four elements, wasn't it: earth, air, fire, and water. The first they liked; the last they hated. Earth was where they got their power from, where they had their secret hiding places, their dungeons, but water could drown everything. It could swallow up air and earth and snuff out fire. Water was the strongest element of all. He stowed the thought away.

'Dunk 'em in the river,' Pike was saying, 'that's what they used to do with witches in the olden days. Dunk 'em.'

When Abe was finally able to get their attention, he told them what Alicia was trying to do. At first they cheered. 'Miss Dunne is number one.' They all agreed with that; Miss Dunne was the biggest Mrs Dunne basher in the universe. But their faces fell when they heard that she was trapped in Oxford and in serious trouble. They wanted to help but none of them wanted to leave London and at first Abe couldn't understand why. They hung their heads, and chewed their lips. Eventually Roberts spoke up. The problem was Jonson. They didn't see why they should listen to him just because he had become a monk. Jack was all right. Everyone nodded. Jack had his bean feasts and was tip-top at bashing the witches. Jack didn't make them do anything they didn't want to do. Jack wasn't bossy.

'You're not listening!' said Abe, throwing his hands up in the air. 'It's not a question of anyone being bossy; Alicia needs our help and this is our one chance. All the witches are gathering to Mrs Dunne and when that happens not even Alicia will be able to hold them off. Oxford will fall and then once that happens every last free city, every last safe house, every last corner of Britain will come under her control. You won't be so free then. And what do you think she'll do with you if she finds you again?' They looked glum. 'Do you think she's forgotten? Do you think witches ever forget?'

They fell seriously silent at this. They knew what she would do if she caught them; she would spell them into a photograph and leave them trapped there for ever and ever. Not a jolly prospect.

He appealed to Jack. 'If we are to do anything, now is the time, attack before she becomes invincible. What do you say?'

Jack looked round the table. 'Miss Dunne is the mum,' murmured Pike, and they all nodded.

Jack smiled and slapped his stomach. 'Knew you'd convince them, skipper McLaddy.'

Abe sighed and sat back. He thought he understood now: being bossy, as Jonson had obviously tried to be, was not acceptable, but it was all right for Abe as skipper to put on a bit of pressure. What a funny old lot they were! The first hurdle was over but now they needed to bring the whole team together. That meant finding Jack Griffin and getting everyone through Mrs Dunne's army into Oxford.

'Oh, I can find Jack Griffin,' said Stokely. 'Leave him to me.'

'What! Are you sure?'

'Oh yes.'

Abe jumped to his feet and was about to give his friend a proper Egyptian hug but seeing the distinct look of worry on Stokely's face as he rushed around the table with his arms outspread, he changed the hug to a handshake. 'You are more sneakily clever and cunning than the great sphinx,' he exclaimed pumping Stokely's hand up and down. 'Now all we need is an army and we shall sweep to victory!'

'Absolutely spot on, skipper, he's sphinxy Stoker all right. Now, how long do we have?' asked Jack. 'A couple of months?'

Abe shook his head and then he painted a picture of the city as it had been when he and Stokely had ridden out two days before. 'Not very long at all,' he said, 'maybe a week, maybe two. It depends how long Alicia, Miss Dunne, can hold them off.'

'I see,' said Jack, and scratched his stomach. 'Better get cracking, eh?' So the team put their heads together and there was fierce muttering and exclamations like: 'Up in Barney's Bunker', 'Twenty in the Gubby hole', 'Wiggy's lot', and then Jack stood up and with an expression of real triumph in his voice said: 'Four hundred, skipper. Will that do you?'

Four hundred against how many thousands of Lakins! Abe closed his eyes: not the best odds. 'It's a start,' he said. 'Could do with a few more though. Any ideas?'

'Um . . . ' Stokely leaned over to him. 'I could get plenty more.'

'Plenty more what?'

'People.' Stokely nodded. 'To fight against her.'

'By when?'

'Seven days.'

'How?'

'Oh, Mrs Dunne hasn't quite tidied up, as she thinks she has,' chuckled Stokely. 'Not quite.' And Abe couldn't get anything more out of him.

And so it was agreed. Within a week, they would all gather at Oxford. Jack would bring the Londoners, Stokely would bring Griffin and his secret reinforcements. They would join together and launch an attack on Mrs Dunne's army. 'Together,' said Abe, 'you will sweep all her Lakins into the sea!'

They liked that. They banged their fists on the table and shouted three cheers for the skipper.

'Together we will pile all her broomsticks and burn them in such a blaze they will be able to see the flames in Cairo.'

They loved that too. They jumped up and shouted, 'Hurrah! The skipper will nip her!'

TWENTY-FOUR

At the end of the feast, Jack, with surprising efficiency, organized the billeting of all the gang members on the various floors of the toy store. Then Abe, Jack, and the others went up to Jack's den.

'We'll talk tomorrow, old man,' said Jack when Abe tried to get them to concentrate on the details of the plan. But Abe didn't think tomorrow would do at all. It was one thing to make speeches and get them all stirred up, but to be successful, they would need to plan. One does not cross the desert without watering the camel. They would need food, they would need weapons, they would need to think of how they were to slip out of London without attracting the attention of whatever witches were left in the city and, most of all, they would need to think of some way of breaking through Mrs Dunne's army so that they could join up with Jonson and Thomas.

'That's the key thing,' said Abe earnestly. Unfortunately every one of them was now very tired. 'Has no one been paying attention?' said Abe.

'The key thing,' murmured Gannet, promptly falling fast asleep.

Abe frowned, aware that, apart from Gannet, the others were all looking at him. He bit his lip. 'But if we get into the city and then into the college, we still don't have Stokely or Griffin.'

'No problem,' yawned Jack. 'We just charge out and join them.'

'Yes,' said Abe doubtfully, 'take them by surprise.'

'No problem, skipper. Leave it to Jack. Jack's got a spiffer of a trick for pulling the wool over Mrs Dunne's eyes.' And with that he yawned loudly again and nestled himself down into a mound of pillows. It was a signal for all the others to follow suit.

'Night, skipper,' said Pike.

'All will be absolutely fine, skipper daddy,' mumbled Chivers.

'Skipper will sort it out,' murmured Bittern, his hands crossed on his chest, his wrinkly eyes firmly closed. A second later he gave a whisperingly light snore.

'What about food?' protested Abe. 'Supply lines; and we need to agree a signal so that we know when Stokely and Griffin are ready to join us . . . '

But they were no longer listening. They were no longer awake. And they were his team, his secret weapon against Mrs Dunne!

'Not to worry, skipper.'

How was it that Stokely could always somehow disappear? Not really disappear, of course, but just become someone you didn't notice.

'Jacko's not quite as he thinks he is, skipper. You'll need to mind him, you know. Don't let him boss.' Stokely unfolded his legs and with a slight grunt got to his feet.

'Where are you going?'

'I have a lot to do.' He nodded and wiped his sleeve across his long nose. 'I am the gatherer, aren't I.' He gave his little wheezy chuckle. 'And Griffin will be expecting me. I'll see you at Oxford, skipper. You get into the city, that's my advice. And then hang on, eh. You keep them all together till I can join you. We'll come from the south, so watch for us, eh. We'll give a signal.'

'What? Which signal?'

'Oh, I don't know yet,' he said, wrapping his cloak round him, and pulling his hood down over his forehead, shadowing his face, 'but you'll know when you hear it.'

'But it's late, Stokely, and dark. Don't you want to wait till morning? We could all set off at the same time?'

'Oh, the dark is best,' said Stokely. 'Nobody can see old Stokely in the dark.' And with that he ducked out of the entrance to the igloo. Abe stood up and followed him out onto the main shop floor, intending to see him off down at the doors, but, although he was no more than five seconds behind his elderly friend, when he got to the top of the dead escalator, there was no sign of Stokely, just the faint hush of the main door closing.

Abe went to find himself a sleeping spot in the soft toy section. It was no wonder that the team were all so strange because everything was peculiar and, when he came to think of it, everything always had been. Would he and Alicia ever be able to sort it all out? 'Sort it all out.' What did that really mean? A battle, the battle of Oxford. And would he be a very great warrior, a warrior about whom songs would be written? A warrior in a pin-stripe suit?

With his nose pressed close to a giant panda bear, Abe fell asleep and dreamed of armies and thousands of stamping feet and the clash of arms and people calling.

And he woke in the half light of dawn, made duller by the dirt-streaked shop windows, aware of voices and movement and then a great booming as if someone or something was banging against the front doors. He scrambled round the counter on hands and knees and glimpsed various small heads ducking down and out of sight behind boxes and pillars and piles of shop junk. What was going on? And there it was again: boom. Boom. He hurried over to the escalator to see and instantly was hissed at: 'Head down, skipper.'

Abe instantly ducked and saw Jack and Roberts standing well back in the shadows, gesturing at him to come and join them. 'What is it?'

Jack pulled a face. 'Visitors. Hurry up, we're going to slip out the back.'

'Visitors?' Abe felt as if his brain was still shuffling off sleep. What visitors would come banging on the front door as if they were knocking at the gates of Hell?

Boom! and then the shivering crackle and smash of breaking glass. Whoever they were, they were in.

Abe peered round the head of the dead escalator and saw them bulging in through the shattered doorway: Lakins! Thirty. Forty. Broad as buckets, grimed with London's dirt, hair lank with foul grease, great fat arms prickled with black hair, and hard grey hands clutching hammers and meat cleavers, thick lumps of wood studded with nails. Lakins and out for serious business.

The first one stepped onto the welcome mat and was instantly dunked in Jack's yellow gloopy booby-trap.

'Ah smell jamboy!' rumbled one of them and there was instantly a belly-fat roar and the whole gang of Lakins lumbered in through Hamleys' main entrance. Abe didn't wait to see where exactly they were charging to; he just hoped that it wasn't straight up the stairs to him. He darted back towards Jack and Roberts and then followed them as they clattered down a fire exit stairwell into the basement again and then out into the back street where a group of no more than twenty or so of Jack's gang of scruffy street children and young adults were casually lounging up against the wall, most of them, it seemed to Abe, gazing calmly up at the sky.

'Is this all there are? I thought you said at least two hundred,' he said as they tumbled out into the street.

Jack shook his head and at the same time gave a thin whistle. Instantly, every single one of the gang, from the youngest, a curly haired girl with eyes as round as saucers, to the oldest, a thin-faced man who could have been any age at all, all turned to Jack. 'North-west,' said Jack. 'Oxford Road but keep off the highway. Lakins at the front, on Regent Street, so watch your backs. Anything above?'

'Nah.'

'One of the sisters round here is a flyer,' explained Roberts. 'They keep their eyes skinned ever since one whole group got snatched.' Of course, thought Abe, that's why they were looking up.

'Well, someone got spotted coming into the store,' said Jack curtly, 'else they wouldn't be here. No time to worry now. Move!'

And they moved, scattering down the street in twos and threes, keeping to the doorways but drifting fast. Like fallen leaves before the wind, thought Abe. Within half a minute the street was empty save for Abe, Jack, and Roberts.

'They were my lot,' said Jack, 'the others left hours ago, 'bout four o'clock this morning. Don't worry, we'll have a couple of hundred. Hope Mr Saintly Jonson will have enough food for us all. Wouldn't want Roberts to fade away, would we, Roberts?'

'Who are you calling fat?' wheezed Roberts hurrying along a couple of paces behind Abe and Jack as Jack hurried them down the street to a garage door which he swung open to reveal Abe's horse and two others stabled comfortably inside. 'I think they've got your scent somehow, skipper,' said Jack. 'So let's go!' They saddled up quickly and then clopped out into the street. Jack kicked his heels into his horse's flanks and broke into a gallop with the other two instantly following his example.

Abe thought he heard someone banging on a window, and a hoarse shout, but he didn't look back. They headed west, riding fast for a good thirty minutes until a breathless Jack was satisfied that no one was in pursuit. Then they threaded their way through small street after small street, past dead houses, and broken down buildings, until late into the afternoon. They saw people now and then, but most scuttled out of their way, fearing that horse riders would bring trouble. Someone yelled out: 'It's the filth!' and one bold boy picked up a stone and hurled it after them but mostly the way was deserted and, as the sun began to sink, they left the last of the outer city behind them.

They rode through the night, stopping every so often

to give their mounts a rest and for Jack and Roberts to ease their backs. It was early the next morning, with the sky wreathed in a hazy gauze of white cloud, like strips of bandage, thought Abe, that they reached the Oxford turning and there they waited for the others to gather.

In bands of three and four and five, they drifted down from the road, from the scruffy copse of woods and rank fields, gathering quietly, and so the small army grew. In came Gannet and Pike, then Chivers and Bittern leading near-sighted Jissop's horse.

Some of the gang members carried long staves of wood, metal bars, chains, and leather slings and there was the glint of blades too, wicked looking knives lashed to poles. These were their weapons. Not much, thought Abe. Not much against Mrs Dunne's massed army and her dark magic.

'No problem,' repeated Jack. 'No problem, skipper. Just leave it to Jack the lad.' And off he bustled having a word first with one group, then consulting with Pike and his group of skinny scruffs. What had Stokely said: Jack's not as good as he thinks he is? Abe followed the stocky, thick-necked joker and tried to get him to listen.

'We would be better to try and slip through Mrs Dunne's army at night. We'll never fight our way through.'

'Who said anything about fighting,' snorted Jack. 'You should know better than that, skipper. Think dodgy, eh.' He patted the edge of his nose and then barked the command to mount up and march off. Abe sighed and scrambled up into his saddle and trotted up to join the leaders of the column.

An hour later, they crested a low hill and there was the vast shadow of Mrs Dunne's camp, like spilt ink across the flat plains to the east of Oxford. And there was the city itself, still standing, college spires and towers spiking the skyline, threads and plumes of smoke from ashy patches which had been abandoned by the citizens. How many had gone over to the enemy? wondered Abe. How many in the fortified colleges were still willing to hold out come what may? What was holding Mrs Dunne back?

Jack brought his horse beside Abe. 'Righto, skipper, ready to visit the bishop?'

'Join Jonson?'

'Absolutementi.'

'You mean just ride through her whole camp? You're completely . . . '

'Bonkers,' said Jack. 'Of course I am. Now what do you think of this?'

TWENTY-FIVE

Jack turned slightly away from Abe and slipped something out from the saddlebag that hung on his horse's right flank. And when he turned back, just for a moment, Abe was looking straight into the face of one of Mrs Dunne's Lakins.

'Eh,' said Jack, his voice a little muffled from the mask. 'What do you think, skipper? I've got a cushion too. Roberts's idea to use disguise but Jissop made the mask after the feast. Looks good, don't you think?'

Roberts's idea was it? Not quite how Abe remembered it. It did look convincing though, especially when Jack pulled his hood up.

'Good,' said Abe, 'but are you thinking of going down on your own?'

'Don't be daft. We all have them. Papier mâché. Brilliant. Good old Jissmop. He's a bit of a genius when he's not trying to add things up all the time. Want to see what we all look like?' Old Jack, white haired, and wrinkly necked, sounded as keen as a schoolboy to show off the trick.

'Of course,' said Abe. It was clever. To cheat a little. To deceive. That was a kind of magic; perhaps it was the right kind to fool Mrs Dunne.

'Tog up,' said Jack to the other team members who were a few paces back from the hill's crest, 'and pass the word.'

There was a rippling movement all along the column as the gang members donned their Lakin masks, and shuffled stuffing under their tunics and threadbare cloaks. And there they were, a small contingent of Lakins ready to march into the main camp, just like so many must have done already, led by sisters answering Mrs Dunne's call.

But this contingent would march right through and into the city.

'It is truly brilliant, Jack. Unfortunately, you appear to have forgotten one thing.'

'What's that?'

'Me. Unless you have a spare.'

Jack made a hand signal and the other team members moved up on either side of them. 'You're our prisoner,' said Jack. 'No offence, old boy, but I think you'll be the icing on the cake. Isn't it you they're looking for anyhow? All the boys being rounded up. You're the bean bag, skipper, the one they want.'

'I do not think I am the bean bag they want,' said Abe. 'They've already tried to drown me once.'

'Spot on. The Stoker told us. It's not just sour grapes, you know. Mrs D must think you're a bit special, skipper, had you thought of that?' said Jack, his face uncharacteristically serious. 'Perhaps you're the business, skipper.'

'Business? I don't think so. I am Nasfali, that's all, trying to put things right.'

'Quite so,' said Jack. 'Quite so.' And he raised his eyebrows as if he didn't for a moment believe Abe.

But there wasn't much Abe could do about that, his attention was on Mrs Dunne's war camp. Far off as they were, he could still clearly pick out Mrs Dunne's shimmering black silken tent, and the square blocks of Lakins, all lined up, presumably waiting for an order to advance on the city. Hundreds of squares, thousands and thousands of Lakins. How could they defeat them? He felt a cold knot of worry in the pit of his stomach but tried to ignore it. Despair did not lead to victory.

'Ready to move, skipper?'

'One moment.' There was something else. Not a single fire was burning, and nothing, nothing was moving. Perhaps they knew all about Abe and Jack and the gangs from London. Perhaps they would simply stand there and wait for them to walk straight into the camp and then

mask or no mask they would snap them up. Mrs Dunne
was a spider, a red-necked fleshy spider. He shuddered.
And this was the web they were about to walk into.

'Well?'

But still Abe waited. A horse snorted. He heard the
jingle of a bridle and a hoof pawing impatiently at the
turf. Something was wrong. They shouldn't go yet. And
then he heard a swelling, grumbling groan as if it were
coming out from the very belly of the earth.

'Pardon me,' said Jack.

But this was no joke. Up from the heart of the camp,
from the black tent, there spun a twisting web of grey that
bunched and writhed and scumbled itself into a vast head,
a dog's head, a ravening hound with black hell holes for
eyes. It seemed to fill half the sky, and the jaw gaped wide
over the city of Oxford as if it would swallow it whole.
And then there was another low moan as up from the
towers of the city there also rose a skein of grey, at first
thin and wispy, no more than a trickle into the hazy dawn
light. But the skein twisted and whipped rapidly round
about itself, and suddenly it was a gigantic coiled serpent,
a hundred times larger than the one that had flashed at
Abe when he had been standing in Jonson's room all those
long days ago. But this serpent had long curved dagger
fangs that were white against the dead grey of its skin and
eyes that burned with the colour of pain.

And as they watched, the serpent ducked and whipped
its head to and fro beneath the hound which snapped again
and again, and the Lakins moaned. Jack's small army
stayed silent and waited, for this contest, they knew, was
a test of terrible power. 'Oh, Alicia,' prayed Abe,
'concentrate. You must concentrate.'

Clearly she did concentrate because, all at once, the
serpent blurred into a frenzy of writhing knots and
suddenly there was the hound, wrapped and trussed like a
chicken ready for the pot, the serpent coiled around it, its
flat head nudging over the hound, its jaw widening and

widening until with a huge gulp it took the shadow hound into its mouth and swallowed it whole. Jack's army watched in astonishment as the vast bulge travelled slowly down the serpent's gullet.

A scream of rage spiralled out from Mrs Dunne's camp.

The serpent flickered over her army, its back undulating lazily, its head browsing down low, its mouth gaping wide again and the Lakins broke and ran, roaring and yelling and shoving each other, this way and that. Chaos.

'Time to move, I think,' said Abe.

'Spot on, skipper,' said Jack.

They moved down the hill in a long column, staring straight ahead until they reached the outer edge of the camp. Nervous guards challenged them. 'Oi, wacher gor in there wiv yer?'

To which Jack replied: 'Out the way, fat maggot. We've gor ve boy and we're bringing 'im to 'er, so move your carcass before the snake gets yer.'

'Awright. Awright. Only doin' me job.' The guard's little pig eyes almost disappeared into his white, oily face but he stepped back out of their way. And though they were challenged at every turn, each time the guards backed away in the face of Jack's snarling responses. Abe, flanked by the eight members of the team, rode with his head slumped forward in what he hoped was the appropriate posture for a miserable prisoner. At the same time he was trying to hold his breath for the camp stank of burnt bacon grease and cats' pee.

Meanwhile overhead the snake flashed and zigzagged and once came low down over them, its long tendril forked tongue flickering inquisitively. Then suddenly it jerked back and soundlessly poured itself back into the heart of Oxford and was gone. Back to Alicia, thought Abe. Everything was falling apart but she was becoming stronger. Perhaps she no longer needed them. Perhaps the team's rescue mission was misplaced heroics.

As they came closer to the edge of the city, they joined trails of Lakin soldiers making their way to their positions; one or two of them stared sourly at Jack's small army.

'Midgets,' they sneered.

'Who's your missis?'

Then a giant of a Lakin stepped out and blocked their way. ''Ere, wha're you takin' that jamboy wiv yer? It's she that wants 'im, innit?' He was twice the size of the others and dressed in a scratched leather apron and a sagging grey chef's hat. 'Well?' A huge forearm gripped a knobble-headed club the size of a parking meter.

'Wa's at, yer girt knob o' ship's grease,' rumbled Jack, in a perfect Lakin imitation. 'The Mrs want this bit of camel droppin' paraded round the city, don't she. So she inside can see him.'

'Er.' The giant nodded his stupid head and his free hand scratched the forest of hair bristling up from the neck of his apron. 'Orright.' And he stepped back.

'Jack,' muttered Abe admiringly, 'you are a veritable genius.'

'The very word,' agreed Jack, as they passed out through the front line and began the last short leg into the city. 'What I've been telling everyone for ages. Isn't that right, lads?'

'Jacko!' crowed the team.

Abe laughed. 'You are not so modest, are you?'

'What's modest,' he said complacently. Then he swung half round in his saddle. 'Tog off, everyone. Don't want Jonno's monks tipping boiling oil on us.'

Their horses clopped in silence on into Headington and slowly they trudged down the hill until they came to the Plain, the roundabout before Magdalen Bridge, where a barricade of carts and beds, and lumps of bricking was strung across the road in a barrier more than ten feet high. There they came to a halt.

Abe cupped his hands to his mouth and called out: 'We're friends from London. Can you let us through?'

There was the sound of running feet and the clatter of iron, and then a strong Welsh voice called out: 'And if you were the mighty devil himself, we would give you a good dunkin' in the river if you so much as put your ugly snout an inch over this wall here.'

It was Thomas. It had to be! 'Thomas, it's us. It's the team! Aren't you going to let us through?'

'Oh, I know you can sound like my sweet Aunt Fanny when you have a mind to, but I know who you are, you are that old ugly witch. You don't fool me for one instant.'

Jack shook his head. 'If that old Welsh goat's not careful, I'm going to charge through and knock him into his own river.'

Abe held up his hand. 'You won't do anything of the sort. Do you hear me? The team stays together at all costs. No scrapping.'

And rather to Abe's surprise, Jack ducked his head. 'Sorry, skipper.'

Suppressing a smile, Abe nudged his horse a little ahead of the others. 'Thomas,' he said patiently, 'you don't even have an Aunt Fanny, so will you stop your bossing and let us through.'

'Jonson said . . . '

'Thomas!' There was a sharpness to Abe's voice that he hadn't intended but it had Thomas bobbing up above his barricade and staring at them like a stunned rabbit.

'Oh, my goodness,' he said. 'I am so sorry. You're who you said you were. That's a bit embarrassing, isn't it? How are you doing, Jack? Pike, old boy, and Jissop, goodness, you're all here, even fatty Roberts, my word, this is a great day, a great day.' And his broad bearded face almost split in half with a grin as long and wide as London Bridge. Then he and his troop were pulling aside a section of the wall and were out there pumping hands and slapping backs and welcoming and double welcoming them to the besieged city.

'And where's the main force?' asked Thomas when all the greetings were done and the last of Jack's column were inside the barricade. 'Positioned them up the hill, have you, because that's what I would have done had we more men.'

Abe shook his head. Then he told him Stokely was their main hope, that he had promised serious numbers, at which Thomas looked rather relieved.

'How is Miss Dunne?'

'Well.' Thomas avoided his eyes. 'Miss Dunne is not really communicating, you might say. Not really. Jonno is a bit worried, but, boy,' he exclaimed banging his stubby-fingered hands together, 'it is a great thing you have come. Do you know, it will be more than fifty years since we were all together. How's that, chaps! A game of footer, maybe.'

'Seven!' shouted Pike suddenly and they all bent over and waggled their bottoms and Pike tried to do a forward roll but he got stuck halfway. Roberts told him that he had the memory of a fried fish because they never did forward rolls with a number seven, and Pike looked sheepish. Abe laughed while the adults in Jack's London troop shook their heads and muttered that the old geezers were daft as brushes but that was the way they were, and they knew a thing or two about dealing with the witches, so as far as they were concerned that was all right.

'Let's go and see Jonson,' Abe said, Alicia too, he thought, if she'll see me.

Then he suddenly gave an involuntary sniff. Was the enemy close? There was no sign of anyone apart from Thomas's men but he didn't feel safe and he couldn't help wondering whether there were witches in the city? Had they grown strong enough to cross the river?

TWENTY-SIX

Jonson, dressed in his brown monk's habit, and flanked by armed citizens, the Greyfriars militia, met them at the gate of the college.

'Look what the old tide's washed up, Jonno,' called out Thomas.

Jonson, standing rather oddly, Abe thought, with his hands behind his back, inclined his head gravely. 'You are all very welcome.'

One of the team, Abe thought it was probably Roberts, suppressed a snort which Jonson chose to ignore. 'My steward will show you to your rooms because you all,' he continued with a completely straight face, 'look old and wheezy . . . '

There was a stunned silence and then: 'He's got a jolly nerve!'

Abe, seeing that a row was about to explode, said, 'Jonson, these are your friends. This is the team, remember.'

'Indeed,' he said, and with a flourish he produced a leather football from behind his back. 'And I have been practising.'

'Blooming well needed to,' shouted Gannet, running in and scooping the ball out of his hand.

Jack gave Jonson a punch on the arm. 'Thought you might have turned into a dull old windbag. Gannet, pass!'

There was an instant scramble for the ball and Abe gave a quiet sigh of relief. They were still funny, still surprisingly quick, still ready to barge and cheat. It was hard to believe they really were old. He looked past them to the doorway on the far side of the quad that led into the garden. He had to go and see Alicia but he found himself reluctant to move. How powerful had she become? That display this morning, a trial of strength between herself and her mother, and she had won, but what did it signify? Mrs Dunne hadn't disappeared; Oxford was still under siege . . .

Standing in the middle of the gateway, Abe suddenly found himself to be the default goalkeeper. Jissop shouted: 'Look out, skipper!' and the next second the heavy leather ball smacked Abe on the side of his head. 'Great save!' The team cheered; but Abe, though his ears were ringing and stinging from the knock, was sure he could hear a different shouting behind the cheers, shouting of a very different order: deeper, hoarser, rhythmic; and he could also hear a thundering clang as of a hundred dustbin lids being smashed with sticks. The sky suddenly darkened. The game froze and a lookout up on the gate tower bellowed out: 'They're coming again!' at the top of his voice.

Three of the militia, who had joined in the game as backs, shoved Abe unceremoniously out of the way and heaved the gates closed and slammed down the locking bar.

Seconds later the attack hit home. The great gates rattled and boomed and the roaring of Mrs Dunne's Lakins turned into a caterwauling din, loud enough to make the air throb and shake.

And then everyone was moving: the militia manned the walls and scrambled up onto the roofs; the more elderly men and women stoked fires and heated vats of old bathwater, and the youngest of the children were hustled down into the safety of the college cellars. Abe was impressed by the organization. Jonson and Thomas had not been sitting in Oxford twiddling their thumbs.

'They've attacked six times now,' shouted Jonson, grabbing hold of Abe's arm and leading him away from the gate. 'Six.'

So the Lakins had crossed the water. Mrs Dunne was not getting weaker at all. 'Any sign of witches when they attack?' Abe had to raise his voice to make himself heard.

Jonson shook his head. 'Not yet.'

'When it's bad like this does Alicia come out and help?'

'Never comes out of the library. But the Lakins haven't got close to breaking in here yet.'

'Too stupid?'

'Perhaps.' Jonson didn't sound convinced. 'Other colleges haven't been so fortunate.'

Abe saw Pike and Jissop scrambling up onto the roof, joining the militia in hurling down missiles, pots filled with steaming grey bathwater, and bits of old tiling and drainpipe. And all the time there was a thunderous banging on the gates. Surely they would burst open at any moment? Jonson obviously thought so too because he hoiked up his habit and, telling Abe he would be back instantly, ran off towards the kitchens.

Abe stared at the gates, willing them to hold. Bang! They shuddered and then slowly bulged inwards; hinges groaned and squealed. Instinctively Abe ran back into the gate lodge and pressed his back to the thick oak, as if he alone could withstand whatever force was being applied from the outside. Bang! Another blow that juddered through the thick wood and jarred every bone in Abe's body.

Behind him he smelt the stink of burning flesh and saw flaming bundles of rubbish, meat wrapped in oil-soaked rags, sailing over the walls and thunking down onto the green of the quad where they spluttered and stank. Small gangs of women and children scurried out from the cellars, dousing fires and scooping up the garbage and filth into bins. Terrible as it all was, Abe was impressed by how calm everyone seemed to be. Jonson was a good leader.

Moments later, Jonson himself returned with a squad of porters, cooks, and town people armed with home-made pikes. Instantly they formed three lines, the first kneeling, the other two ranked behind them, and they stood there like the prickly back of a porcupine. Any Lakin who hurled himself through the gate would be most uncomfortably skewered. 'All right, old chap,' said Jonson, 'I think you can let this lot take over.'

'Not bad,' said a short-of-breath Roberts trotting up to Abe and Jonson. 'Not bad. Hope for you yet, Jonno. But I think we need a hand on the side wall, they're using ladders there.' But even as they spoke there was a high, thin, squealing sound and suddenly all the shouting died. By the time Abe and Roberts and Jonson had found themselves a vantage point from which they could peer down onto the street, they could just see the last fat-bottomed Lakins lumbering away, some of them, they were pleased to see, limping and clutching their heads.

'Ha blinking ha,' jeered Roberts. 'Showed them what's what, eh. Nothing like a bit of a scrap to give a chap an appetite. When's tucker?'

Jonson ignored him. 'Look over there, skipper,' he said pointing back towards the city where a thick pall of smoke was pouring greasily into the sky.

'It's over near Magdalen, isn't it?'

'It is Magdalen,' said Jonson grimly. 'We survive but the other colleges do not. Each time we have been attacked, one of the others has fallen. That's seven gone, and there were only ten fortified to begin with. There's only Balliol and St John's and Worcester left. The attacks on us, I think, are just distractions. It feels as if we're being saved till last, skipper, and last isn't going to be more than a few days away unless Miss Dunne comes up with something more than that smoky snake of hers.'

'You mean we haven't won?' said Roberts, his fat face paling. 'I thought that was the big battle. Didn't we win, skipper?'

'Not yet,' said Abe.

'Oh gloom,' said Roberts. 'Gloom and despondency. Can't you do something, skipper, you and Miss Dunne?'

Jonson looked at him. 'If anyone can talk to her, it's you, isn't it?'

Of course it was him. She was his cousin, after all. In a way she was his responsibility. 'I shall go and see her now,' he said.

'Splendid,' said Jonson. 'I must go and do my rounds. Roberts, you can come with me. See you at tucker, skipper.' And with that the two of them headed off, leaving Abe to make his way to the library. What worried him was what he would find there. Would there be anything of the old Alicia left? Or would he find some ashy-faced sorceress spinning smoky magic?

Stepping out into the high-walled back garden, Abe was immediately aware of some subtle change having taken place, though for a second or two he couldn't put his finger on what it was. The grass was green, the shady trees were still in leaf, ivy grew thick along the outer wall, everything was as he remembered it, everything except for that part of the garden which butted directly against the old library itself. There the flowers looked as if they had been scorched; they were black and withered and the old wisteria was burnt into black, twisty stumps that looked disturbingly like the stringy limbs of old men.

What had she done?

'Well, what did you expect me to do, Nasfali?'

Abe almost jumped out of his skin. He spun round and then back again. Expected? He had not expected this. Where was she hiding? Her voice was so close it was as if she had been standing beside him; he could almost feel her breath on his ear.

'Up here.'

His eye travelled up the side of the building and there she was, standing at the upper window, her face a hazy faraway moon; her hand pressed palm forward on the glass of the window.

'So, Nasfali, you came back.'

'Of course I came back.' It was hard not to feel cross: he had ridden halfway across the country, avoided being mashed to pieces by rolling-stomached monsters or thrown into a witch's prison. He was tired, sore, and half of Oxford was tattered and ruined, and here she was, her voice as cool and imperious as ever, as if he was the one who had casually deserted her. 'I gathered the team, nearly all of them,' he said, and then corrected himself. 'Stokely is the real gatherer, he's getting Griffin.'

'Griffin. Yes, of course.'

'Shall I come in?'

'No!' and then a fraction softer, though Abe was too out of sorts to notice. 'No, I think you had better not, not just now.' What he did hear, though, was a distinct ring of excitement in her voice. 'You saw my creature, Nasfali, the great serpent? It beat my mother's saggy hound.'

He expected her to say it was 'wicked' or 'deadly' but it wasn't just that her voice sounded different; she wasn't even talking in the way she used to talk and it startled him. 'There will be a reckoning, Nasfali, a red dimmed reckoning. What do you think of that? It will be pointy and hard for the witch, my mother. It will be—'

'Alicia! Don't talk like that.' It wasn't just the strangeness of the words, but he felt he could hear a snakiness in the way she was speaking, a faint hiss, and it was frightening him. 'Why won't you let me come in and see you?' he said, though he wasn't at all sure that he wanted to get too close to her, not if she was in some strange mood.

It was as if she hadn't heard him. 'I am prepared, Nasfali. It will happen soon. Tomorrow early. It will come down and there will be a fierce reckoning. If you have the courage, you will share the triumph, Nasfali. Rise up, when you hear the call, rise and lead a great charge against my mother's army and we shall see then who holds the power.' And when she said the word power there was a positive thrill trembling in her voice. Power, this was the only thing that Mrs Dunne and her sisters existed for, nothing else mattered. Had she begun to be like them? 'When you hear the call, Nasfali.'

And that was it. Silence. The pale face at the window gone.

What call, exactly? Who would call whom and how? Would it be the same calls as the one Stokely would give? Why couldn't people be more precise? He turned away, and a little later, when he had tracked down Jonson and the others sitting around a table in the great hall, he reported to them what Alicia had told him, though he decided not to mention the disturbing way she had spoken, nor the way she had refused to let him go in and see her, nor the way that everything that grew round the library was now dead. Perhaps that was why she wouldn't let him in, because to get too close to her now would be dangerous. Perhaps he would shrivel and burn. He shuddered. What was going to happen? What was going to happen if she was right and they did triumph over her mother?

Still, the team were cheerful and this was good. No one had been hurt in the last attack; the college walls were secure. They had shovelled away a plate of what Roberts called 'tucker supreme' and they were, for once, ready to listen. In fact, though Abe didn't register this, they were surprisingly sensitive and saw immediately that Abe was deeply worried about something. Jack came and patted him on the shoulder. 'Are you all right, skipper? Look as if you have sniffed a maggot.'

'All will be well.' It was Abe's automatic response. He didn't see Roberts raising his eyebrows, or Jissop giving Gannet a slight nudge.

Jonson cleared his throat. 'Did Miss Dunne say exactly when the call would come?' he asked.

'Tomorrow.' He looked up. 'This will be it, I think,' he said. 'I shall lead a charge—this is what Miss Dunne wants. Everyone shall take part in the charge. It will be glorious.' He spoke without great enthusiasm but the team seemed quite bubbly with anticipation.

'Then we had better prepare. Thomas, if you would organize the college, I'll take Jack, if that is all right, Jack.'

'Absolutimento, Jonson, you worshipful boiled egg.'

'And whoever else wants to come. We'll warn the free colleges because it seems we should all move at the same time. One sharp blow . . . '

'One giant step for mankind,' said Jissop.

'Exactly.'

They got up and divided into two groups, most of them electing to stay with Thomas and organize themselves for this last battle. 'I want something really long, with a bonky thing on the end,' Bittern was saying. 'Not too heavy, of course, because the old arms are a bit weedy thin, but I want a bonky thing on the end so I can really do some serious whacking.'

'I have exactly the job for you, boyo. I'll show you . . . ' said Thomas putting his arm round elderly Bittern's skinny shoulders. 'The very thing.'

Abe stood up. They made him feel better. Odd that. Such a headache they had always been, but when they weren't breaking wind or barging each other they were somehow as comfortable to be around as a warm hot-water bottle on a cold night. He would go with Jonson.

TWENTY-SEVEN

A small troop of the toughest college soldiers were mounted up to accompany Jonson on his round of the free colleges. Abe hadn't realized but this was part of Jonson's daily routine. A sombre and dangerous task since every day Mrs Dunne gradually ate away at the city. It wasn't just the shrieking cleaver-wielding Lakins, but also a seeping despair that floated down into the city with the sour smell from the cooking fires of her besieging army.

Greyfriars' gatekeeper gave the all-clear and they rode out onto Iffley Road, once a long residential road but now nothing but rubble, rats, and rubbish. Greyfriars was a lonely outpost on the edge of the city.

They rode down to the Plain. The barricade where they had been challenged by Thomas had long been torn away. Keeping close together for fear of ambush, they crossed over Magdalen Bridge. As Jonson had predicted, Magdalen, the huge college that dominated this entrance to the town, was a wreck. Every window was broken, the gate on Longwall Street hung open, off its hinges, and the great wall was breached; the hewn blocks of stone tumbled down into the street as if a giant had flicked the wall over. Of the garrison of this huge, fortress-like college and its hundreds of refugee families, there was not a sign. Only shadowy figures flickered here and there across the doorways of the ruined college. Scavengers.

'They're bypassing Greyfriars,' observed Jonson. 'I suppose we're just small fry. They're picking off all the important colleges, one by one.'

'Or perhaps,' suggested Abe, 'they're leaving the hardest till last.'

'Well said, skipper, you little Egyptian trumpet.' Jack slapped his belly. 'Onward and upward, Jonno. Griffin never let us get gloomy, even when we were stuck in the photo.'

'Onward,' agreed Jonson, though his expression remained serious.

They rode up Holywell Street. New College had fallen and to their right they could see the smoke pouring up from a burning Wadham. Broad Street was silent. The smaller colleges to their left that fronted on Turl Street looked secure though deserted. Jonson didn't stop to investigate but led them straight up to St Giles, the very heart of the city. The old Church of St Mary's had been gutted but from the northern corner of Balliol a seriously impressive barricade stretched right across St Giles to the Ashmolean museum. This wasn't a case of turned-over carts and old mattresses but a steep earthworks, topped with wire and spikes of iron and punctuated every twenty feet with timber watchtowers. In front of the barricade the road had been broken to make a deep ditch brimming with scummy water. The whole earthworks bristled with armed men who glowered down at them until Jonson was recognized by the captain of the guard.

They exchanged information and the man promised to report back instantly to the master of Balliol who was leading the defence of this part of the city. 'A call, you say, but one we'll recognize. I'll take your word for it, Abbot Jonson. For my part I'll be only too glad to lead the men out of here, the city sickens and decays around us and I even begin to feel it in here. A last charge. Very well. Good luck to you.' And so saying he turned away to deliver his message while Jonson and the others wheeled their horses about; but instead of taking the way they had come, Jonson led them south down St Aldates to Christ Church.

Jack started making odd beeping sounds.

'What are you doing?' asked Abe.

'Danger warning. Danger warning.'

Abe felt eyes watching them. A stone pitched down, hitting one of the horsemen, who clutched his arm, and cursed, and then swung his horse round in a tight circle. But there was no enemy to be seen; just long slashing streaks of graffiti slapped bloodily across the ruined buildings' walls. The same thing over and over again: 'slave', 'slave', 'slave'.

They kept going but when they came abreast of Christ Church, a gang of rough-looking men sprawled out across the road in a loose line. Abe gave an involuntary sniff: there was the stink of witch about these men. Their eyes were dark, their faces hollowed out with a hunger no food could satisfy. They hadn't come to parley either. One of them stepped ahead of the others, tilted back his head and gave a growling animal roar that was echoed by the others. Then there was the hissing flash of metal and Abe suddenly saw that each of them was carrying a long thin-bladed knife.

'Ham knife,' observed Jack with odd calmness. 'My auntie always used those for ham, not surprising really . . .'

'Shsh!' Jonson held up his hand and their troop reined to a stop and stood silent. Another stone clattered on the street, missing Abe by inches. What was Jonson playing at; they should back off immediately. In the silence, he heard a scutter of feet and turning he saw that they were cut off by another line of starved renegades. 'No hesitation,' said Jonson calmly, 'and keep as close to me as you can.'

And with that he kicked his heels into the flanks of his horse, which responded with a high-pitched whinny and lurched forward in a clattering, shoulder-heaving gallop. Abe, Jack, and the men instantly spurred their horses too.

'Could do with one of those long poky things,' shouted Jack.

'Lance,' shouted back Abe, keeping his head down along the flank of his horse's neck.

'Lance! Splendid. Knights of the Round Table, skipper, that's the job for us.'

What these renegades expected was anybody's guess. They slashed wildly with their knives but there were too few of them to frighten the horses and disrupt the charge. They were simply spun and buffeted out of the way and the riders were through, with only a couple of cuts to show for it. The man beside Abe had a tight expression of pain on his face. Blood stained darkly down his right leg.

'Will you be all right?'

'I'll get back, don't you fret,' he replied through gritted teeth. 'Take more than them witches' starvelings to topple me.'

They cantered over Folly Bridge and Jonson reined them in again. 'I've seen enough,' he said. 'This is it. All the outer colleges are gone, only Greyfriars is left and despite what you say, skipper, they'll pick it off easily enough in the end.'

'Can't see why Mrs "Thing" doesn't have her army occupying all the bits of the city she's already sacked,' said Jack. 'She must be as thick as two tons of horse manure, if you ask me. Is that your college over there, Jonno?' he asked pointing across Christ Church meadow.

'That direction, yes.'

'Are we going to go back along the river?'

'Yes.'

Abe was half listening as he looked down at the wide, slow-flowing river. He knew why the Lakins didn't stay in the city; it was the river. They could cross it all right but they didn't linger because they were witch spawn. Witches couldn't abide water. Gold of the desert, thought Abe, that's what it was. And then it came to him what they must do: they must make Mrs Dunne attack this way, over Folly Bridge. A fine name for a valiant last stand. Yes, the bridge was where the people of Oxford should hold the line. Then the men of Greyfriars could stream south across the meadow and whack into the witches from the side. And then maybe with whatever Alicia had planned and with Stokely and all his promised fighters attacking from the outer edge of the witches' camp, maybe then they could sweep Mrs Dunne away. The claws of a crab, thought Abe.

But how could they make Mrs Dunne come this way?

What would his father do?

He thought of the strange man, his father, the keeper of the great book that Mrs Dunne and his own mother had gone to Egypt to steal. He had been clever. He could make things seem different without really changing them. Like with Jack's masks. Fool them, it wasn't so hard. Dangerous, perhaps, but not so hard. Sneak their way into the heart of Mrs Dunne's camp and the moment Stokely gave his great signal they would strip off their masks and then run like jack-rabbits for the bridge. Mrs Dunne would be in such a rage seeing them that she wouldn't even think; she would come full tilt after them, straight into their trap.

'My goodness, skipper,' said Thomas, when Abe had outlined the scheme, 'you have a brain the size of . . . well, all of Wales, really. That's a mighty, mighty plan.'

Everybody nodded. Everyone was excited. This would be it.

'It!' shouted Jack for no reason.

'But didn't she, Miss Dunne, I am most fearfully sorry, didn't Miss Dunne say that the call would come today,' drawled Gannet, pushing his flop of grey hair back from his eyes.

They all instinctively turned towards the window where the late summer sun was slowly settling into the murky haze that lay perpetually now all along the horizon; the murky breath of Mrs Dunne's camp.

'No,' said Abe. 'She said tomorrow. There is always tomorrow.' He had a feeling that he had heard that on an old film on television. It didn't seem particularly wise but the team nodded their heads in satisfied agreement.

'And,' said Jissop gobbling up his words hurriedly, 'tomorrow is another day.'

'Jiss-hop,' said Jack, 'if you were the Duchess of Timbuktoo, I still would not marry you.'

They returned to Greyfriars, then broke for the night, agreeing that all the team apart from Jonson would disguise themselves as Lakins and with Abe leading them, sneak their way into Mrs Dunne's camp. Claws of the crab, they liked that. Jack liked the idea so much that he gave Roberts a sharp pinch. 'Just practising. Just practising, old chap,' he said backing away from his angry victim.

At this point, Abe slipped away to get some sleep. He did not feel quite so confident in his plan as the others appeared to be. But it was the only scheme there was. The only one he could come up with. 'It will have to do,' he said to himself, and he looked across the darkened quad towards the library where she who had been the vision of his prep school days laboured over the book of secrets. The scheme would just about do, if Alicia had the power and the will still to fight with them against her mother, and if the team could run fast enough.

They would have to enter the camp on foot. If they were lucky they would be able to tether the horses in one of the ruined houses on the outer edge of the city. If they were unlucky they would end up having to run all the way home. I, thought Abe, am swift on my feet. Many times have I won the sprints on sports day but the team . . . He pulled a face. His good friends, however, had old legs and wheezy chests. He had heard Roberts puffing and panting and that was just after the horse ride of the afternoon. Perhaps he shouldn't come. Perhaps none of them should come.

He looked out of the window and saw Gannet and Pike talking together down in the Quad. They were fine. They were very fine but for them this plan would be too dangerous. Wouldn't he, Abe, be better off on his own? It was him that Mrs Dunne hated, and Abe's mother too, she despised him. Seeing Abe right in the middle of their camp would do the trick very well. They would come slavering like wolves and then there would be such a chase that songs would be made up about it afterwards. The great run of Ebrahim Nasfahl Ma'halli, the wily fox of the desert. He liked that. And it would be better not to tell the others. He, Ebrahim, would make the run; he would go on his own.

TWENTY-EIGHT

It took till midnight for Abe to complete the first part of his preparations. He checked his horse, brushed her down, and made sure she was well fed and watered. He scavenged a bundle of rags and carefully bound each hoof so that he wouldn't make a din either leaving the college or when approaching Mrs Dunne's camp. He went down to the kitchens and armed himself Lakin-style with a long meat cleaver and a giant ladle, though what use a ladle would be if he had to fight it out in the middle of a host of Lakins was more than he could imagine. Then he told himself not to be so stupid; he had no intention of fighting anyway; these were just for show. Trickery, he muttered to himself, merely trickery.

He swiftly tucked both implements under his arm, scooped up a fist-sized ball of blackened grease from the cooking stove and hurried off to the steamy laundry room where he scavenged pegs and towels and a pillowcase and then down to the cellar where he knew wine was kept. He opened a couple of bottles, poured away the wine and went off with the corks. Then, stuffing all his bits and pieces into the pillowcase, he made his way back to the stable, dropping into the gate lodge where he warned the guard there that he would be leaving at first light and told him he must oil the hinges of the gate so that Abe could slip out silently.

He dumped the laden sack behind the stable door and plopped the ball of grease onto the windowsill. With the first and easiest part of the mission completed, he leaned back against the wooden stall to rest for a moment, and felt the warm breath of his horse nuzzling him at his neck. This was where Stokely slept; stooping, solitary Stokely, the gatherer. Abe found himself wishing his old travelling companion were here now. It was one thing to make a bold decision when you have company all around you, and the night doesn't seem so dark nor so threatening, but here with just the shuffling, heavy silence of the horses, he felt less sure. Would he really be safe with this disguise? And Alicia's promise of triumph, did that really mean that they would win and that they would all be there to share the victory? It didn't feel like victory, not yet.

He stepped out into the night again and looked towards the library. A single light glowed creamily in the upstairs window. Did she ever sleep? Did she know what he was doing or planning to do? Probably. She had a knack of always knowing. For a moment he was tempted to go and knock on the library door and tell her, but then he would have to shout out to her and half the college would hear. Where was the glory if he went looking for support? The great trapeze artists do not need a safety net, he told himself. I, Ebrahim Nasfahl Ma'halli, do not need a safety net.

And so he turned away and set off to complete the second part of his preparation. The team, Jonson included, were sleeping up in the gate tower. The slight hints of jealousy or suspicion that Jack and the others seemed to have had of Jonson had gone. They liked being together. They liked jostling and teasing and poking each other in the ribs. The threat of Mrs Dunne didn't seem to bother them unduly. They looked forward to the return of Stokely and Griffin. Abe suspected that they were actually looking forward to a real showdown with Mrs Dunne.

From halfway up the stone stairs he could hear the thick rumble of their snoring. How could they sleep? Still, it made his task easier. Shielding the candle he was carrying with one hand, he nudged open the door and slipped inside. They were all scumbled together like a contended litter of pigs. He could just make out Jissop, his bare foot sticking into Gannet's neck; Gannet's elbow lodged in Jack's eye; Roberts's round belly rising and falling like a gently swelling sea, a lulling pillow for Pike.

Quickly Abe scanned the debris of their cast-off clothes and boots. As he suspected, they had simply tossed their Lakin masks onto the floor. Some of them had already been trodden on and were useless but it still didn't take him a moment to scoop up one that would serve him well.

'Hello, skipper,' murmured a sleepy voice. 'Come to tuck us up?'

Abe looked back to the bed and saw Gannet with half an eye open. 'Soft dreams,' he whispered.

'Absolutely, old man. Absolutely . . . ' and his eyelid slowly drooped down.

Abe kept very still for a moment, then backed out of the room and softly pulled the door closed behind him. He listened but there was no stir, nothing but the same regular whistle and rumbling snore of the sleepers.

Down the stairs he went and back to the stable. There he bulked his body up with towels pegged together behind his neck. He wadded straw into the pillowcase and strapped that round his middle, giving himself the trademark barrel chest of a Lakin. He smeared the grease onto his hands, forearms, round his neck, and into his hair. He fitted the Lakin mask over his face and, in the candle light, he looked at himself in the little mirror he had propped up on the sill. It was possible he would fool them, if they were sleepy enough. He pulled on a cloak, letting the hood fall low on his ugly mask. Better, much better. He would do.

He led the horse across the quad and through the gate, the guard wishing him luck. Then he mounted and rode slowly up the long, dark, ruined Iffley Road. Nothing stirred but ahead of him was the camp; he could already smell the thick sour smell.

When he was close to where he imagined their front line to be, he dismounted and led his horse into a roofless cottage and tethered her there. She tossed her head and pawed the ground. Evidently the smell and atmosphere of the witches' camp was as unpleasant to animals as it was to Abe. However, he settled her down, giving her a lick of salt and then patting her nose and promising her he would be back to take her away. Then he squared his shoulders and set off for the last stretch of his journey on foot, the stretch that he hoped he would be sprinting back along in a couple of hours.

''Ere, warra'r you, eh?' The large black shape of a Lakin loomed out of the darkness.

Abe shovelled the corks into his cheeks and when he answered he managed a pretty good spitty, Lakin-style answer. 'Shove orf, yer,' he growled. 'I'm looking fer mea', ain' I? Rat or rabbit, eh.'

'Gi' us some, yer squat-legged little run'.'

Abe had been worried that he wouldn't be tall enough to fool them; he was a good foot shorter than any Lakins he had seen but this one sounded almost friendly. 'Ge' yer own grub, yer fat great slug a' lump o' lard.'

'Her-her,' rumbled the Lakin, waving Abe on.

'Hur-hur,' mimicked Abe. It wasn't so hard, this looking like a Lakin, not hard at all, and he strode out with renewed confidence down a wide track dimly lit by the glowing embers of the camp fires. He passed lines and lines of makeshift tents and tin hoops inside which he could just see Lakins beginning to stir. As he walked, a grey light inched into the eastern sky and he wondered quite how far into the camp he should get before revealing himself and beginning the chase.

Around him he could hear moaning and the occasional crack and snap of a whip followed by a short yelp. He saw the bent shapes of slaves wheeling laden carts. Something, too large for a bat or bird, hissed by low overhead and Abe flinched and snatched at the handle of the meat cleaver he had tucked in his belt. A witch? Had Mrs Dunne sensed him? His confidence ebbed. How near to her tent should he go?

The thick smell of the camp clogged his nostrils and made it hard to breathe and there was such a heavy feeling of despair pressing in on him, it even seemed to have infected the ground on which he trod, seeping up through the soles of his feet, slowing him, making him doubt. Was there really any point in doing anything against her and her kind?

He slowed. His own breath felt stale against the mask. Supposing he could never lift it off? Supposing the mask became his face? He stopped and as he did so the reluctant dawn finally broke greyly across the sky and there, no more than twenty paces in front of him, was a great, black, silken pavilion and at its entrance stood Mrs Dunne herself.

For a moment Abe thought it was him that she was waiting for. There was a low murmuring from every part of the camp, swelling and dying like wind sighing along a sea shore. Mrs Dunne held out her hands, palm upwards, as if she were carrying an invisible bowl, and out from the space between her hands a cloud trickled and thickened and streamed and piled into the sky, turning and boiling into a serpent such as the one that Alicia had conjured the day before, but this one was so very much bigger. It was a dark, smoky cobalt, and its body, that wound in titanic coils around and above the camp, was thicker and longer than a train with a hundred carriages. Mrs Dunne had learned from her daughter and with this monstrous piece of magic would surely bear down anything that Alicia could send against her. This serpent with its tongue flickering like black lightning could devour entire cities.

Abe heard a quiet moan and realized that it came from him. Around him, however, and rippling out through the camp, were hoarse yells of triumph and the clash of metal on metal.

Pull yourself together, Nasfali. Do not despair.

Without reflecting where that thought had come from, he straightened his shoulders. Was this the time to move?

Perhaps if he distracted Mrs Dunne, broke her concentration—he knew how important concentration was for Alicia's magic—perhaps if he did that this serpent would shred into wisps of cloud. Was there anything to lose?

He lifted a hand and gripped the corner of his mask. Now! He snatched the grotesque face away with one hand and threw back his hood with the other. 'Mrs Dunne!'

Her eyes were fixed on the sky serpent.

'Mrs Dunne!' He stripped away the pillowcase of straw and ripped off the thick wadding of towel until he stood there clothed only in a thin cotton under-tunic and his pin-stripe trousers.

For a second her eyes flicked towards him and then her crimson mouth pulled back into a high, piercing, scream of rage. But Abe realized she wasn't looking at him at all: swooping down from the height of the sky was Alicia's answer to her mother's magic—a smoky eagle whose wings seemed to ripple and snap with silver fire and stretch so wide that they outspanned the length of Oxfordshire. It wheeled and banked and its talons hooked the serpent by its head and tore it up into the sky, higher and higher until they both diminished into black dots and then were swallowed in cloud.

Mrs Dunne's scream doubled and redoubled, hitting Abe with the force of a stinging slap. He staggered back a pace and clamped his hands to his ears. And it was as well that he did for, as if prompted by the witch's scream, the very air was crushed by a deep reverberating sound, a long, painful mocking 'Hroooom'. It was a sound such as Abe had never heard before but it made him think of a hunting horn, or perhaps a thousand horns. Stokely! Stokely and his secret army. Stokely and Griffin. This was it. This was the call!

He spun round on his heels but could see nothing but tents and Lakins and Mrs Dunne, of course. And all the time the air juddered and shuddered with the booming

calling of Stokely's horns. Lakins twisted and clutched
their heads. As for Mrs Dunne, her face flattened and
stretched as if a gale were blasting her. Abe's eyes streamed
but he knew what he had to do. As soon as the horns'
sound died he called to Mrs Dunne again.

'Mrs Dunne!' But his voice sounded thin and silly in
the gasping stillness. He heard a cough behind him and a
'Waz 'im, there?' He closed his eyes and concentrated. He
must be bigger, stronger, and with a deeper, more
powerful voice. He took a breath and when he called his
voice emerged with such round booming tones that he
startled himself.

'Mrs Dunne!'

Now he had her attention.

'I, Ebrahim Nasfahl Ma'halli am come. I am your bane,
Mrs Dunne.' He liked the word bane and had been
wanting to use it for some time.

Mrs Dunne's mouth seemed to gulp for air. 'You!' she
finally spluttered.

Abe looked past her. 'Mother!' he called. 'Come out!'
and the tent flapped and there was the slim, dark figure
of his mother. 'Run,' he boomed, 'run before you are
swept—'

But he had, once again, slightly overstepped the mark.
Mrs Dunne's eyes blazed; his mother's face was a painted
mask of rage, her eyes glittering black with dislike. 'Run?'
said Mrs Dunne. 'You tell me to run? You . . . '

Abe knew exactly what was next. He had come too
close and stayed too long. A serious error of judgement,
he said to himself, as Mrs Dunne slowly, magisterially,
raised one arm, stretched out the finger on which she
wore the blood-red stone ring and spat out the next
word: ' . . . worm. You worm, Nasfali. On—your—
belly!'

Abe felt his legs snatched away from under him and
he fell smack down into the dirt, sensing Lakins slowly
edging in around him.

'Jamboy,' he heard them muttering spittily. ' 'S jamboy . . . '

'We'll boil you, Nasfali, and bake you.' Her voice softened and her words oozed like rotten fruit. 'And give you to my chefs to skin and put in a pie. What do you think, sister?'

But Abe's mother never had a chance to answer. Abe suddenly found he could twist his head and he could see Alicia's glittering eagle come sweeping down out of the clouds, tearing the air with its great wings, scattering huts and tents and carts and people in its slipstream. Mrs Dunne and Abe's mother both shrieked. A rush of icy wind poured over Abe's back and, released from Mrs Dunne's spell, he bucked into the sprinter's starting position and then sprang forward and ran for his life.

Would they follow?

Of course.

But it was indeed such a run about which songs are sung. He ran so fast his knees nearly clipped his chin. He ran in the white heat of instinct, his feet flying over the ground. Had he wings on his heels he could not have run faster.

Both Lakins and witches followed blindly, furiously, like a herd of buffalo. Abe threaded his way past or through every obstacle. He side-stepped a monstrous mountain of fat and ducked under the outstretched arm of another. He leapt a guy-rope and vaulted a tipped-up cart. He ran like the wind. His heart pounded and his arms pumped. How far now? Not so far. Eyes streaming. Not so far.

Where were Stokely's riders? Were they already attacking the outer edge of the camp?

The air thrummed and thrashed over him as the eagle swept by again and, left and right, Lakins were tumbled to the ground. Blessed Alicia, he panted. Blessed she who watched over him.

And then he was out of the camp. One last sprint.

There was the old cottage; and then, with his legs buckling under him, he was scrambling through the broken doorway where he had tethered his horse. The unfortunate animal was panic stricken but he had no time to settle it; he snatched the rein free and somehow slung himself up onto the horse's back. 'Go!' he breathed. 'Your legs are wings: fly.'

The horse, from a standing position, launched herself through the opening, scattering the first of the pursuers left and right and then, cutting west and south, Abe spurred his mount in the direction he wanted Mrs Dunne's army to follow.

It was a break-neck ride and behind him all the time, rolling like a dirty avalanche, was Mrs Dunne's army, a vast sea of chefs, no longer yelling and hoarsely calling but pounding heavily and determinedly after their prey. Above them, like storm crows, flew Mrs Dunne and her sisters.

Abe's horse stumbled and at the same moment Abe heard a grunt and felt the clutch of a hand on his leg. He swung round and lashed out with his fist and his leg was free. Ahead, he could make out the hump of Folly Bridge and charging towards him the unbelievable sight of nine horsemen. The team! Brown cloaks streaming, long poles lowered like lances. Within seconds they were round Abe, piercing, poking, roaring and shouting, and belabouring the exhausted Lakins and then sweeping Abe up and galloping him back to the bridge. They all swung off their horses and, with Abe at the centre, they turned to face the Lakins pounding heavily towards them.

And so the great battle of Folly Bridge, as it came to be known, began.

They held the bridge, just keeping the Lakins at bay with lances made from sharpened punt poles and metal-tipped oars. Brave and strangely powerful as they were, their thin line couldn't possibly hold back the weight of Mrs Dunne's army for more than a few minutes. But that was long enough: surging up from Christ Church Meadow came the Greyfriars men, while from the north came every single soul from St Giles. The claws of the crab. 'They are pinched!' shouted Abe and it's true the Lakins were squeezed tight as an accordion and they howled and screeched with frustrated rage and renewed their attack, shoving out their barrel bellies and pushing their way into the defenders' line.

Then, at last, Abe and the team saw Stokely and his wild army crashing into the back of the Lakins. 'Stoker!' roared Jack, whacking his punt pole down onto the blunt head of a scowling Lakin. 'It's the Stoker!'

And there he was, bristling white eyebrows under the hood of his cloak, one hand gripping the reins, the other holding a thin pole with a stripy pennant fluttering from the tip. No, not a pennant, Abe suddenly realized, but a football shirt, one of the shirts they had worn in the great match at Giza. Where had he kept it all these years!

Streaming in behind him like a river in spate came his ragged army of out-people, bearded and brawny, packs of savage hunting dogs bounding beside them, hurling themselves at the enemy, and wiry freed slaves from Brighton; and there, right in the centre of the flood, was gnarly Aunt Ida riding a home-made chariot, grim-faced, a match for any witch that stood in her way; she would snap them away with a cut of her tongue. And flanking her were Ralph and his out-riders. They had all come! All of them. And Abe tried to fight his way forward to greet them. For a moment he lost sight of them and then the battle shifted and wheeled like a lop-sided scrum and they were all there. Ida beside Stokely, Griffin on the other side of her, and tucked in close, the young men, her homesteaders.

Safely through the defenders' lines, Stokely's troops swung down from their horses and threw their weight in behind the townsfolk. Stokely appeared beside Abe. 'Are we the stitch in time, skipper?'

'You are indeed, Stokely, and you are more than that
. . . ' Abe skipped, ducked, and thrust, and a Lakin
billowed out his cheeks like two fat balloons and collapsed
to his knees. ' . . . you are a miracle. You are the claw of
the crab.'

'Always glad to help out in a pinch.' And Abe just
caught his happy chuckle.

But there were so many of the enemy. They just kept
coming. For each Lakin the allies felled, another swelled
into his place and so the battle heaved to and fro. Men fell,
the renegades who haunted the ruins of Christ Church
threw themselves against the defenders but were beaten off
by the furious men and women of Balliol. Witches spun
and lashed their magic down, sometimes scorching a
militia man, sometimes frying one of their own. Bodies
tumbled into the deep water of the Thames and from time
to time there were cries of triumph when a witch was
tumbled from her stick and plunged screaming into the
water.

But slowly the allies were beaten back, step by step,
until the bridge was lost. The enemy paused, some
looking skyward to see if the hated eagle was hurtling
towards them, fearing a trap. Then with a grinding
rhythmic grunting they moved forward. The defenders
knotted together into one tight group. Abe, bruised and
exhausted, was shoulder to shoulder with Thomas and
Roberts, both of them as weary as him. No clever tricks
now. No suddenly shouted numbers and jumping forward
rolls or scissor jumps. This was no football game in which
they could cheat their way to victory.

'Chin up, skipper,' said Roberts, 'it'll soon be time for
tucker.'

If only, thought Abe, side-stepping a blow from a club
nobbed with sharpened spoons. Then he thought, if only
Alicia could do something, right now.

And she did.

TWENTY-NINE

Had Abe been able to see the city from the air, perhaps from the back of that eagle, he would have seen the battle as a shifting and heaving black shadow pulsing around Folly Bridge; he would have seen the smoking ruins of fine buildings and the tangled thread of brick and debris-strewn lanes; and, he would, perhaps, have seen a single figure high on the roof of the Greyfriars library; a bony-thin girl with straggly, black, uncut, unkempt hair, narrow wrists, a face hollowed out from lack of food and sleep and glittering, black, deep-staring eyes. He would have seen the girl turn slowly, arms outstretched; he would have seen her back arching, and crackling lines of blue light, streaming from her fingers, filling the air around her in a web of fine blue veins. He would have seen all the waters of the rivers and streams and ditches that half surround the city piling up into peaked waves that raced towards Folly Bridge, growing taller and taller the nearer they came; streaming white foam and towering over the bridge.

What he did see as he dodged out of the way of a steaming great Lakin stinking of onions was Mrs Dunne, caught in the middle of the bridge, unable to move because of the thick press of men and Lakins around her, and a huge tidal wave towering over her. 'Oh, blessed Alicia!' he grunted, whirling the broken punt pole he had been using as his weapon, and cracking it down with as much force as he could manage into the back of the Lakin's head. Blessed, blessed Alicia, she had indeed come up trumps. He quickly wiped the sweat from his face, dodged out of the way of a nasty looking spear made out of flattened baked bean tins with a razor sharp point; saw Mrs Dunne stretching and growing upwards, her arms flailing like tentacles, as she tried to rise up above the wave; saw the sky over Greyfriars crackling and splitting with a thousand threads of lightning; saw the dead stone eyes of the bearded man gripping the spear turning towards him and then Roberts and Griffin bursting out of the thrashing mess of the battle skipping about like mad monks in a frying pan.

One of them had a rusty sword—that was Griffin—and the other—Roberts—had two metal dustbin lids which he was using like a giant pair of cymbals, cracking a Lakin between the lids and then tipping his head back and yelling: 'To me! To me!' while Griffin poked and pranced and shouted: 'To him! To him!' The bearded spear-holder gazed with his dead pebble eyes at Abe, pulled back his spear ready to thrust, when he heard the clash of the dustbin lids and Roberts's ear-piercing yell. He hesitated and that was it for him: Griffin's rusty sword swooshed down and chopped the spear in half, and the dustbin lids clanged with juddering finality on either side of his head. The bearded man sank to the ground without a sound.

'I'm a whopper with a chopper!' shouted Griffin.

'To me!' yelled Roberts, giving Abe a wink. 'How are we doing, skipper? Ready for a bit of a charge?'

And at that moment, Abe saw the wave spin up way into the air above Mrs Dunne. Her power was no match for that of her famished daughter. Then it came thundering down onto the bridge, sweeping Mrs Dunne and all those with her into the torrenting river.

Indeed, thought Abe, a charge would be the very thing. He saw Pike and Gannet, and Stokely and Thomas forging their way towards them, Stokely still on horseback and Ralph riding close beside him. This was the moment!

'Follow me!' shouted Abe.

'Follow him!' shouted Griffin, and Roberts gave a triumphal clash of his dustbin lids.

And somehow, Abe, and the small core of the team, like a shining pebble flung from a sling, burst through the attacking ranks, and as they did so, the town's defenders, seeing this crazy charge and also the violent effect of Alicia's tidal wave, suddenly took heart and began to surge forward towards the river-soaked enemy.

The extraordinary thing was there was almost no resistance. Lakins buckled and slumped, a mere shove and they tumbled to the ground, and those slaves who had been witched into Mrs Dunne's army stared in a puzzled way at the weapons they were holding and, one by one, let them drop to the ground.

Abe, however, saw little of this. He ran as fast as he could, Thomas and Griffin on either side of him, down to the flooded bridge. Below them the grey and turbulent river was awash with the bulky bodies of drowned Lakins. It was a grim reckoning. Abe turned to the others. 'If we can find Mrs Dunne, we'll have won the battle,' he panted. 'She'll have been washed downstream. Come on!'

They ran, slipping and slithering through the soggy field, scouring the bank for their enemy. They found a black-haired witch sprawled face down in a muddy ditch, still breathing, so they quickly bound her hands and feet before she regained consciousness and was able to cause more trouble. They bundled her up onto Stokely's horse and then almost seventy yards down from Folly Bridge they saw the unmistakable form of Mrs Dunne, half of her body trailing into the current.

As they drew closer, she lifted her muddy face and gave them a look of exhausted hatred. 'Nasfali,' she said, little bubbles of river water spilling out of the corner of her fleshy mouth. 'I should have twisted you into a knot and burned you in an oven. You will suffer for this.' There was such venom in her voice that Griffin and the others froze. Abe, though, did not. He went right up to where she lay and stood over her.

'Watch out, skipper,' muttered Jack. 'You don't know what she can do.'

'She can do nothing,' said Abe.

He didn't know why he knew this, but he did. He sensed an emptiness behind the poisonous words. Her face glistened with wet; her fat hands were slimed with mud and the blood-red ring she always wore on her finger had lost its fire. Mrs Dunne was no longer what she had once been and Abe knew it. And he knew that it was the water that had done it. Of course, he thought, it is so simple; a river is life and this river had washed all Mrs Dunne's strength and power away from her. She was nothing. And it was Alicia, the great Alicia, who had done this thing.

'Take her arms,' he said. Stokely and Pike grabbed an arm each and hauled her out of the sludge and up on to the bank. 'You're our prisoner now,' said Abe.

'I'll turn you into a frog,' she snarled.

'I don't think so,' said Abe.

Griffin cocked a white and bushy eyebrow. 'The skipper don't think so, old girl.' Stokely chuckled and Mrs Dunne mumbled and snarled and spat out her curses and nothing happened.

Abe gave an elaborate shrug. 'You see. You are nothing, Mrs Dunne. All you needed was a good bath.'

She shuddered.

The team were impressed. 'Bravo, skipper!' They clapped and laughed and Jack tried to do a handstand and didn't manage it. Then they all spontaneously made a circle with Mrs Dunne in the middle and, linking arms, they did their version of a Highland fling, whooping their joy while Mrs Dunne, slowly realizing what had happened, turned ashy grey.

And this was how the great battle of Folly Bridge ended.

★ ★ ★

Of course there was the tidying up that had to be done; there is always tidying up after a battle. While Abe and the team brought Mrs Dunne and the other witch they had found back into Oxford and bundled them both unceremoniously into the buttery cellar at Greyfriars, Aunt Ida's horsemen and the out-people hunted down the scattered stragglers of the witch army.

All up and down the county they rode seeking out the Lakins and rounding up bedraggled witches. These they bound tight with cords and unceremoniously dragged them back to Oxford and herded them into the great cellars of the colleges.

Abe and the team, however, did not take part in this hunt. As soon as they were through the gates of Greyfriars College, Abe had said: 'Wait here. I shall get Alicia; she'll be happy to see us all back and safe.'

'And her glum mum,' offered Jack.

'And her glum mum's chum,' added Roberts.

Exhausted as he was, Abe ran for the library. This time there had been no barrier to him climbing the stairs and the upper room, where she had remained for weeks on end poring over that hateful book the witches had stolen from Abe's father's care, was empty. A bookcase had been overturned and a makeshift stairway of tables and books had been made up to the ceiling where she had broken a way through into the attic and from there up onto the roof. He called out. He even went up onto the roof himself, and, clinging dizzily to a chimney stack, scoured every bit of the college that he could see from up there; but there was no sign of her. Where was she? Where had she gone?

Slowly he made his way back down to the quadrangle where the team, immediately seeing that something was very wrong, gathered round him.

'What is it, skipper, old chap?' asked Roberts.

'She's gone.'

'Miss Dunne? That's not possible, is it? Can't just

disappear like that.' But they all knew she could. Stokely turned away and walked slowly towards the stables. The team suddenly seemed very old. 'It takes the fizz out of it all really,' said Pike.

'I am just so tired,' said Gannet.

'Me too.'

Griffin and Roberts sat down on a bench. They both looked miserable; not even the prospect of tucker cheered them up.

Of course there was feasting and celebration in the town. Barricades were pulled down and trestle tables set up. There was dancing and music; but though Abe and the team were fêted as heroes, they found it hard to join in properly. They just got on with things. However, as days passed, a kind of order was restored. Jonson, the first of the team to pull himself together, called a meeting of the surviving college masters and reformed the council. Aunt Ida was invited to join them and she did for while, helping to organize work parties to clean up the city and make arrangements to care for the wounded. She sent out Ralph and his riders north, south, east, and west to see the state of the land. When the reports came back they learned that all the sisters of Britain had either been with Mrs Dunne in the battle at Folly Bridge, or had gone into hiding. The country was still dangerous to travel through but at least it was free of witches.

The next problem was how to deal with all the prisoners. After some discussion, Jonson set up a court in the Sheldonian building where he and the masters dispensed brisk justice to the captured sisters and their followers.

'Send them as far away as you can,' advised Abe when Jonson came to speak to him. 'Somewhere where they are surrounded by water.'

'The Lake District,' said Jonson.

'Are there islands in the middle of the lakes?'

'Oh yes, I should think so.'

'That'll do then.'

'Capital,' said Jonson.

So, one after the other, Mrs Dunne and all her sisters were banished to the faraway north, where each would live alone on a wild, rocky island in the middle of a cold mountain lake with nothing but the wind and rain for company and comfort. And it was no more than they deserved, that was what Abe felt, as he watched them booed out of the court to their waiting escorts of grim-faced young men, one-time out-people who had no time for witches or any of their kind.

This was the triumph, Abe knew; it just didn't feel like it.

'We have so much to undo.' That's what Alicia had said and that was why he had come back with her from Egypt. Undo their magic. Break their tight grip. Well, that's what they were busy trying to do, but Abe felt it would be a long, long while before everything would be back to normal.

'Whatever is normal, old boy?' drawled Gannet who was squashed in next to him in the hall watching the trial. 'There was only awful school—that was hardly normal—the awful inbetween time (most of the team couldn't bear to refer directly to the long years when Mrs Dunne had spell-bound them) and then sixty-odd years of dodging Mrs Thing and her ghastly sisters.'

Abe wasn't entirely sure what normal was either. It didn't feel very normal sitting in the Sheldonian, watching the trial and judgement of a bedraggled Mrs Dunne and of his own mother. He felt empty.

Why?

Because Alicia had disappeared.

It was Stokely, of course, who pulled Abe to one side, one evening, and said, 'I think we should be off, don't you, skipper?' and Abe had known exactly what he had meant. If she had disappeared, she had disappeared to somewhere and they should find her. Of course they should be off. This he should have thought of himself.

Needless to say, the team agreed instantly. 'Good old Stoker,' said Jack. 'Brain sparking on all four cylinders for once!' They made hurried preparations and the next morning they rode out from Oxford in four separate directions. Abe, Stokely, Jissop, and Chivers headed for the west country; Jack and a couple of the others rode east for London; Griffin and Roberts went south, and Thomas, Bittern, and Pike took the road north.

To Abe it really did seem as if the tight grip that the witches had held on Britain was truly broken and in its place there reigned a fragile, trembling peace. Those who had been slaves suddenly noticed that they could go where they wished and they walked away; the southern counties saw trailing groups of men, women, and children criss-crossing the land, heading for their lost homes.

For Abe and the team it was a time of hard travelling, strange encounters, dangerous pockets of spent magic fouling dens and thickets that had to be avoided, and all the time, the constant asking: Had she been seen? Was there word of her?

It was Stokely who kept urging them westward. 'Hunch, old boy,' was all he would say.

When they passed the free town of Shaftesbury and there was still no sign of her, Abe started to argue and say that Alicia would hardly have managed to travel that far. Chivers pulled him aside and just said very quietly that it was best to let Stoker take the lead. This was what he was really good at. It was true; he was the gatherer. But why did Stokely want to keep heading west?

'Arthur country,' said Chivers. 'He's got a bit of a passion for all that old round table business. Never really grown up, has he? Awfully sorry, skipper. You probably think none of us have, don't you? Should have, of course, got the old bones and the aches. But the thing is, my mother and father were a very dull lot when they were grown up; wouldn't want to be like them, would I.'

Abe smiled at the old winger. What a raggedy, stooping scarecrow he was. But he was still fast on his feet and in the middle of the battle Abe had been astonished to hear him actually singing as he exchanged hammering blows with a rubbery-faced Lakin. When Chivers had suddenly shouted his chorus of 'Coocoocachoo!' the Lakin had gawped, taken a step back and dropped his guard; at which Chivers had nipped forward and dealt him a swingeing blow to the side of his head. The Lakin had keeled over neat as a slice of bread.

They did find Alicia eventually, curled up in the corner of a darkened and deserted cottage. Her skin was cold and damp, her eyes glazed, and she was muttering all the time, a kind of muddling of Arabic and nonsense, punctuated with frightened exclamations of 'No. No. No.'

She neither recognized them nor reacted to them in any kind of way at all. The old woman who had told them about the sick beggar girl had also told them that she had tried to feed the girl broth but she would swallow nothing but the water the woman had dribbled into her mouth.

They gave Alicia clean dry clothes and wrapped her up in soft wool cloaks. They found a cart and made her a bed of straw. Then they laid her down and began the long journey back.

In Oxford, she would let no one but Stokely and Abe come near her. Day after day they tended her, taking it in turns to sit by her bed, bathe her face, and offer water to drink. Gradually the strange muttering died away, and her unseeing eyes began to focus.

On the fourteenth day of her return, she suddenly gripped Abe's wrist as he was tilting a glass towards her mouth. She pushed the glass away. 'You are going to wish you had never brought me back, Nasfali.'

'This is nonsense, Alicia. Why should I think that? You saved us all.'

'I saved you from my mother, that's all I did,' she said. 'Who's going to save you from me?' Then she had lain back and closed her eyes.

'You're making a joke, aren't you?'

'I don't make jokes, Nasfali. You know that.'

This was mostly true. In all the time he had known her, she had only made one joke and it hadn't been particularly funny.

'Leave, Nasfali. Go back to Cairo,' she said. 'Find your father. Before it's too late.'

'Why should I do that? There is much still to be undone here. You yourself said that.'

'Can't you see? Can't you tell?' She sounded both impatient and exhausted. 'I wanted to go away, to be lost. I don't want to be me any more, Nasfali, but you brought me back and there will be no stopping me now, no stopping me at all.' She appeared to fall asleep and Abe quietly left the chamber.

Indeed, she was not being humorous, and he knew very well what she was saying. She thought she had finally become like the mother she had defeated; but he couldn't believe it. She looked like her old self; frail, yes, certainly frail and her voice was soft, softer than it had ever been; and she didn't seem bossy at all, and she had always been bossy. Was that a good sign? He didn't know.

Abe kept his worries to himself, not even saying anything to Stokely who was gently nannying Alicia into better health; and when she finally got out of bed, it was Stokely who walked beside her, she leaning on his arm, like father and daughter.

She began to attend the council meetings, at first merely to watch, but then as she grew visibly stronger, the men and women of Oxford who had positions on the council begged her to join them. Abe watched her closely: she always seemed to be merely listening, hardly ever speaking, unless her opinion was asked for; and yet, increasingly, her opinion was asked for, until no decision was taken without her approval. Then it was somehow a short step before she sweetly—and that was not at all like the old Alicia—agreed to become the council leader.

The next day workmen were building a dais and skilled joiners were making a suitable chair for her.

'They want to,' said Alicia when Abe asked her what this was all for.

'To me,' he said carefully, 'it seems very like a throne, Alicia. I did not think you would wish to have anything to do with thrones.'

She looked at him coolly. 'Things are not very often what they seem, Nasfali. I have told you that before. It is about time you understood.'

But Abe still didn't quite understand.

Meanwhile, Alicia presided queen-like over her councillors. She was never imperious, never threatening, never shouted or bullied and yet everyone naturally agreed with everything she had to say. Ruined Oxford was her city but gradually her power began to extend outwards. Who was to say that this was bad. Abe had to admit that things did get done: workers came to rebuild the burned-out homes and colleges, roads were mended and farms produced food which was brought into the market.

Griffin and the team, however, had nothing to do with the meetings and government. 'Boring,' said Jack. 'More of a skipper's job, thank you very much.'

'But Alicia is changing. We should all talk to her.'

They didn't want to.

'Miss Dunne usually knows best,' said Jonson. 'Give her a little more time.'

Stokely nodded. 'Miss Dunne is clever, skipper. And it is peaceful, don't you think?'

And it was. Except that when he was up early and watching the carts being driven into market, Abe noticed that the men and women who were busy working at mending or building or driving the carts had the hurt look in their eyes that the witches' slaves had had; and when he tried to talk to them, they looked away and once he was sure he heard one of them muttering: 'I hurt. Oh, how I hurt.'

Everyone else, though, appeared content.

'Don't meddle, Nasfali,' said Alicia when he asked the council how all the work was being paid for.

The councillors tutted and looked at him as if he shouldn't be there.

'Foreign-looking people on the council,' sniffed a sour, thin woman, a woman Abe was sure that he recognized as having been one of the city leaders who had been in the pay of Mrs Dunne all those months ago before the city had really started to crumble. What was she doing there?

'But everyone has a right to be paid for their work,' said Abe. Indeed, this was an important principle to him. Always he had made money from his schemes. And someone who worked should have money for his labour. 'If they don't get paid they are no better than slaves.'

'The work must be done,' said Alicia, 'and therefore people have to do it. You could do some work, Nasfali, perhaps.' Her eyes gazed at him, and he had the most uncomfortable feeling that she was somehow viewing him differently, as if he were someone whom she could well do without.

He made as if to go but Alicia said: 'Not yet. I have an important announcement to make concerning my mother. It is my view,' said Alicia, looking directly at him, 'that we could get things done much more quickly if I had my mother and my aunts back here with me.'

'You can't be serious!'

'I would, of course, make sure,' she said to her assembled councillors, ignoring Abe's interruption, 'that their power was only used for the common good. Think how much we could achieve. We would have the whole country back to rights in no time at all.'

They all nodded. All but Abe.

'How can you do this?'

She turned slowly towards him: her face waxy pale. All her studs and nose-rings were gone now as were the pixie points in her hair and the dark lipstick and black-painted fingernails, but around her forefinger was a large blood-red ring such as her mother had always worn and around her neck a blood-red scarf. Where had both those things come from?

'It is good to keep your friends close,' said Alicia, 'and your enemies closer.'

As if this were a pre-arranged signal, there was a thunderous knocking at the council room doors and Mrs Dunne, followed by all the banished sisters, walked in and stood before the seated Alicia. Then, as Abe, stunned and incapable of speech, watched on, they kneeled one by one before the girl who had defeated them and been their bane.

'Hello, mother,' said Alicia. 'Are you ready to do our bidding?'

Where had this royal 'we' come from and the equally royal 'bidding'?

'Are you willing to use your magic only in our cause? Are you willing to forgo all other spells . . . '

'We are very ready,' said Mrs Dunne.

Abe could stand it no longer. 'Who are your friends, Alicia? Your mother?' He pushed back his chair. 'This is—' What was it? 'It's a betrayal, Alicia. I did not expect this from you.'

For the first time Alicia's control snapped. She smacked the table with the flat of her hand. 'Good!' she snapped. 'I warned you but you would not listen. I am now what I am, not what I was. So go. We no longer want you with us, Nasfali. Go to Cairo. The team may stay, but you, you are banished! You have till sunset. Go!'

And he found himself being propelled rapidly towards the large double doors which swung open for him and then slammed shut as soon as he passed through.

Then the pressure on his back suddenly ceased and he staggered slightly, caught his balance and looked back at the doors closed against him. Not a very dignified exit.

'I wish we'd never bothered to look for you!' he yelled. 'I wish we'd never brought you back!'

The two armed guards standing outside stepped towards him. He looked at the tips of their razor-sharp spears and backed away. She seemed to have become a full, cold-blooded, un-human witch. The Alicia of his adventures really had disappeared.

He walked slowly down to Magdalen Bridge. The sun was setting, a dull and lonely dark red blob on the edge of the world. He leaned on the balustrade and looked down into the water and thought of the winding River Nile. How very alone he was. He thought of that mother of cities, Cairo, on the edge of which were the Pyramids and somewhere between the three points of those great triangles was the vanishing point into which his father had run. Should he look for him? Could he ever find him again? Would his father be able or willing to do something about these witches, about Alicia?

Perhaps some things cannot be truly undone. The sun had half sunk into the horizon. He would have to leave the city soon otherwise she would have her guards after him and what then? A witch's prison? Anything rather than that. I need a scheme, he thought, such a scheme as only I can dream up.

'Indeed you do, skipper,' said a sing-song voice behind him. 'And I'd say that you could count us all in, isn't that right, boys?'

'Thomas! How did you know what I was thinking! Stokely? What are you all doing here? I thought you were with Miss Dunne . . . '

'You're the skipper,' said Jonson.

'She brought us back,' said Jack Griffin, 'but you are the skip with the schemes.'

They were all there, all eleven, dressed in brown monks' cloaks, each holding the reins of a horse, apart from Stokely on the far right who had been leading his own and Abe's.

They had come for him and this was a good thing. 'How could you be so quiet?' said Abe. 'I didn't hear you at all.'

'We have got particularly good at creeping,' said Jack. 'So what are we to do? Even an egg basket like Roberts knows that things have gone a bit whoopsy all of a sudden.'

Yes, thought Abe, they had indeed gone whoopsy, whatever that meant. 'We shall,' he said, 'have to unwhoops them but first I think we should . . . '

'Run away?' suggested Stokely.

'Exactly,' said Abe.

'You mean,' said Thomas, 'that good old discretion is the better part of valour.'

'Of course,' said Abe, not entirely sure what this meant but rather liking the sound of the words. 'And in my scheme,' he said, as they trotted up the Iffley Road, 'we re-group. We re-form. We rise up.'

They liked that.

'We jolly well rise up!' they agreed.

Yes, they would indeed rise up, thought Abe, and it was now coldly clear exactly what it was they would have to do: by hook or by crook they would steal that book from Alicia and return it to his father. Then, perhaps, Alicia might become what she had once been and he could forgive her for this betrayal. As for Mrs Dunne, he knew exactly what her fate must be but that scheme he would keep very, very secret until the time was right. 'We shall rise up,' he murmured.

'King Arthur,' chuckled Stokely.

Abe looked up to see the last sliver of the sun disappearing. 'We ride for the west country,' said Abe.

'Of course we do,' said Stokely. 'Where else?'

But Abe wasn't really listening. 'We shall be,' he said, 'the princes of sunset.'

'Very good,' said Jissop.

'And we shall put things right.'

'You mean sort out Miss Dunne. Make her like she was.'

'Yes,' said Abe. 'This is what we shall do.'

And with this they were content.

So they rode through this strange land and into their sunset, eleven of them with creaking bones and wheezy chests, and one with a head full of schemes.

'We shall be called "Ebrahim's Team",' said Abe. 'Is that not a fine name for us?'

Jack said, 'Oh yes,' and then snorted with laughter.

'I prefer the one with princes,' said Jissop.